# FOR THE LOVE OF
# MUSIC

## Interviews with Ulla Colgrass

Toronto   New York
OXFORD UNIVERSITY PRESS
1988

Oxford University Press, 70 Wynford Drive, Don Mills, Ontario, M3C 1J9

Toronto  Oxford  New York  Delhi  Bombay  Calcutta  Madras  Karachi
Petaling Jaya  Singapore  Hong Kong  Tokyo  Nairobi  Dar es Salaam
Cape Town  Melbourne  Auckland

and associated companies in
Berlin  Ibadan

CANADIAN CATALOGUING IN PUBLICATION DATA

Colgrass, Ulla
For the love of music

Includes index.
ISBN 0-19-540665-6

1. Musicians – Interviews. I. Title.

ML385.C64 1988     780'.92'2     C88-094399-8

# Contents

# Acknowledgments

I am most grateful for the generous co-operation I received from the twenty-two musicians interviewed here. I also greatly enjoyed collaborating with photographers Walter Curtin and Birgitte Nielsen, whose many photos in these pages reflect their sensitivity to music. Both the Canada Council and the Ontario Arts Council gave essential support to *Music Magazine* and thereby made this book possible. My co-publisher Anne Barrett was an indispensable partner, as was editor Richard Teleky, of Oxford University Press, who tackled the project with energy and imagination. My most valued support, however, came from my husband, Michael Colgrass.

# Photograph Credits

ARTPARK: Christopher Keene. WALTER CURTIN RCA: Maureen Forrester, Anton Kuerti, Arthur Ozolins, Jon Vickers, Edith Wiens. WALTER CURTIN, RCA, NATIONAL PHOTOGRAPHY COLLECTION, PUBLIC ARCHIVES CANADA: Istvan Anhalt, Glenn Gould, R. Murray Schafer, Teresa Stratas. ERNIE COX: Erich Leinsdorf. VIRGIL FOX SOCIETY: Virgil Fox. PAUL HOEFFLER: Rivka Golani. BILL KING: Yo-Yo Ma. MARC MILLER: Orford String Quartet. BIRGITTE NIELSEN: James Campbell, Kyung Wha Chung, Robert Aitken, Wynton Marsalis, Richard Stoltzman. PETER SCHAAF: Elly Ameling. CHRISTIAN STEINER: Pinchas Zukerman.

# Introduction

"What musicians are and what they do is almost incomprehensible to a vast portion of our audience. . . . Just hearing that a musician can actually speak the English language and that he can make fun of himself and be human can dispel the image of the musician as a tall, austere person with white hair." So said American conductor Christopher Keene in our talk, which is part of this book of interviews.

For years I had observed this gap in communication between musicians and their North American audience, and it eventually inspired me, in 1978, to start *Music Magazine*. As a European I had not been intimidated by the "classical" world, but knew musicians as people of great diversity, warmth, humor and creative strength—much the way many people on this continent appreciate writers and actors. Music criticism alone was apparently not bridging the gap between musicians and listeners here, so co-publisher Anne Barrett and I chose to make *Music Magazine* a forum for musicians to speak about their art and lives, confining critical views mostly to the pages of record and book reviews. The interviews in this book were chosen from among some fifty conducted during my decade as editor of the magazine.

Fortunately there are now many avenues of information that combine to change the public's perception of musicians. Television especially has brought them into the realm of ordinary mortals, several publications like *Music Magazine* have spring up, and even newspaperc print occasional profiles on classical musicians.

In these interviews I wanted to probe the creative process and learn about the external forces that make for a great performer. Glenn Gould, Elly Ameling, Wynton Marsalis, Kyung Wha Chung, Jon Vickers, Teresa Stratas . . . what a rich and deeply personal world each had created. And instead of being aloof, they seemed eager to talk about their work and ways of life, always giving generously of their time and thoughts.

The circumstances of these interviews were sometimes unusual. I was surprised when I had to meet composer R. Murray Schafer at a distant lake in Ontario at four in the morning to properly appreciate his work. He was producing one of his environmental pieces, which involved trombones, wildlife, theatrical effects and the special acoustics of the lake as the sun broke through a frosty haze. After a warming breakfast, Schafer poured out his passion for nature and his iconoclastic views on art.

Pianist Glenn Gould set a different kind of stage for our meeting—he wouldn't meet in person at all. Normally he did not give interviews, but he had always been supportive of the magazine and consented, though on his own terms. I knew from experience that he had to be one of Bell Telephone's best customers, so I gathered plenty of tapes and rigged my tape recorder to the telephone. He always spoke very fast and precisely enough to be quoted verbatim, sometimes playing devil's advocate with opinions like, "There is the funny assumption that wallpaper music is very harmful. I don't think it is harmful at all." (His colleague Anton Kuerti, on the other hand, said that Muzak "goes in one ear and out some other opening.") After more than two hours and no apparent slack in his concentration, we stopped when the tape ran out. He asked to see the manuscript before it was published, and although this was an unusual request, I was fascinated to see how he would deal with his own faithfully transcribed comments. In a long, late-night telephone session he requested 150 changes! He was not at all patronizing and did not alter a word of my writing, but his own words were refined and reworked in much the same way that he was known to work with the technicians on each of his recordings. In retrospect, it was as much fun working with Glenn Gould the editor as it was to interview the pianist, and as a bonus he improvised some of his hilarious impersonations of well-known people.

My interview with Elly Ameling was held under the worst circumstances, over a hasty breakfast in a noisy hotel restaurant. It might have been a superficial chat, were it not for the extraordinary concentration and attention to detail that is built into a lieder singer's psyche. After half an hour under the spell of the soprano's intense brown eyes, many of the mysteries of a concert singer were unravelled to my satisfaction. Yet Ameling called me the next day from Washington, D.C., to make sure that she had made a certain point completely clear. I then realized that she alone decides what is superficial, and that one reason why she is so successful is the perfect match between her personality and the art of lieder. Ameling got rather agitated at Gould's remark that concerts were "an utterly wasteful activity." To her "there is no better place to meet for the spirits of us earthlings . . . you never get that with a record."

Nearly every musician seems possessed with the need to teach. This urge to bring along the next generation is a curious trait—it is as if musicians feel bound by an unspoken vow to pass their knowledge on to others. The foremost soloists are extremely busy, of course, but still they inevitably apologize if they cannot squeeze teaching into their schedules. The preoccupation with teaching springs naturally from each musician's background. All the people in this book talked at length about their training and early years of performing, which makes these interviews a useful reference in the survival techniques and psychology of performing.

Our great soloists feel tremendously indebted to the teachers who sent them on their way, even though some of those mentors could be terrifying. Pianist Arthur Ozolins had a running battle with Nadia Boulanger in Paris. Clarinetist Richard Stoltzman says that Kalman Opperman "dragged me down and put my ego way low." Kyung Wha Chung's first response to Joseph Szigeti was to feel as if she "had fallen into a bottomless pit." Yet they all revered their teachers. Their mutual goal, ephemeral and elusive, lay beyond personal considerations, but each knew it was worth the struggle.

The search for perfection is a way of life for musicians, and many remarked playfully that they would always be students. "It is the knowledge beyond the notes that you are constantly searching for—that's a need like having to eat when you are hungry," said Pinchas Zukerman. Cellist Yo-Yo Ma is always re-evaluating his work and finds strength in approaching music through words as well as in sound: "To be able to articulate something gives you one more thing to latch on to." Stratas, on the other hand, said, "I hate analyzing what I do, because I think a person can talk and talk a thing away. So my work is like my religion: I don't like to verbalize it."

Many of the careers of these prominent artists were launched spectacularly—some won major prizes, others overnight celebrity as last-minute replacements—but initial success does not always guarantee smooth sailing. Each has experienced highs and lows, and some have even considered opting out of their careers. For some, weaknesses or bad luck have caused physical injury—Stratas' battle with tuberculosis, Chung's accident with her fingers in a car door—but psychological problems can be just as debilitating. In order to perform at their best, musicians often devise their own strategies. Flutist Robert Aitken, for instance, returned in his late thirties to his teenage philosophy of life by deciding to perform the best he could without looking past tomorrow; he also learned self-hypnosis in order to relax. Clarinetist James Campbell is modest offstage, but recommends: "For the few minutes you are playing onstage, convince yourself that you are the best in the world and afterwards congratulate yourself."

Everyone offered advice with a seriousness that emphasized how vulnerable a soloist can be. Concertizing is often a lonely existence, and some very strong personalities have developed through sheer necessity. A touch of eccentricity sometimes comes with the territory, but that too may be an essential element in giving the very best performance. The notion that musicians are interested only in their own world seems ill-founded. They are often closely involved with other art forms and hold strong views on worldly matters. In their leisure time they enjoy farming (Vickers), painting (Chung and Rivka Golani), writing (Schafer) and fishing (Aitken), among other pursuits. All twenty-two musicians described a personal life beyond music.

My main purpose in these interviews was to listen and pose some of the questions that concertgoers might ask. I did not place each musician in critical perspective, since that has been done at great length by others. Most readers have undoubtedly formed an opinion of these artists already through concerts and records, so the following pages are entirely a forum for the musicians' thoughts on their work and lives.

Just as we appreciate these outstanding performers, they never fail to mention the fresh inspiration that we, the audience, contribute to this symbiotic relationship. The late organist Virgil Fox captured it exuberantly: "When you finally align with what you know is right for your usefulness, it is a marvellous sensation. You really do soar."

# Robert Aitken

When I talked with Robert Aitken in 1981, the flute was just about the most popular instrument around, and James Galway was all the rage. Granted, the flute has always had its faithful followers, but at that time many more people developed a taste for its lilting sounds. Today the air of show biz has worn off, but the instrument's popularity remains high, and Robert Aitken is very busy as Canada's foremost flutist.

Aitken is originally from Kentville, Nova Scotia. Today his main address is Toronto, but he is music director at the Banff School of Fine Arts in Alberta and of Music at Shawnigan, a summer festival in British Columbia. He also spends about three months a year touring in Europe and is right now testing a more permanent life there as flute professor in Freiburg, West Germany. If he likes it and the work is compatible with his solo career, he will be the third Canadian musician interviewed in this book to move abroad (following violist Rivka Golani and clarinetist James Campbell). "I would like a bigger presence in Europe," he says.

Aitken is known for his exceptional technique and wide-ranging repertoire. The Swedish BIS label carries several of his records, among them all of the Doppler brothers' charming nineteenth-century flute music. At the same time Aitken is an avid spokesman for the music of his own time, having played solo recitals at the Pompidou Center in Paris and being the co-founder of Toronto's New Music Concerts. In fact, Aitken is well known in the close-knit contemporary music circles and travels widely with his own compositions and those of his contemporaries. The recent Concerto for Flute and Orchestra written for him by R. Murray Schafer was played with great success with the major orchestras across the country, starting with the Montreal Symphony Orchestra under Charles Dutoit. (It's due out on a CBC SM 5000 record.)

Approaching his fiftieth birthday (in 1989), Aitken appears modest and easy-going. A few questions, though, soon ferret out his strong opinions about flute music and the ways of the music world. In a recent conversation he was particularly incensed that the Canada Council had cut off all support to summer festivals, so that Music at Shawnigan was threatened, although it eventually went on with a generous donation from Taiwan.

*Colgrass: Your career has really accelerated in recent years. Do you think there is room in Canada for a topnotch solo flutist?*

Aitken: There is probably room for several. People really flock to flute concerts now. The instrument seems to be the right one for the age, and so many young people have been playing flute now for quite a while. It's managers who don't always have faith in the instrument. Very often they say, "Well, we can't have more than one flute player in the symphony season because they won't attract people." But I haven't been to concerts with good, mediocre or poor flute players that weren't pretty well packed.

*Are you kept busy in Canada, playing from coast to coast?*

The possibility is there, if the people responsible would be willing to hire solo flutists often enough. I think it has reached the stage where most of the orchestras have one flute soloist a year. Certainly the country is big enough to sustain a flutist's solo career; our orchestras need only hire a Canadian flutist every other year and foreign ones in the years in between. There are some major orchestras in Canada I haven't played with yet. [Thankfully, by 1988 that is no longer the case.]

*Are they unaware of you?*

I don't know. Maybe they have flute soloists of their own. As a flutist you always have a problem, because the orchestra will always consider their own flutists first, whether or not they are of the caliber to play solo.

*You are more versatile than most flutists, playing a wide repertoire reaching from early to contemporary music.*

Well, I haven't played jazz for a long time, and I don't think I could do it. Hardly anybody plays jazz and classical music equally well because the rhythmic responsibilities are entirely different. In classical music you spend your entire life playing exactly the rhythms in front of you—almost like a machine—while in jazz you spend your life not ever playing the same.

*Wouldn't it be helpful for a classical musician to learn jazz improvisation?*

Sure, because it gives you a lot of confidence.

*You have played a great deal of new music in Europe.*

That happened in the beginning through the New Music Concerts in Toronto. But most of my concerts in Europe are with traditional music and all of my eight recordings on BIS are with traditional repertoire.

*Do you think there are too few and too dominant influences in our musical life?*

Perhaps—but I think we suffer more from lethargy than anything else. That's an unfortunate part and perhaps a Canadian trait. Perhaps I shouldn't use the word "lethargy." It is more a lack of confidence and believing in what you are doing. Every country has some kind of special problem. At the moment Sweden is becoming too safe and people there complain about everything being decided for them, right down to the number of bottles of liquor a person is allowed to buy each month! That is looking after you in the extreme. Despite our own complaints, I still think that if you believe in what you are doing, you can do it here. The trick is to maintain the momentum.

*Do you feel that more energy might be the answer to developing a richer musical life in Canada?*

I think we do have a very lively musical life in Canada—I can't imagine what we need. Per capita, Toronto is probably second only to London in musical activity. Often it is the lack of performing space that restricts the number of performances.

*What made you take that step from orchestra musician to soloist?*

I tend to let things happen to me in typical Canadian fashion. [Smiles.] When I was playing in symphony orchestras—first the Vancouver Symphony and then the Toronto Symphony—I counted during that last season that I had taken 103 airplanes to play solo concerts as well as playing three symphony concerts a week. Obviously it had just reached the point where something had to go. Since I also enjoy teaching and composing, the least flexible—the symphony orchestra—was the thing to give up. For the next five years [1971-76] I was teaching at the University of Toronto, where I had tenure.

*You have said that you changed at the age of thirty-seven—in which way?*

I went back to my teenage philosophy of life, which was to do everything the best way I could without looking past tomorrow. When you are ambitious and want a certain kind of career, you tend to think that things will happen because "good work is rewarded," but good work is not necessarily rewarded. If you play a fantastic concert and you know that a certain manager or conductor is present, you hope that it will result in another concert. Well, it may not happen, and it can get very frustrating. Then over a period of time you can become very negative, and a bit of that was happening to me between the age of thirty and thirty-seven.

I was determined to find a way through this maze. Now when I play what I feel is a good concert, I scarcely even look at the reviews or anything else and go on to the next concert. I'm much happier and everything seems to be going better—maybe I am, in fact, playing better.

It's always a question whether you play better when you are playing for somebody special in the audience. I discovered little by little that if I was playing in some town where I didn't know a single person, I had quite a good time by myself on that stage, and I think now that my best concerts are when I don't know anybody in the audience.

*Is the audience important to you?*

Very much so. I get everything from the audience when I feel they are right with me . . . I feel the audience, but I think of the music. What I find interesting in terms of programming is that I seem to get even bigger applause when I play solo without a piano, perhaps because it is more direct and focused and less watered down. A few years ago I played a concert at the Liszt Academy in Budapest. That place was packed, although they didn't know me. The program was just solo flute, and I thought, "How will they stand this?" Well, I had to play five encores, and more and more this trend is happening.

*Do you think there is too much show biz in your field?*

Sure there is, but that will pass. Actually I'm surprised it has sustained itself as well as it has, because the political pendulum has already swung to the right, as has the compositional pendulum, going back some eight years. In the arts you find that the trend often follows politics; then the audiences follow, always being last.

*What has that done to your New Music Concerts?*

Strangely enough, it did cut back the audience a bit. There was really no reason for this because the music itself had already become tonal again and was quite accessible. Nevertheless, people's interest dwindled for a while, nostalgia became fashionable and it was a time of entrenchment and re-examination of old values. When the money is short, people begin to ask "why?" In the seventies or sixties did you ever hear the question "why?" It was always "why not?" So for a while it became rather unfashionable to go to New Music Concerts, but now our audiences are fine again.

*Doesn't it depend on who is on the program?*

The star system, unfortunately, always works. I have been reluctant to go that route, but we have been forced into the star system to make sure people would come. However, the ticket sales account for very little of our expenses—twelve percent or less—and I have for this reason always wanted to give our concerts free to the public.

*Do you think people appreciate something they don't pay for?*

For new music it's different. We just want to get people into the hall and get them exposed to it. I wouldn't advocate giving classical music concerts for free, though.

*Why do you think so few of the established composers attend the New Music Concerts?*

Perhaps some of our composers don't want to expose themselves to other influences—they are content with what they are doing, so they stay away. Maybe they are afraid, but I think that creative artists should expose themselves to new things. I compose myself, go through a lot of new scores and play many new works. Those things excite your imagination and give you ideas, so I feel that some of the composers are shortsighted not to come. I think we are among the best in the world in terms of performance standards, and we are really besieged by composers from all over the world who want their works played.

*How do you find time for composing?*

Now I program it into my schedule. The performing and composing is not such a problem—it's the administrative work related to New Music and my own career that is a disaster. Just composing and performing be a schizophrenic existence, because when you compose you turn inwards and when you perform you have to be an extrovert. Now, when I compose I also find myself worrying about who is going to play E-flat clarinet next week, let alone the financial aspects.

I do my best practicing when I'm away. Often, on tour, I feel that I play my first concert so terribly that I wonder how I'll get through it [laughs self-deprecatingly], but by the end of the tour I'll be playing really well. Even when I'm well prepared, I get on stage and wish I had practiced more.

*When do you find time to relax?*

Well, after I became self-employed everything changed. I take the concerts as they appear. Let's say that I set aside two weeks for skiing in March and then a concert comes at the end of it. There goes the vacation, because you have to practice for the concert.

*Do you feel there is a conflict between quality and quantity of performing?*

Sure, there can be. But you have to plan in advance. If you know that a program is very difficult you have to make space for practicing and try to build up your resistance if it's a long program as well. I have at times been practicing and rehearsing six hours a day and then was expected to be fresh for playing an evening concert.

*Do you ever feel completely worn out?*

No, not any longer. I think you reach a point where you are always in control. A few years ago I wouldn't have been, not for physical reasons, but mentally I have learned to control certain things—and you realize that you can only do your best.

*When I asked you before about what it takes to become a soloist, I wasn't thinking primarily about the musical requirements, but more about the perseverance and psychological state, which I presume is most important.*

Definitely! How to control your body with your mind is really what it comes down to. How to make it go when you are very tired and how to think clearly when you are just off the plane in a different time zone.

*Do you have special tricks of the trade to pass on?*

I use my mind very much for relaxation in the area of self-hypnosis, which I learned from a medical hypnotist in Saskatoon eight years ago. It is a very useful thing for a musician to learn.

*Yet it's not used much.*

I think many of the great musicians always used it, maybe without knowing it. It can have very specific uses—even speeding up a trill. [Laughs.] They say that Paganini played concerts in a hypnotic state, but I tried it and found that I wasn't really there and therefore it wasn't successful. To do that successfully may require a strange mixture of neuroticism and relaxation.

*That label doesn't seem to fit you.*

I'm sure many of the best sight-readers are quite neurotic because the nerves are right on the edge.

*I know that many flutists despise James Galway. Why is that?*

How tricky. [Laughs.] You don't give me a chance to say that I don't despise Galway! Well, I don't. I think he is a fantastic flutist. At the moment he wants to be accepted in every household, so he is watering down his repertoire to the extent that everybody is going to like him. But there are many flutists in the world who have very high ideals for their instrument, and who would like to stay with the repertoire which is composed for it and not lower the flute to any level in order to get admirers.

*In other words, you think Galway is cheapening the instrument?*

I don't think he is, but that is what a lot of people say. Of course, he is so overworked that it's hard for him to be on top all the time, and he now shows a bit less respect for the audience than before.

*About Ransom Wilson . . .*

He makes a great sound, but he likes to do things in unconventional ways and probably feels that flute pieces have been played in a certain way for so many years and that he would like to change the tradition. That makes him very original, but it is diametrically opposed to my thinking—there is only one way to play a certain work!

*How is that?*

I feel that any artist with ethics should feel that there is only one way to play a phrase.

*Who, then, determines the right way?*

He does. There may be more ways, but he, as an artist, should feel there is only one way and all his concentration and effort should be confined towards that end.

*So when two flutists don't play a work the same way, they may still both play it right?*

No.

*You mean that only one got it right?*

Maybe neither! [Laughs.] If I said that each of them could be right I wouldn't have any artistic integrity. If I know a work and I know it well, there has to be one way that's better than another.

*I would not like to go to a concert and know what to expect . . .*

I would hate to go and hear a concert where the soloist was just making up how he was going to play a certain movement. I would like to know that he had thought it out and believed very much in his interpretation and that he was teaching this piece to me. I think the easiest way to overcome nerves—not just for younger players— is to go on that stage with your music, determined to teach it to your audience. Say, "Here is a fantastic piece of music and here is the way it should be played." In that way you don't feel you are standing there being judged by them, but you are giving them a very positive picture of the music. That's the kind of performance I like to hear.

If you hear Rudolf Serkin in a concert, you know that he isn't inventing that phrase for the first time while sitting right in front of you. But if you go to many flute concerts with some prominent flute soloists, you know they are making that up when they are standing right there, and the next concert you come to will be entirely different. The argument for that is, "Well, it's always fresh!", and that's why some of these people put me off artistically. It has nothing to do with their flute playing, because those you mentioned are great flute play- ers, but artistically it's a different story.

*Nonetheless, you constantly change as a player?*

Yes.

*So there can't be one set way to play a work when you keep hearing new things?*

There can't be a set way, but you should try to find a set way to play it. The same applies to composing—I like to know that note is there because the composer thought about it, and not because he didn't have any time and just put it there.

*Have flute styles changed?*

They have changed somewhat, because there was a school of flute playing in North America that came almost exclusively from William Kincaid [Hawaiian-born teacher and prominent flutist, 1895-1967] and now we are into another generation of students who are taught by students of Kincaid, so it's more watered down. Also many more European flutists are coming to North America.

*Have there been any great technical changes in the flute?*

They are always trying. They are moving the scale all over the place and lots of things that the public doesn't know. But in the end, a good musician can play on a piece of pipe. [Laughs.]

*Are you planning for any major changes in your career?*

It's probably a bit late for me now. I'm just letting it happen to me—but sure, I would love to have a big career.

*Is it a drawback for you to be a Canadian?*

Oh sure! We instantly suffer a forty-percent discount. The minute somebody wants to hire you and hears you are Canadian, they expect you can't be as good as anyone else. Let's say that an impresario wants to put on a concert with a trio and there are three available from London, Paris and Toronto. He would definitely not take the one from Toronto even if he knew it was the best, because he has to also convince the public that it is good. Now, he can take an unknown group from Paris, London or New York and the hall will be filled.

*I thought this prejudice was mostly in Canadians' own minds . . .*

Oh, it's more in the eyes of the world. They still view us as a colony.

*Is this a result of the isolation Canadian artists have suffered in the past?*

Well, the more we go out to perform, the more things will change. The situation is the same for New Zealand and Australia. Let's say you are going to pick a group right here in Toronto and have the choice between ensembles from New Zealand, Australia, London and Paris [laughs at the irony] . . . when did you last hear Australian musicians in Toronto?

*We are even hesitant to use Torontonians at times.*

So you see, there really is a battle. We can use government money to play in other countries, but the minute they print that sponsorship in the brochure we are in trouble. Those subsidies should be hidden to make it look like we are there on our own merit and not because of government subsidies.

*Yet many Canadian musicians have made great careers abroad.*

But they didn't come back here and they didn't live here.

*Do you think you would do better if you didn't live here?*

Definitely. I should never have moved back when we lived in Switzerland and I was quite well accepted everywhere. I am not unhappy, but I was chauvinistic enough to think that I could possibly have an international career out of Canada. Now I know it isn't so.

At this moment I am in one of the best frames of mind ever. I am overworked, yes, and I could take six weeks just to answer correspondence.

*You play a wide repertoire, from early music to contemporary. Can it be confusing to play both in one concert, for example?*

No, I think it is very good to play both. I used to want to do just one or the other, but I had heard Heinz Holliger [prominent Swiss oboist] play both so well, so in that way, too, he has been a big influence on me. If you pick your contemporary pieces well, then the most staid of audiences will get very excited.

*Theoretically there is a resistance to contemporary music. In which quarters do you think it's most pronounced?*

Oh, among educators. I don't find anything negative about contemporary music. It's just a matter of getting it before their noses and then it's okay. It is very hard to get it into the schools because the teachers are very reserved.

*Children are more open to new music than they are to, say, Beethoven, because they understand the sounds.*

That is true. But on occasion when we have had a bigger hall than usual for our New Music Concerts and wanted to paper it with young people, we would phone a few teachers to offer free tickets and perhaps end up with ten students from five high schools! So I suspect the teachers themselves didn't promote it.

Once we offered a practically free concert of zippy new pieces to a music educators' conference and they turned it down. None of that really bothers me as long as the music is there for those who really want it.

*How important has New Music been to your career?*

Some people think the series has been very important in making my career, but at the moment it is the opposite. It pulls me down. I have had to turn down many important engagements to take care of the series. If I could put the energy I put into New Music into my own career, there is no telling what I might be able to do. But if you start something, you must act like a responsible person.

# Elly Ameling

To the connoisseur of lieder, Elly Ameling is the consummate artist. Wherever she appears around the world she is showered with superlatives, and her recordings are spread over a bountiful thirteen labels. Although she does sing oratorio and the occasional opera performance, lieder is her pre-eminent expression, which makes her a rare artist indeed. "Besides having a beautiful and minutely equalized voice over which she has absolute control, she projects a hundred shades of color, never sings a strained or ambiguous tone and never takes a breath at the wrong place," wrote a reviewer in *High Fidelity*. Moreover, she achieves that most delicate balance, maintaining technical perfection while keeping her songs vibrantly alive, be they her favorite German lieder and French *mélodies* or her wide and varied international repertoire.

In 1981, I had met Elly Ameling after a Schubert recital with accompanist Rudolf Jansen in Toronto. She is a small, attractive woman in her forties with dark, sparkling eyes and a ready smile. Yet she exudes a certain formality, and there is the sense that what she says is carefully considered. (She made a follow-up phone call from Washington, D.C., to make certain that a particular point had been clearly explained.) As she wraps her listener in an ambiance of detail and perfection, it becomes evident how her talent and the art of lieder were destined for each other.

Ameling is the recipient of an array of honors, among them the Knighthood of the Netherlands (her native country), the Grand Prix du Disque and Preis der Deutschen Schallplattenkritik. Still, she acknowledges with excitement that the University of British Columbia awarded her with her first honorary doctorate. Ameling has had a love affair with North America ever since her debut in 1968 at Lincoln Center in New York. She continues to tour around the world and has recently produced an all-Ravel record with pianist Rudolf Jansen and

a *Soirée Française* of *mélodies* with the Leipzig Gewandhaus Orchestra under Kurt Masur. To encourage and perpetuate the great art of lieder singing, she has established the Elly Ameling Lied Prize to be given annually at the International Vocal Competition of 'sHertogen-bosch in the Netherlands.

*Colgrass: Do you think a special kind of intelligence is required to be a lieder singer?*

Ameling: You can't be dumb, of course. [With a smile.] But I do think it requires a special kind of insight—although that sounds so intellectual—a feeling for what is possible deeply inside the soul of a human being; really deeply and in the smallest nuance. You also have to have a psychological insight when you do the role of Aida or whoever, but it is more obvious in opera and in the development of one character.

In lieder, you have so many different songs in one evening and all these songs have a different personage. Sometimes it is just in the atmosphere, the lyrical description or whatever—but most of them have a little personage in them, and you have to point out what moves this person in the smallest detail from the bottom of his heart. So I think you need a feeling for detail . . .

*. . . as well as literary interest?*

Yes. You have the music and the beautiful literature, and that makes it easier to grasp the whole thing.

*Did you develop your literary interests through lieder?*

The music came first. I have played the piano since I was six years old and I have sung Schubert since I was twelve. This opened the poetry for me. But the initial acquaintance you make with a piece— also now that I more or less know what I'm doing [laughs]—still is in its totality. I must say that I don't understand exactly what I do when I first look at a lied, but I do it . . . I play it, I sing it and intuitively revel in this experience. Here you get your inspiration which you will never lose in the time that you study and dissect the song. Some people may get stuck in the dissecting and lose the inspiration—that's a danger.

*So after the initial intuitive thrust comes the fine intellectual "tuning."*

Yes, and when I know the piece by heart, know it so well that it falls from the lips, then this thrill can come back every night. I can feel the goose-bumps when I sing a song like "Seligheit" or "Ständchen" . . . real goose-bumps!

*It is obvious that you recreate a song every time . . .*

There you come to a point where I want to react to what Glenn Gould said in your magazine. [Gould found playing in concerts "an utterly wasteful activity."] There must be other people who think the way he thinks and hopefully more people who think the way I think. It's so strange what he said about the utter waste of doing a concert with an audience, because I think there is no better place to meet for the spirits of us earthlings, and the spiritual realm where the composition was born long ago, than the moment we are all present in the flesh. We have to be present and we can't help it that we have just this flesh! What you can get under the most favorable circumstances— not always, but often—are the unseen waves, what I call the "fluidum" that comes from not only the artist, but from the audience. When those waves meet, you form a *happening*, that nice English word. You never have that with a record.

*You don't see recording as your favorite medium, then?*

No, certainly not. I love doing it because the sense of perfection is appealing. We can do it again and again. We always want it perfect, which is impossible, but the striving is beautiful.

*Do you do patch a lot, or do you use long takes?*

Well, this is a strange thing . . . the most emotional passages of a work I usually do in the first or second take and it's used as a whole. When it is something for the heart to say, it loses some of its expression if you have to do it again and again. You must do it in your imagination as if an audience were present. I remember once working with Jürg Demus at the piano and I said to him, "I don't know how to sing this moving song—there's no audience." He replied: "But Elly, I'm your most grateful audience," and that solved the problem. When you have a good crew in the control room, they can all be with you and that helps a lot—I can't be without that radiance back and forth . . .

*. . . the interaction.*

Yes, but "interaction" sounds so corporeal. What I call "fluidum" happens in spite of the fact that you don't see or hear it happen. I see very little because I wear these spectacles in daily life, so on stage I see just enough not to stumble—knock on wood! But I feel it from the first few measures if the audience is already awake, so we really do it together. It's not only from us.

*How do you feel about singing lieder in a very large hall?*

From the aspect of viewing, it is almost always a setback. As for the sound, it doesn't have to be a setback at all. Our next concert will be at the Kennedy Center which seats over three thousand, and every time I have sung there, I have felt that the audience grasped what I did in detail, right back to the last row.

*You don't feel a loss of intimacy?*

Not necessarily because of the size. There are small halls that for some reason are not communicative, not only acoustically, but for this special communication. Concertgebouw in Amsterdam, for instance, seats over two thousand, but you feel right in the middle of everybody and the audience feels very close to the person on stage.

I do think that facial expressions in a *lieder abend* or a recital of French *mélodies* are very important and people should be able to see you react. From that point of view, a large hall is always a setback.

*How do you adjust vocally to a large hall—do you project differently? And does the accompanist make adjustments as well?*

Yes, I think the accompanist always has to listen to how far the sound goes into the hall, and I think I do indeed project a little further. There are halls where I say, "Tonight I can take it easy vocally"— though never spiritually—because the sound comes out so directly. But there are larger halls where you give a little more.

*Do you think lieder singing is the most demanding form of singing in terms of energy and concentration?*

In a way yes, but in other ways no. We can go to the hall just thirty minutes beforehand, put on a simple dress and some makeup, whereas in the opera you have to be there two hours before curtain. They make you up, put on costumes . . . it takes much more time. Then you have all those lapses where you don't sing and are sitting offstage.

*In terms of concentration, though, you are always the center of attention in recitals.*

Yes, but this is very uplifting. The audience feeds you—if they are nice [laughs], and they always are on this continent. It strikes me they are so open here to beautiful music.

*Is that not the case in Europe?*

No, it is different. I think in Europe there is a certain sense of, "How good will she be?" rather than, "I come here to listen to beautiful music." I have the impression that people on this continent come to listen to beautiful Schubert, and when the singer is good, they react to that.

*But they don't compare you to yourself or others.*

That's it.

*Maybe it's because we are not so sophisticated in this part of the world?*

You can call it sophisticated or you could call it a little blasé of these Europeans! Though there are differences—it's not so much the case in London as it is in Paris.

*I can't imagine you ever having a negative audience.*

I would have to think back a long time. Again, why shouldn't they open up and listen?

I have toured Japan often and people there are different in a way

I had to get accustomed to. Like many Orientals, they don't show their feelings easily. For me, that was not easy the first time I sang there. I thought, "My God, something is wrong. Perhaps the voice is not projecting in this hall—but I feel fine, so what can it be?" Then at the end I got the real enthusiasm, and it was explained to me that they don't want to break your concentration with applause. They are so considerate.

*One thing that must be very difficult for a lieder singer is to expand into other nationalities. Not only must you learn the music and the language, but you must absorb the national characteristics. How do you master that?*

I don't know how it works, but I do know that Holland is just a borderland between two big national influences, the Latin and the German. We speak languages easily and when I was in school we had German, French and English for five years.

*How about Spanish songs?*

They are a little more remote for me. I sing them, but perhaps I should travel there more often.

*Are you interested in the other arts pertaining to those countries?*

Oh yes, I think it helps to gain a total view of a country, its art and religion. I love to travel. I was just three months on the road with accompanist Dalton Baldwin—first to the east and west coasts of America, then I stopped in Hawaii where my husband came and we had a lovely vacation; then on to Japan where we had three days in Kyoto and could see all the temples at ease. I take slides and try to make them as beautiful as possible. After that we stopped for seven days in India.

*Do you think it is possible to give an artistic expression of something that you have not developed in yourself?*

Oh yes, so much the more. I have no children because I didn't dare take that task on me, too. But in *Frauenliebe und Leben* where I sing about the child, I feel it so much. You must always consider that people sing their hearts out about what they miss and not always about what they have.

*You evidently have developed a love of children. I was referring to something you have not felt emotionally yourself.*

When you do develop in all areas I think in some way, generally, it becomes audible in what you sing—the way you give it depth. You cannot say, "She sings 'Gretchen am Spinnrade' because she has seen the pictures of Terborch"—it's not that explicit. But an overall depth dimension is added to your performance.

*The recital world has diminished somewhat in recent years.*

There are fewer recital singers. Where is the golden time of the young Schwarzkopf, the young Seefried together with Souzay and the young Pears and Fischer-Dieskau?

*Does that worry you?*

A little, but not too much because they have said, "The art of the lied is dead" for fifty or sixty years. I don't want to sound proud, but how can this be when the halls are full and people do come to hear the lieder? You see the interest in it from the younger singers who come to master classes and have a real wish to be good at it. They study the languages, which on this continent is not so easy. There are great talents among those young singers. So maybe we are going through a narrow passage with not too many lieder singers. It could be because we live in a time of total disorientation. We are in every aspect in a vacuum, economically, politically—there is a big question mark about everything. So it is not so logical that people will look for the small detail—they go easier for the more obvious big orchestras, big opera. With a time of restfulness there might come a return to lieder.

*Don't you also feel that the art of the lied flowered in the nineteenth century when literature reached a high emotional peak that spilled over into the songs? For us today that's almost distasteful, because we are so reserved and cut off from extrovert emotions.*

That could very well be. Right after the war in the fifties and early sixties, there was great attention paid to lieder because most people were not yet so spoiled. They wanted to go into the details of the poetry.

Now the big opera houses have concerts where the opera stars perform so-called lieder recitals, but what he or she sings is mostly arias with piano accompaniment. That, of course, disturbs and spoils the taste of people, and the young people who have not yet formed their tastes hear these flop-flop-flop piano accompaniments. It is not beautiful, of course—it should be sung with an orchestra.

*Was there a good climate in Holland for your art when you started out?*

Yes, certainly. I do think the Dutch have a great attention for detail. Look at our pictures! The seventeenth-century paintings have great inner radiance. You can hardly call Rembrandt's pictures miniature, but they have an attention to detail. We are all great admirers of chamber music.

My studies in Holland were short, maybe only three years, but I was very lucky to have a good teacher, an old lady [Jacoba Dresden] for vocal studies. After forty-five minutes of technique, she would go to the door and call: "Father, can you come for a moment?" and her husband [Sam Dresden] would come and teach me the principles of

Debussy, Mozart, Rachmaninoff and a great many other composers. He pointed out exactly how to follow a composer, how to read behind the notes—but for only two years and that was about enough.

I don't give many master classes, but sometimes I see people who have been studying for years and years, and I think, "My God, go on the stage and do it! That's where you get the real experience." My first accompanist was Jürg Demus who is, of course, very much a solo pianist. He brought his approach to the art of the lied from his instrumental point of view. It was very important for me to learn how important the piano part is. Demus also developed in me a sense of poetry and the nuances in the German language.

Dalton Baldwin, whom I also work with, gave me a sense of French music. In those days I was still very energetic in my way of singing, but Baldwin radiates such calm love and he made me able to relax enough to get the feeling for singing a cradle song. You do the real learning with your colleagues. Then, of course, I've toured with Erwin Gage and Rudolf Jansen. If I sing a tone a certain way, it's very strange with Rudolf, he knows how I'll do the next one and when I'll bring it.

*Do you learn new songs by yourself at the keyboard?*

Yes, you must be able to play yourself, perhaps not perfectly, but enough to see what's in the notes.

*Have you had accompanists that you didn't feel that comfortable with?*

Those that I mentioned here I feel very comfortable with. I like to give them all the space to have their say, because nothing is more uninteresting than the kind of singer who says, "I'm doing this and I want you to follow me!"—because if you follow me, you are already too late, it can't be done. I think the accompanist must have the space to take his own chance and when he does that in a beautifully inspiring way, then I can answer him and both of us fly higher and higher. If you don't take any risks, people say, "She was perfect, but we weren't excited." Then better do something wrong.

*What happens when you forget the text?*

You do sometimes forget the text, especially in these constructions of German poetry, but you just sing whatever comes out of your mouth because you always have the melodic line to hold on to. But I have never had a total blackout, knock on wood!

*That special soaring quality you have in the upper tessitura, is that a gift from nature or is it something you have developed to gain that riveting musical expression?*

The expression you want is given to you by your mind, by the soul, and then at last, hopefully, you will soar like that. I don't think I could always do that. When I studied, I really struggled to develop that. I hear from people, and I hope it's true, that the deeper voice is coming along now—that comes with age.

*How do you keep body and soul together when you travel so much?*

Soul is easy. If you look for beauty, you'll find it anywhere. I was at the Van Gogh exhibit today where I had too little time, but I could still drink some in. I walk a lot and avoid taking taxis—and I wouldn't miss my cold shower in the morning, although some people think it is uncivilized. [Laughs.] I replenish in the simple nature where I live— you know the flat country with the windmills [between Amsterdam and Rotterdam]; there is a little stream by the house and a big piece of grassland where I roam with the dogs.

*Is your husband in the arts?*

No, he's not. He does everything that I need when I'm home or away from home, so he makes everything possible.

*He is your manager?*

No, not manager, but he takes good care of me. I'm very fortunate, because not every husband would be content with his wife being away sometimes for three months at a stretch.

*He must admire greatly what you do.*

I think he does, although he doesn't say it often and I think that is right, too.

*You don't seem to be a nervous person—do you ever suffer from nerves?*

Real nerves? No, as a performer I don't know what it is. I'm so lucky. Of course, I do think you have to be so concentrated that you can't be nervous. You have to be very well organized before a concert—here is my comb, there's my brush, here's the lipstick, there's the banana that I eat before a concert, there's the hot tea. There is so much to do that there is no time to be nervous. But I must say I'm kind of tense like a horse before the jump, and that is good because without that tension I would feel flat and nothing would come out.

# Istvan Anhalt

A dreamily introspective person, Istvan Anhalt is on solid ground when it comes to composing. His early works were firmly rooted in serial technique, but his curiosity about new expressions, such as electronic music, has freed him from any one stylistic harness. Anhalt, who was born in Budapest in 1919, was a student of Zoltan Kodály; although he sincerely admires the famous scholar and composer, he has avoided the folksy or temperamental traces that sometimes flavor Hungarian music. He also composed and studied at the Royal Hungarian Academy, and for a while was assistant conductor at the Hungarian National Opera House. He arrived on these shores in 1949, and now follows his own intense, lyrical temperament. He has written some twenty finely crafted works and his latest compositions, done since our interview (at his home in Kingston, Ontario, in 1980), are of increasingly lush textures and grand scope. Among them are his "interior operas," based on interesting personalities of the past, but involving no visual effects or action onstage. "They are really like historical pageants. The music is very dramatic and you have to imagine the events," he explains.

Anhalt is a small, precise man with a gentle nature and a touch of sadness in his eyes. Fortunately his lively intellect makes way for a warm sense of humor that allows him to laugh easily at his own foibles. And Beatrice, his delightful wife, undoubtedly lightens his serious temperament.

Anhalt creates his highly personal musical world by meticulously compiling and polishing the fine details of his work. The result is often sombre music, densely textured and burning with characteristic intensity. His early works in the 1950s were for orchestra or chamber ensembles, and less complex than the later compositions using pre-recorded tape and voices. Seven works are recorded on RCI and Columbia Records.

At the time of this interview Anhalt had already been working for five years on an elaborate work entitled *Winthrop* after its main character, the visionary first governor of Massachusetts, John Winthrop. The main reason for the long gestation was Anhalt's duties at Queen's University, where he was head of the music department from 1971 to 1981 (he retired in 1984). By 1983, the completed score to *Winthrop* had grown to two-and-a-half hours of musical drama for symphony orchestra, two choirs and a cast of six singers. It was performed in the fall of 1986 by the always adventurous Raffi Armenian conducting his Kitchener-Waterloo Symphony Orchestra. Word must have spread, because the hall was packed with the musical cognoscenti from far and wide.

It is worth noting that Anhalt has escalated his output since he became a full-time composer. Although his 1983 book *Alternative Voices* received fine notices in academic circles, he won't spend time writing another. However, he happily writes poetry and texts for his own works, such as his recent duo-drama for soprano and piano called *Thisness*, built on nine poems. A recent orchestral work, *Similacrum*, has already been played by several orchestras.

*Colgrass: What motivated you in your youth?*

Anhalt: For a long time I was very envious of those boys who belonged, who were not Jewish, not persecuted, but simply accepted as belonging to the majority, sharing a historical past and the symbols of Hungarian history. They were the ins, I was the out. I have never really received a Jewish education, so I couldn't even pit my Jewishness against them. I only had little myself, so I had to develop little myself.

*Unlike many well-known Jewish musicians, you didn't escape to North America at the beginning of the Second World War.*

I would have liked to leave as well, but I was trapped. I was in my early twenties and had no money, so I ended up in a forced-labor camp, digging ditches, unloading grain, chopping wood and building some ridiculous fortifications that were supposed to stop the Russian tanks. They did nothing of the sort and the Russians must have laughed.

*But you managed to survive with both your health and sanity intact?*

I was mad as hell and scared—also resentful. I thought it was the worst possible place to be, but after the war when I heard of the British soldiers marching through the jungles of Burma, American soldiers having to storm Iwo Jima, and the concentration camps, I realized we were quite well off. We had two or three meals a day— not much, but something.

When the war was over I felt such an incredible relief. I was twenty-six and found life beautiful. I just had to write something jubilant because I survived. But what came out was, according to others, terribly sad and brooding. I couldn't understand that. My pieces had to do with death, like *Three Songs of Death* and *Funeral Music*.

*Can you explain your creative process?*

The antenna is a beautiful metaphor to me. I don't know how a composition happens, but the sensors bring information. I have no explanation for that and I'm quite happy that I don't.

*That might remove the magic?*

Those unexplainable impulses or happy accidents can be the most exciting. Once I was looking for something simple and dreamed about practicing Czerny's études as a boy. That was the clue and I'm grateful for it.

*It must have been difficult to work as a teacher and administrator while you're composing.*

If I don't find time to compose, I get so nervous and unhappy. On the other hand, nothing is more stimulating for a teacher than a student who looks at him with a blank face.

*Why didn't you pursue a career in conducting?*

Who doesn't want to conduct? [Laughter.] Waving a stick and playing God! It's easy up to a point, but to know the scores inside out and hear everything is a tremendous effort. A conductor also has to keep abreast with new repertoire.

*Including contemporary?*

Oh yes, although I must qualify this—I'm speaking of an ideal conductor. He ought to learn. We are all specialists in a way, and a conductor might say: I'm specializing in the nineteenth-century repertoire and there is so much to do that there is no time for other things. So I can't set an impossible task for them. Only a few lucky ones are able to interpret a very catholic repertoire.

*You studied with both Kodály and Nadia Boulanger. . .*

Kodály was very aloof, almost to the extent of being unapproachable, but he was a great man and a profound scholar. Boulanger was entirely different. She was very approachable, very warm, understanding and interested in the students. The great musical mother.

*How did you become interested in electronic music?*

I heard a broadcast in 1954 with a few compositions by Stockhausen for the electronic medium. The sounds were really unlike anything I had heard before, not only the physical beauty of the sounds but the effective range that explored some realm or feeling in music that I thought had not been explored elsewhere. I thought: what a privilege it must be to work with these marvelous machines. One must be a mathematician, an engineer, a physicist and composer all rolled into one. I thought I had to find out about what I imagined to be a huge room full of equipment.

*Where did you study?*

With Stockhausen in Cologne. I was led into a room [Stockhausen's studio inside a radio station] which was not much larger than our bathroom and I asked: where are the machines? The assistant explained that they had three tape recorders, two oscillators and a few disheveled old bits in a box. So I realized that those sounds were really produced by enormous labor and not by the machine.

*Later you studied electronic music at the National Research Centre in Ottawa and the Columbia-Princeton Electronic Music Center in New York, even established an electronic music studio at McGill University. You must have been pretty dedicated.*

I found out about cutting tape into little bits and spending hours and hours splicing them together. [With a forlorn smile.]

While I was working with electronic music, I received a letter from a professor of psychiatry that said: "Dear Mr. Anhalt, I understand that you are a composer of electronic music. I'm working with some mental patients and I need some stimuli that will disorient them. Could you send them some of your music?" I did send him some, but never found out the effect.

After I learned how to make these machines work for me, I accepted that I could write for the electronic medium, for an orchestra, a violin or voices, and I could combine them all, as I have. While I'm a bit sceptical, I think it might be possible to program a computer to generate some kind of music.

*Does a faithful adherence to the twelve-tone row act as a straight-jacket for a composer?*

It seems to me that we are structuring our lives according to certain programs, accepting the rules. These allow us to behave in a certain way and impart a certain order. Now this doesn't mean that it's a straight-jacket. In the same way, the twelve-tone system is one kind of constraint which a composer creates for himself artificially. We could create half a dozen other constraints that would allow him to impart a certain personality in his composition.

I could compare the pure twelve-tone system to a monastic order where people work for the same purpose and adhere to the same theology. They choose to exclude a tremendous amount of stimuli from their lives for the sake of this simpler, different kind of existence. The musical analogue would be to listen to a Webern piece, an austere, short, rigorously constructed serial work—for most people probably not for an ordinary dinner but for an occasional lean breakfast.

*Is there more freedom of musical expression today?*

Freedom leaves the question begging. Does it mean there is no system and no constraints? The answer in my opinion is no, there are even more complicated constraints, a whole counterpoint of constraints.

*What was it like, being an immigrant in Canada?*

I immediately felt very good here. At that time there was no flag, no national anthem that everybody could sing. Also, people made fun of nationalism in those days, which was very refreshing, and I felt that nobody could really do any harm to me under these conditions.

There is probably more vigor because many of us had to start anew. I felt that I could make something, and that's a good feeling.

*Recently you've been using history as a catalyst in composing. How did that happen?*

John Roberts, then of the CBC, asked me to write a work with the theme of man's search for order in life through the focus of religion. Very specific. I thought, my God, he must have sent the letter to the wrong composer. [Laughter.]

*What made you select Marie de l'Incarnation?*

She established a Catholic order in Quebec in 1639, but she was also a mystic, a business woman, a writer and a doer. This woman, who was a mother, wife and widow as well, left everything behind in France and went to the end of the world—yes, Canada was really the end of the world in those days. Now did she leave because of self-realization or a sense of mission? I'm interested in people who go somewhere new, which is the visible part of seeking something.

There are some people who have utopian ideas that they attempt to reconcile with their personal ambition. You might say they are people who would like to save the world—well, perhaps not quite that foolish, but they try to make an input.

[The resulting hour-long work, *La Tourangelle*, was premiered in 1975. It is scored for chamber orchestra, five singers and tape, with a text assembled by Anhalt from the subject's own writing and from contemporary documents.]

*What drew you to John Winthrop?*

I thought I would like to write about an English Protestant, a puritan, who settled in America and Canada in the early seventeenth century. John Winthrop was a very interesting man, also a mystic and a seeker with a utopian vision. He established a community in the Maritimes and wanted to do good and improve conditions for everybody—make a model for the future. Yet within a few short years he became an oppressor, the establishment, the King. He prosecuted people who didn't conform, and to be expelled at that time in North America was a very perilous business—it was a wilderness, a bush.

That, of course, posits another question: is there such a place as an ideal society that will satisfy everyone? Is one forced into oppressing people with dissimilar views? That's where the tragedy lies.

*Finally, what are you working on now?*

I have another orchestral work on the drawing board right now. Its called *Sparkskraps*. [Chuckle and significant pause.] Have you spelled that backwards yet?

# James Campbell

When I met clarinetist James Campbell in 1984, he was in his mid-thirties and had played more than a thousand concerts around the world as soloist with orchestras or as a chamber player. Yet when asked to pinpoint the time when it became clear to him that he had joined the upper echelon of musicians, he said, "I'm still trying to realize it. Fortunately, as your reputation builds, so do your standards and your desires—not in terms of fame and career advancement, but in terms of music and development. I'm certainly by no means finished. I feel I'm just beginning, really. Maybe I know a little bit about the clarinet repertoire by now."

This may sound overly modest from a musician who replaced an ailing Benny Goodman in a series of concerts with the Amadeus Quartet and was described by Terry McQuilkin of the *Los Angeles Times* as "an extraordinary clarinetist. His creamy, bright sound and ample vibrato remind one of some British players, but his superb control, smooth technique and immaculate phrasing mark the Canadian as an international virtuoso." Spanish newspapers pronounced him "one of the great clarinetists of our time" when he played a Weber clarinet concerto with the Spanish National Radio-Television Orchestra for broadcasting throughout Europe. And Paule Tran wrote about Campbell in the Belgian newspaper *La Libre Belgique*: "He blends fluid technique, a line as natural as breathing, and superb, precise articulation with irreproachable musicality."

Campbell has become known for his superb collaborations with famous chamber players—the Orford, Amadeus, Guarneri and Allegri quartets, the Borodin Trio and, of course, the Camerata ensemble that he founded with five Toronto friends when he was just twenty-two years old. Camerata was appreciated not only for its high standards but for its innovative programming and youthful exuberance. As an added bonus from Camerata, Campbell met his wife who came

from England to manage the group. Later, he formed the ensemble Da Camera along with violinist Moshe Hammer, pianist William Tritt and cellist Tsuyoshi Tsutsumi, and they still perform on rare occasions. He has played in twenty countries in major halls, but did not find the right venue for his New York debut until 1986 when he was invited to Town Hall with his friends from Da Camera. Now he plays more in the U.S.A. than in Canada, and New York management is in the offing.

After years of listening to James Campbell's fluid, refined sound, I was eager to get to know him. He has a slightly austere stage appearance and always seems in total control during concerts, so I anticipated a somewhat formal person with careful responses to my questions. Instead I found a relaxed and informal young man who had just returned from a long stint at the Festival of the Sound at Parry Sound, Ontario. He was chatting cheerfully between bites on a sandwich in the kitchen of his comfortable home in the Beaches of Toronto, where he lives with his wife Carol and daughter. (The family has since added a son.)

Since our meeting, Campbell has won a Juno for his album of light repertoire, *Stolen Gems*, and he has produced a stream of recordings on several labels (during one month last spring he did five!). He has expanded into jazz of the Swing era in collaboration with pianist Gene DiNovi. The University of Indiana in Bloomington has enticed him to join its distinguished faculty, though Campbell wants to try it out first during a year as visiting professor of clarinet. He wants to make certain that such a move will not hamper his concert career.

During our meeting, there was a suitcase to be packed for a three-week trip to China, starting the following morning, and one more interview to be squeezed in. The excitement of seeing China for the first time was the immediate subject of conversation. Campbell had been asked by the Canada Council to put together a group of musicians to give master classes and eight concerts in Beijing, Guangdong and Wuhan. But the China tour is just one of many plums that have fallen to James Campbell in his brief career. He seems mildly surprised at the unusual turns his life has taken since he first picked up the clarinet to join the school band in his small home town of Leduc south of Edmonton. His family was a musical one, with his father singing in the local choir and his mother playing in the church where her mother had been organist before her.

*Colgrass: Did you always know you wanted to be a musician, even when you were growing up on the farm?*

Campbell: I feel that in my career most things have happened to me, so I can't tell exactly when I knew that I was a musician. When you are raised in a small town, you don't really know what is out there.

I had to get up at six to feed the calves, even in the winter. But I would always do it quickly to come back to practice the clarinet. Playing was easy and that appealed to me. My parents were very supportive, even when it became quite clear that I was not destined to take over the family farm.

I certainly wasn't a child prodigy. They worry me anyway because they sometimes start to associate success with being loved, and that is a dangerous connection. Feeling loved by being on stage with people applauding you is the old clown syndrome. To this day my parents and family think of my work: "That's nice, we like it, but it's not the be all and end all."

*You received a degree in music education from the University of Toronto . . .*

Because of this degree I have learned to superficially play a number of instruments. It was helpful in developing an ear for color, although playing the trombone doesn't help your clarinet embouchure, but it does make you think like a trombonist.

My goals have changed along with the opportunities that were offered me. Just as I began to think that it might be nice to get a job in an orchestra, the solo offers started to come in. So I thought, "I'll do this for a while and then I'll get serious." Well, I'm still doing it. [With a laugh.]

*And while you were a student, one of your solo engagements came from Glenn Gould.*

He may have heard me on the radio. Although he wasn't playing in public, he knew what was going on and what everybody was doing.

*You did some TV concerts with him. What was it like?*

Working with him was the biggest thrill of my life. I don't really want to talk about Gould too much, because everybody seems to have a story about him and wants to benefit from his reflected glory. I will just tell you that our first rehearsal took place over the telephone—no instruments involved—as we sang Debussy's *Première Rapsodie* back and forth to each other. Just playing with him and experiencing his strength was exhilarating, and I liked him very much as a person. [Campbell was offered a place in the orchestra that Gould set out to conduct shortly before he died in 1982, but turned it down for lack of time.]

*It's unusual that you formed your own group [Camerata] when you were only twenty-two.*

It was very lucky, because there is a difficult period just after you finish school. Because of Camerata I didn't suffer these traumas. It was terrific, it was fun. We learned together and it shaped all our careers.

*And then you formed Da Camera.*

Chamber music is really the heart of my playing, more so than solo work. Soloing is great for the ego and brings in higher fees, but chamber music is more challenging.

*Camerata was admired not only for its high standards but also for its innovative programming. Do you think musicians have enough influence on the programming of concerts?*

Here you have to make a distinction between commercial success and artistic success. Both are necessary, but not synonymous. However, the concert organizers have their business to run and have to think commercially. It is a very big business, and I would like artists to have more to say without taking over completely. Of course, nobody can make you play something you don't want to play unless you care only about money, in which case you'll play anything.

*Do you think that luck plays a part in building a career? Being in the right place at the right time . . .*

Last season I happened to be booked with the Amadeus Quartet to play the Brahms Quintet at Roy Thomson Hall in Toronto. Benny Goodman was supposed to play with them the following week in Los Angeles and San Francisco, but he canceled because of illness. That was my luck. However, the woman who booked the Quartet into Davies Symphony Hall in San Francisco wasn't so sure—after all, there are three thousand seats to fill and I'm not known like Benny Goodman—so she flew over to hear me play with the Borodin Trio in Stanford, California. All these events led to my San Francisco debut.

*I heard the Trio got snowbound, and you went on with very little rehearsal time.*

There you do the best you can. We rehearsed till midnight. The concert could probably have been better, but it was adequate because they were very experienced musicians. Sometimes such circumstances can make for a better performance, more spontaneous. But I wouldn't want to make a record that way.

When one rehearsal is all you get, you prepare by studying the score so you know where to listen and what to listen for. In chamber music, that is the most important thing. I often play the Mozart or Brahms quintets with established string quartets. We all know these works well and one rehearsal is often all we get. On the other hand, it is possible to over-rehearse.

*Has touring changed your attitude towards your work?*

It has given me more confidence. I know now that I can play with anybody.

*The clarinet doesn't figure prominently among solo instruments even with your catholic repertoire. Is this an obstacle?*

At this stage I find that my management has to sell the clarinet more than me. Of course the repertoire is nothing like the violin repertoire. If there were twenty-four clarinet concertos by Mozart then you would see clarinet players touring the world. The flute, of course, has become very popular, but that is not because of its repertoire, which is worse than ours. It has happened because of personalities, with Jean-Pierre Rampal blazing the way and now James Galway. Richard Stoltzman is doing very well for the clarinet and I'm glad he is out there.

*Do you play all the standard repertoire for clarinet? Didn't you once say you hated Carl Nielsen's Clarinet Concerto?*

I loathe that piece. Well, maybe that is too strong, but I don't like it well enough to learn it. [He has presumably modified his stance, as he has since played the work with the London Symphony in Ontario.]

*Historically the clarinet covers a wide territory—jazz and ethnic music . . .*

I admire the gypsy clarinet players from Hungary. They really rip into the music and I love to hear them play—for about ten minutes. [With a laugh.]

*Who is your favorite classical performer?*

Harold Wright [first clarinetist of the Boston Symphony Orchestra]. He seems to be able to do almost anything, but he is such a self-effacing guy that few people have heard of him.

*You've searched beyond the conventional clarinet training.*

The control, including breathing, really starts in the ear. But there are important techniques, and probably the biggest change happened when I began working with M. Cohen-Nehemia who opened up a lot of technique by teaching me the Alexander Method. It involves controling the quality of breath and freeing the muscles so that I am not working against myself. By manipulating the body of a player the strangest things can happen to change the sound. It's something I have been using in my workshops, which I call The Sound of the Body.

What you hear in your head goes into the clarinet, not the other way around. It doesn't work for me to duplicate what other people play. In fact, most of my work takes place away from the clarinet, studying the score. I try to get in the ear what I want to hear, so that when I pick up the clarinet I go for it. I enjoy the luxury of not having to conform to a particular sound, as many orchestra players must in order to fit in.

I'm not really interested in the clarinet as an instrument—fixing reeds, worrying about how this and that key goes. There are clarinet conferences where these technical matters have gotten to be almost a mania.

*What about building stamina and psychological well-being?*

The psychological aspects are probably more important than stamina. For the few minutes you are playing onstage, convince yourself that you are the best in the world, and afterwards congratulate yourself. This is common practice among athletes to maintain a good psychological state. Then the next day when you are rehearsing, you know that you have to strive to be better.

I found that if musicians get nervous to the point of ruining a performance, it's because they are so concerned about what people think of them. But if you can become really immersed in the music and think instead, "What can I give them?" then it becomes a question of giving rather than a judgment. This is when you can give your best.

*Why did you decide to replace Anton Kuerti as director of the Festival of the Sound?*

I'm doing it to learn. My measurement of success is: can I grow? That is my only yardstick—not financial reward or fame. When you are twenty you want to be famous, but as you mature the internal growth as an artist becomes most important.

*Has being Canadian influenced your career in any way?*

People may say that they are not appreciated in their own country, but that is not my case. Being a Canadian soloist is advantageous in many ways. I have gotten plenty of support from the Canada Council and from our music community, which is so small that everybody knows everybody. Where would we be without the CBC? And now I'm going to China thanks to External Affairs. The disadvantages of being Canadian occur when, for example, an Australian music director gets a brochure from a German clarinetist and one from a Canadian. Chances are that they will choose the German.

That doesn't mean that people's minds are closed. Once I play somewhere, there is no problem and I'm often invited back. If you play well, people really don't care where you come from. Canadians seem more concerned than anyone else about nationality. Why, I just heard an announcement on the radio about an upcoming festival in Edmonton which said, "Appearing will be Canadian and international artists." I don't think they mean to put Canadians down, but it is ghettoizing. I like to think of all musicians as belonging to one musical community.

*How can you enjoy a family with a growing career like yours?*

It is as important to me as music. There is as much work going on in the family as there is in my career outside. I'm glad that women's lib started about ten years ago and that we are now beginning to see the results. It's freeing men as well. Bringing up children is wonderful and I don't know why anyone would want to miss it.

I look at my family background and see very few people who ever worked for someone. I think that is deeply instilled in me. I balance out the busy periods with the dry spells and sometimes say no to engagements that interfere with my family life. There are more important things than the material.

# Kyung Wha Chung

Kyung Wha Chung was sent from her home in Seoul, Korea, to New York's Juilliard School of Music when she was just thirteen years old. While studying with the renowned violin teacher Ivan Galamian, she convinced him that she would not "run off with boys at age sixteen," as he had predicted. Instead she excelled in chamber music with her fellow students Itzhak Perlman and Pinchas Zukerman. Her stepping-stone to world-wide acclaim was the first prize in the Leventritt Competition in 1967, which was such a bumper year in young talent that she shared the prize with Zukerman. A spectacular debut in London, performing the Tchaikovsky Violin Concerto with André Previn and the London Symphony Orchestra, launched her international career. Within three days, thirty concerts were booked throughout Britain, ten in London alone. Her many records on the London label bear witness to her artistry in concertos, solo and chamber music.

Twenty years have flown by since Miss Chung's career was launched. She has grown as an artist, but looks as young and exotically beautiful as ever. After concentrating on her career for many years, she married quite late and now enjoys family life in Chelsea with her husband, an English businessman, and their young son. When this interview took place in 1984, she was pregnant and had just performed with the Toronto Symphony wearing a beautiful gown that she had made herself, to make certain that she would look elegant. She did. On her next return visit, she had baby and nanny in the dressing room, as she had told me she would. But whether she can combine her status as the foremost female violinist of her generation with the creation of a new little chamber group of Chungs remains to be seen. She comes from a large family that is rich in musical talent. The Chung children were among the first in a wave of Oriental musicians who now enrich our musical life: conductor Myung Whun Chung, cellist

Myung Wha Chung, and flutist Myung So Chung, in addition to Kyung Wha.

*Colgrass: Can you solve for me the mystery of name-giving in Korea? It appears that your brother and sisters have the same first name.*

Chung: Six of us have the same first name. In large families we often give all the children the same first name or else the same middle name. The combination determines whether the name is male or female. We were seven children in my family.

*Did you all play?*

At first, yes, but only four of us became professionals. My mother played both the guitar and piano.

*How did that influence you?*

We were very close, played together and openly criticized each other's playing. It was never a question of unpleasant competition if one of us did especially well, nor was there jealousy in any way. It was extremely constructive.

*How are you placed in age?*

My cellist sister, who lives in Rome, is the oldest; I'm second and my brother, who conducts and lives in Paris, is next. My younger sister, the flutist, lives in Los Angeles.

*Did you give concerts as a child?*

Yes, I started very young. I first played in public after I had studied the violin for two weeks. [Smiles at the memory.] I was playing a few songs by ear, and as I faced a thousand kids in the school auditorium I thought, "My goodness, this is what I want to do!" My first real performance was in a young people's concert with the Seoul Philharmonic when I was eight years old.

*When you came the great distance from Seoul to New York City to study at Juilliard, did your entire family move?*

No, my parents first sent the two oldest children—the older brother who didn't want to pursue music and went to MIT and my flutist sister who went to Juilliard. I was next in line [in 1961], along with my cellist sister.

*It must have been quite a project to educate children so far from home.*

It was actually very, very brave of my parents to send us. I was only thirteen years old then. Eventually the rest of my family emigrated and settled in Seattle.

*How was music education in Korea at that time?*

Well, the reason they decided to send us to America was that the situation in Korea was limited. My mother knew I was very gifted. I was determined to study with the best and actually requested to go to Paris before I was nine years old—I was so serious about playing.

*You studied with Ivan Galamian at Juilliard, a man who nurtured many great violinists.*

I have gone through several stages of development by now, but Galamian [1903-81] remains the most important influence. You see, when I was a child it was very important for me to become a famous star; I imagined myself standing on a beautiful stage, playing my heart out to thousands of people. But like all childhood fantasies it faded. Mr. Galamian gave me that solid foundation. He taught me the essentials of how to handle the instrument in the sense that technique serves to make beautiful music. He didn't just devise a method and stay with it for years, but always revised as he went along.

*He was not a performer himself.*

No, and maybe that was why he never affected a gifted player's personality. For someone who had never been on stage, he still knew what worked, and for him projection was terribly important.

*Was he tough?*

Oh yes, he was a very tough disciplinarian. He used to make me cry during lessons, and at the end of the lesson he would pretend he hadn't noticed it. At the same time he had infinite patience.

That was a fascinating time at Juilliard because we had a wonderful group of students—Pinchas Zukerman, Itzhak Perlman, James Buswell, Young Uck Kim and so on. We all played chamber music together under the guidance of Josef Gingold. Hal Makanuski, a fantastic player and musician, taught me contemporary music, which Galamian didn't teach; he concentrated more on the violin repertoire.

*Are there other guardian angels in your career?*

Yes, I studied with Joseph Szigeti up till the time I played in the Leventritt Competition, and it was a fascinating experience. He opened me musically. It was the most shocking eye-opener to be around Szigeti. He was such a thorough musician, not just knowledgeable in music, but in art and literature and other fields. He would incorporate everything and taught me that everything is related. Before that, I concentrated on learning to play the violin and playing it brilliantly, but that is not enough.

*Isn't that the Juilliard approach?*

Not just Juilliard—it's the American approach to develop a brilliant technique. It is a sort of Heifetz and Horowitz disease that Americans have. But one must realize that Horowitz and Heifetz have European culture in their system. For a young player it is essential to get a strong flavor of Europe.

*This great specialization and exclusion of other aspects of life is common to many professions in North America.*

That's right, but I'm encouraging players to expand their world. Having the skill to play an instrument is terribly important and it can be learned only when one is very young. Physically it's impossible to wait. But to become an artist and to find happiness, the child must have a wider view.

When I went to Szigeti, I felt like I had fallen into a bottomless pit. I realized that the world is full of artistic riches and became terribly depressed because all my efforts so far seemed not even like the minutest beginning. Where was I going to start? I felt so terribly limited and at one point thought of giving it all up.

*So what did you do?*

Because I was so impatient, depression took over. But looking back I'm rather proud to say that I'm slowly learning patience. I started by doing simple things, like opening up a score. Previously, when I studied the Tchaikovsky Violin Concerto I never once looked at the orchestral score.

*Didn't they teach you to study scores at Juilliard?*

No, the training there was concentrated on playing the right notes most brilliantly. I find that the Juilliard kids today are very knowledgeable about what managements exist, what recording companies and other commercial arrangements. It's quite shocking. When I grew up there, we were much more sheltered and innocent.

*I understand that you, your brother and cellist sister have started your own school of music in Monticello, New York.*

That was quite spontaneous. In our family, when we decide to do something it has to be done right then and there, and these things should probably be planned much more carefully. We all had a full schedule when we decided in 1982 to have a summer school. The family put everything together at the last minute and opened the school in upstate New York with twenty-five students.

What it takes an experienced teacher a few minutes to say may take me half an hour. I was experimenting and had so many ideas. If I had four students to teach in a morning, I would end up teaching one—it was terribly exhausting. Also, by teaching the whole summer I was hardly able to prepare the program for the coming season.

*Are you particularly interested in teaching?*

I never thought I could be so interested. I have been asked in the past if I would ever teach and said, "Absolutely not." It is a completely different field.

*A great performer is not necessarily a good teacher.*

That's right. But teaching is so rewarding. As I grow older I'll probably do more.

*Do you ever feel pressured by being a commercial entity?*

Yes, but in the beginning of your career there are certain things you can't dictate, so you have to go along. But I have several times said, "Truly, I'm not prepared to do these works at this point." I was considered a very conceited young girl, because I dared turn down such honorable engagements. Now, if I had played something I wasn't ready for, I would have felt I was cheating—not only other people, but most of all myself. I would sometimes have nightmares that I would make a complete fool of myself. So I lived under a tremendous amount of pressure.

Of course, my attitude affected my professional life. Music directors would say bad things about me. But only time takes care of that. Ten years later they have nothing to say—what can they say?

*You have amply proven youself.*

I have. And I have never turned down a concert date for superficial reasons. A manager might say, "This is too terribly important, you must do it." If I feel that it is so convincingly important to play that engagement, then I'll give my utmost to somehow come up to that level. A lot of times such a situation can actually be beneficial, because you have to drive yourself.

*So your early success was a mixed blessing?*

Well, it is never like it looks. When you make your debut and everything goes well, you are the most recent news and are booked immediately. That was one of the hardest times of my life, because there was pressure every time I made my debut in a different country with a different orchestra. Even more difficult was my second engagement in London, for instance. I was completely paralyzed, because everybody was there. At my debut I didn't realize it was supposed to be so hard, so I just played.

As far as public recognition is concerned, I soon realized what a superficial aspect this is to a career. The minute I received the first prize at the Leventritt Competition, my idea of this being the ultimate success disappeared . . . the bubble burst and nothing existed. Finally you learn, little by little, when you have succeeded in combining the cultural and the physical in playing. Some people are tremendously good at the technical side. Everybody is built differently—and this violin is a terribly awkward instrument!

*You don't seem bothered by that. In fact, you seem to fuse with the instrument and play with a natural assertiveness.*

I'm not at all aware of my style. Only when I walk on the stage at Carnegie or Avery Fisher Hall I say to myself, "Here I am walking on stage in New York where I grew up and suffered all these fears about whether I could succeed."

*Does it get easier as you get older?*

No, but psychologically it gets more stimulating to work. In my twenties and teens it was more physical. There will come a time when everything blends and a totally different plateau is reached.

*Have you always toured alone?*

Always. Looking back on my life, I don't know how I did it. Yet I never felt lonely and I love my profession. I don't get any more depressed than people who sit in their office eight hours a day—that must be terribly boring. But nothing is easy, and I have my difficult moments.

*While touring, do you have time for making friends?*

Basically, I'm not very sociable. I keep in close touch with very few people, mostly my family. I used to think that I would never get married because I saw no way of blending it with my career. All my life I have acted by gut feeling—that has been essential—but when I met my husband I realized that this could work. I was ready for a change, because I was tired of just thinking about myself. As an artist you have to know yourself and how you function. When you are on stage you can't say, "Ladies and Gentlemen, I'm terribly sorry . . . ." I have to present the music, so I have always been thinking about myself. Now the idea of having a family is terribly exciting and I look forward to someday traveling with my children.

*How can you plan for family life when you are booked years in advance?*

I dislike very much to plan years ahead, and I'm now talking with my management about reducing my number of concerts to a drastic degree. Some people find it very comforting to be booked four years from now, but how do you know that's what you'll feel like doing?

*Yet this long-range planning seems built into a high-level career . . .*

I hate the idea that a career is controlling my life. It should certainly be the other way around, once you have proved your worth as a performer.

I used to think it was terribly special to be creative—as a composer, a writer and so on—because as a performer I really feel that we are just filling the gap. I know that when I perform, people do appreciate it and enjoy it. For the next generation there will be another performer to fill that gap. A composer, on the other hand, is forever living. I don't believe that performers are the most important. All I believe is that I have a certain talent and that I always crave to express it. If I don't stand on the stage for a while there is some frustration, which means I'm a born performer.

The rest of me also has to be satisfied. I am a very private person and I have some very ordinary interests—I sew, I cook, I knit, everything that female instinct supposedly dictates. In my new life I'm much happier than I have ever been, and my husband fully supports my desire to perform.

*I understand you also paint?*

It started a couple of summers ago when I was expected to play at the Edinburgh Festival. By accident I got two fingers on the left hand caught in a car door! Just a few months before that incident I had said in an interview in London, "If something should happen to me so that I'm physically unable to play the violin, life is so full of interesting things that my time would be well occupied—I would be very happy." Well, when the door closed on my fingers, and I knew they didn't break but would put me out of commission for a while, I cried, "Oh, my concert!" and became very upset. One really doesn't know until one faces reality.

Eventually it became a very interesting situation, because I felt totally free all of a sudden. There was a perfectly good excuse not to play, so I started to paint and enjoyed it thoroughly. Since that time I take time off to paint, as I take time for courses in languages and literature.

*You have won acclaim and many awards for your recordings, most of them on the London label. Do you enjoy the process?*

I dislike it intensely, although not as much as I used to. I got into it by accident. If I had known beforehand what it was like, I don't think I would have had the nerve to do it. Someone had canceled a recording date (Tchaikovsky and Sibelius) and I stepped in.

It happened right after my London debut. I had no idea that Decca had been looking for years for violinists, and they auditioned almost everybody who came to London. So I had a half-hour audition with an upright piano that was at least a quarter tone flat and I had never seen the pianist before. I took this as a joke, but shortly afterwards I received a telegram asking me to record. I flew back and I was so frantic that I practiced in the London Airport. When I told André Previn, who was conducting, that I had never played with an orchestra before in my life, he turned gray . . . [laughs], but it turned out fine.

I have been asked to record certain repertoire and turned it down because I was not ready, but I have said, "You know, so-and-so would be wonderful for this." The company has taken my recommendation and with very successful results. Does that mean I'm getting fewer recordings? No! Ever since I was a child, playing has only been worth my while if I have done my homework. Some people have worried that if you don't take a certain engagement somebody else will and perhaps have more of a success. But that is absolutely untrue. Talented people simply don't come by the dozen, and even if they did, every one of them would be different and have different things to say.

*Aside from time limitations, what would be valid reasons for you to turn down a concert engagement?*

Very often I turn down orchestras that are not up to a certain standard. On the other hand, I also say yes to orchestras that fall very short of the standard when the people are so incredibly devoted that I know I will be working in a wonderful atmosphere.

*Do you offer orchestras a choice of your large repertoire?*

No, I play only what I choose and have done so for many years. In this way I can prepare myself fully.

*I recently heard you play the Dvořák Violin Concerto in A Minor with the Toronto Symphony under Andrew Davis. Where does that concerto place in your affections?*

Affections? It is difficult to even place it in that category. Although I love the piece, this concerto has given me more aches and pains than any other concerto. When I first started to learn it, I thought it would be just another addition to my repertoire, but I quickly realized it was not like other concertos. Thematically it has such beautiful material, but structurally it is most awkward and technically it's very difficult to put together. It must have the right Slavic flavor and you can't pretend to do that—you have to feel it.

This concerto is not in the standard repertoire, so it is difficult for the orchestra to reach the point where it is full of joy and singing. I have been playing it for over twenty years and it has driven me crazy. I would leave it for a couple of years and then pick it up again. On this North American tour I will play it a dozen times. I'm determined to have a crack at it.

*Do you ever venture into unknown territory?*

Well, I have had people approach me about writing repertoire and that has frightened me so much. First of all, would I be able to live up to it? When I learn repertoire, it takes me a terribly long time and I have never accepted engagements where I have had to learn something in weeks or even one month. I learn it, live it and study it very hard for two to three months. So, I would only work with new composers without any obligation to perform the piece.

*What is your most recent chamber-music repertoire?*

Oh, Messiaen—I did *Quartet for the End of Time*. That's a wonderful work.

*Looking at the possibilities that are offered young violinists today, what advice would you give a very talented eighteen-year-old?*

If young people want to be performers, they really have to be completely crazy about it. They have to be almost abnormal, thinking that it is what they want more than anything in the whole world. To succeed they must be extremely sensitive, gifted, intelligent, devoted, diligent and disciplined. However, if you really have to force yourself to go on stage—a lot of soloists suffer terribly from nerves—it may be too painful to go through your life like that.

*The way the music business is structured, do you think it is possible that a talented player might not be properly appreciated?*

Actually no. People are more aware nowadays and talent is difficult to hide. There are more people training to be in this profession, but ironically that doesn't mean there are more gifted players appearing. Gift is some incredible phenomenon. It won't blossom by itself. A gifted person needs a lot of support from the environment, family, teachers and so on. But I don't think that a person with an incredible gift can hide—quite the contrary. There is more of a chance that such a person would be exploited. By the way, being a woman in this field is completely different from being a man.

*How?*

One does suffer from being a female artist, because society is still structured in favor of men. Women are subjected to much unpleasant destruction, although it's better now than before.

*Don't you have the same opportunities as a man of equal talent?*

The same chances. But would somebody say, "He's a tough guy" if a man is simply concentrating on his career? There I was, determined to become a concert artist and I know people have called me tough. What they actually mean is that I'm strong.

Still, the idea of what a female being is has changed in the past twenty years. When I first went to Mr. Galamian, he didn't take me seriously. He was the first person whom I had to convince that I could do it, and it was such an effort. He had had so many gifted young female students and they never went past age sixteen in their studies. "They ran off with boys," as he expressed it, and to him it was the greatest disappointment. Now the situation is quite different.

*Due to social conditioning?*

Absolutely. Years ago women expected to be married in their early twenties. There is nothing wrong with being married, but at that time marriage meant a new career. That is wonderful if that's what you want, but if you are a specially gifted musician, very few men would understand and support you.

*Have you helped young performers in their careers?*

Yes, I do help as much as I can. When I hear young musicians I like, I recommend them to others. However, it is difficult to recommend someone, because it carries with it a responsibility. Now there are a lot of talented people coming up, mainly Orientals. I feel one must help talent get ahead.

# Maureen Forrester

After forty years in the public eye Maureen Forrester is almost a cultural institution. Now in her late fifties, the singer can look with pride at the life she has spun around her sumptuous voice, from her working-class beginnings in Montreal to a place among the world's foremost contraltos. A repertoire of lieder and oratorio with the occasional opera thrown in is not usually the ticket to great popularity, yet Miss Forrester is probably the best known "classical" musician in Canada. For several decades, her cheerful stage presence and unaffected manner have captured audiences of all levels of sophistication, inviting everyone to enjoy her extraordinary artistry. She began as a soprano in church choirs and later excelled in the dark mezzo repertoire, until she finally found her unique power as a contralto. Her voice has great subtlety and strength, impeccable pitch, and, of course, the depth that lends her Mahler interpretations such beauty.

It would fill several pages to recount the artistic milestones and honors in Maureen Forrester's eventful life, not to speak of her numerous associations with the world's pre-eminent musicians. During the ten years that divide the two conversations that follow (1977 and 1987), her life has not only been more of the same, but has sprouted new shoots. She has become chairman of the Canada Council and is now the grandmother of a growing flock. She also published her memoirs. Her energy undiminished, she often invites her five children with their families and her ex-husband Eugene Kash to her country place, and spends her spare time fund-raising for the Kidney Foundation, battered wives or AIDS patients. She is constantly on the move and sleeps only five hours a night. When the pace gets a little dull, she is known to move and create another elegant home for herself.

*Colgrass: With all this energy, did you ever turn down a job?*

Forrester: Many times. I remember when I first sang with Ormandy as a young singer. He had a great knack for finding young talent— they are cheaper, you know—and he immediately offered me to open the next year's season with Bartók's *Bluebeard's Castle*. I studied the score but refused, because I couldn't sing it in those days. He admired my decision and promised to use me in the future.

*How did you become a Mahler specialist?*

That is a very interesting story. Way back when I was doing my little Handel, Schumann and Gypsy songs, I didn't even know the name Mahler. I had somebody write every conductor in America, asking them to hear me sing, and as a result I got a personal note from Bruno Walter saying, "I'm always interested in young people and would love to hear you sing." He asked me to bring some Bach and Brahms, which I sang for him while he played everything too fast on the piano. He right then invited me to sing Mahler's Second at his last performance with the New York Philharmonic and to make a recording. He had a way of picking a color he wanted in a voice. Still, it wasn't love at first sight. He said, "Young lady, you sing too intimately." But somehow, through osmosis, you got from that man what he wanted if you were on his wavelength. Casals and Szell had the same ability. They said very little, but you felt instinctively what they wanted. Looking back now, I guess that Mahler just appeals to me because I'm very melodramatic.

*Would you recommend that a performer establish a family of five children?*

I would say that if you are going to have a family, line the nanny up first! When my children were young I had the most phenomenal nanny, which meant everything to me. The times she was not with us, I was really not happy on the road. You know, I'm a people watcher and I see many unhappy, lonely women sitting in coffee shops with their cup of tea, hoping the waitress or somebody else will talk to them. Then why is it that we don't have more nannies? Nobody works slave labor any more, and they would belong to a family. Our Tetta came to us at age sixty—a very small woman, but she was like a field marshal.

In general, though, it is a strain on the family when the mother is away a great deal of the time. As you know, I no longer live with my husband.

*Singers are notorious for their temperament . . .*

No! Temperament is to me an excuse for singers who don't know their parts or simply have bad manners. Time nowadays is a lot of money and managers don't re-engage temperamental singers because they can't afford to waste the time.

*How long do you expect your voice to last?*

I don't think your voice gives out if you have a good technique and you don't force it.

*Lois Marshall changed from soprano to mezzo. Where will you go?*

Well [uproarious laughter], I don't think I'll end up as a bass!

*Do you find Canada insular in matters of art?*

I don't think the public is. It is the second level of artists who are insular, but what they don't understand is that they improve themselves by working with the better performers. It brings the whole level up. I fear that their attitudes will spill over into other areas, so that we can't show Picasso here, thank you very much, because we have our own painters, or De Bakey is not welcome because we have our own heart specialists. It's a terribly chauvinistic situation.

*Are our young performers willing to go out on a limb?*

Well, many will come up to me and ask, "Shall I become a singer?" And I say NO! If you have to ask, you don't want it badly enough. The young are afraid of criticism and expect things to be handed them on a silver platter. When I was young, I would get an occasional bad review, criticizing my diction or talking of a hot potato in my mouth. Well, I didn't go off and cry in a corner, I repaired the problem.

*Does financial support create singers?*

I don't think money helps at a very early stage. A scholarship becomes important when you have almost made it. When a trained student is ready to become a performer, financial help becomes very important, simply because it will enable the person to accept all the engagements that cost more than the fee covers. If a singer can't afford to work, it can become very depressing.

*What is the ideal start for a singer?*

The main thing for a young singer is to find the best teacher in Yellowknife or wherever she lives and learn what she can. The next step is to have the courage to leave and go to a big center to find a teacher who is on your spiritual wavelength.

*But an outstanding talent, such as yours, has special needs.*

Don't you feel that if an outstanding talent lives in Medicine Hat, the powers-that-be will know it? They will somehow help that person get educated. When I toured Saskatchewan last year, a young man travelled 200 miles to come and sing for me. I said, "That is the sexiest voice I have heard since Pinza!" Well, he left the pig farm he worked on and he is now studying in Toronto on a scholarship. But he is twenty-nine and that is already quite an age. He should have been picked up much earlier, at around twenty-two.

*Who helped you?*

When I was a young singer living in Montreal, I was earning about $35 a concert doing Jeunesses Musicales concerts. The person who made the difference was J.W. McConnell, a fantastic man and great philanthropist who owned the *Montreal Star*. He had educated many young people, but never someone in music. He had me investigated—he was then eighty—and finally called me to his office and said, "Young lady, you can have as much money as you want for as long as you want to stop performing and concentrate on studying." But I was not at that point in my career. What I really needed was to accept the $200 engagement in Vancouver that would cost me $800 in expenses. So he paid all my musical deficits for two years and I kept it quite separate from my living expenses, never taking advantage of the situation in the hope that he would do the same for someone else. Believe it or not, it cost him $20,000 over the two years to enable me to accept every engagement.

*Do people realize how much it costs a singer to function?*

Ooohh! [Eyes fixed to the ceiling.] To make my kind of fee, which admittedly is high, I need a manager, a PR person, a business manager, a secretary and a housekeeper. And I pay for gowns, travel, hairdresser and more. Sometimes two hundred kids will write and ask for photos and resumés as part of a school project. They are very sweet to take the interest, so I can't say no.

*You have paced your career in a very deliberate way.*

Yes, for years I did oratorios, recitals and symphony dates, going along at a comfortable pace. People said, "Look at that lovely lady up there." But one day I said, "Maureen, do you know what is wrong with you? You neither excite nor disturb!" The breakthrough came when Mario Bernardi asked me to do the witch in the opera *Hansel and Gretel*. After that, everybody said, "This is a screwy dame."

*Now you love opera.*

I love it simply because I enjoy being with other singers. Remember, a recital singer's life is quite lonely.

*Are you interested in teaching?*

Yes, but I'm afraid I don't have a great deal of patience if a student doesn't catch immediately what I'm saying. I teach very little and I teach differently. I was once asked to change the whole singers' curriculum at the Philadelphia Music Academy where I taught for a few years. I was flattered to death—you know that I left school at thirteen—but I know how singers should be taught. What they need is repertoire. They shouldn't perfect it at the conservatory because they are not ready vocally. I told them to graduate with five or six recital programs, five orchestra works memorized, five or six chamber music pieces, forty oratorios and three operas cover to cover. Then you have a basis to build on.

What happens is that these kids spend four years in school and graduate with one recital program which they have perfected because they worked on it so damn much that they can sing it in their sleep. They get engaged and do their program and when they are invited back, they panic because they don't know anything else! The teachers didn't share my views in Philadelphia and I finally left.

Another thing I demanded was that the students sing in front of their class so as to be corrected not only by the teachers, but by their peers. If their friends say, "I can't understand a word you sing," they realize they have to work on their diction. Just making beautiful sounds without any interpretation becomes like wallpaper after a while.

*What is your advice to young opera singers?*

I don't believe you have to go to Europe and apprentice yourself to a small opera house. I can't tell you how many tenors I have worked with whose voices were burned out in ten years because they went to Europe and sang every role. You need a mentor to guide you or else the courage to say no.

\*

Ten years have passed. Maureen Forrester is sitting in her newly decorated Rosedale home in Toronto, her usual mega-energy focused on what has taken place since our first interview. Her children are grown and she now has four grandchildren. Forrester has lived at numerous exclusive addresses, all decorated to her exacting taste, as if she would grow stagnant living in the same place for more than a couple of years. She is still singing internationally, though less than before, and has turned out to be a natural policy-maker as the chairman of the Canada Council. The 1986 publication of her fascinating memoirs, *Maureen Forrester: Out of Character*, removed the last specks of stage glitter from her persona.

*Colgrass: Since you have been chairman of the Canada Council, have you gotten a different insight into how our artists fare internationally? They are often griping.*

Forrester: Yes, but artists all over the world are griping. At first I had no idea about the Canada Council, never having applied for a grant, and I didn't know that the staff of over a hundred worked so hard. They can only give one in five grants, so they have four very disappointed parties whenever a grant is awarded. We may be losing that talent because people get discouraged—though I don't feel all talent should be subsidized, that could make for laziness. Still, a dancer has to dance every day.

*Do you think it's right to present the arts as "industries" to the government, just to make politicians understand their importance? Isn't there ample historical evidence of the value of art?*

It is all important. People often say, "You are always looking for money." And I look them square in the eye and say, "You are only saying that because you don't have a talented child." If you have a talented child and an average income to put a daughter through dance training or allow a son to spend ten years in a studio to become a painter, it costs an enormous sum of money. People don't like to subsidize the learning process, yet they appreciate artists when they become famous.

*How can we make people aware? Politicians seem particularly remiss.*

Trudeau was an exception, and if it is any consolation, Ed Broadbent loves opera. Overall, it is very sad that we still consider artists to be people who merely indulge in their hobby.

*Do you ever hear, "Well, artists may not make much money, but they are compensated by enjoying their work so much"?*

Yes, my son was just lamenting that fact. He recently returned from England, where they had a successful run of a play, and he was absolutely broke. So we helped him out.

*Right now our best young musicians go south to Juilliard, Eastman or Bloomington. Shouldn't we have an equivalent school here?*

We should—something like the National Ballet School. We should take the cream of the crop and polish it up, not just artistically, but teach them how to be clever about a career. I think it should be a government-funded school, though I don't think the present government would be interested. I'm not a political animal, but it is good to remind every politician that there are a lot of artists in this country and they are very vocal, especially if something like the "arm's length" were taken away from the Canada Council. I hope that when I retire the Council will get someone as fearless as I am.

*You still find time to sing?*

Oh, I give close to a hundred concerts a year, and I have just returned from Hong Kong and Wales. Also, I have just recorded yet another Mahler's Second with the London Symphony.

*Elly Ameling told me that she has to practice more as she gets older to keep her voice in shape. Is that necessary for you?*

I never ever had to vocalize, but don't forget that I sing in my natural speaking range. I no longer sing out and with full emotion at a rehearsal if I have a concert the same day. It takes the bloom out of the voice. After all, I'm fifty-seven and I'm lucky to have as much voice left as I have. I have engagements booked till 1990 and 1991, and I said to my manager, "How about putting in fine print: 'If I still can'?" [A rippling laugh.]

*I admire your book for its candor and integrity—besides, it is very entertaining. I did hear remarks like, "Do you think she should have talked about something that private?"*

I get at least ten letters a day from women who say, "I admire your honesty" or "I cried," but I tell them that everybody has problems. The one thing I don't do is dwell on them. If you don't tell the truth in an autobiography, somebody will find the truth and distort it.

*What do you consider the greatest threat to music at the moment?*

Because of television the taste of the public is not improving enough. We tend to think of the sale of tickets rather than the quality of the music we are performing. When I sing, I often talk about the music first—the composer, the piece, the poetry—and then the audience enjoys it more. It's a little like a lesson at the same time.

# Virgil Fox

Virgil Fox was the virtuoso and *enfant terrible* of the organ. He was adored by audiences, envied by many colleagues and disliked by defenders of the historically correct. However, he was never merely tolerated. That would have been too lukewarm a response to this feisty organist who successfully converted rock fans to Bach and who shot straight from the hip at his baroque-minded colleagues: "I notice that they do not ride in ox carts. Yet they want to grovel around in the dung of two hundred years ago, when they could be riding on the inspiration of what now exists." Each blast was followed by his infectious laugh.

The man knew how to celebrate. During concerts of Heavy Organ with Revelation Lights, he sent youngsters into a frenzy yelling "B-A-C-H" in pep-rally fashion and shouting "A minor!" towards the stage where he was bathed in changing lights, swaying his torso, hands bouncing in the air—even changing stops cross-handed.

Then there was Virgil Fox who was organist at New York City's Riverside Church for a decade, mastering its magnificent 200-rank pipe organ. He was also the soloist of many a symphony concert where his own light was enough to brighten the stage.

Shortly after our 1979 interview, which was enjoyed by a slew of people packed into a New York hotel room after one of his concerts, Fox became ill. Only his closest friends knew that he had suffered from bone cancer for several years, but his spirit had kept the demons offstage. Certainly there were no signs of diminished vitality on this occasion. During 1980, will power alone carried him through concerts, and the last took place with the Dallas Symphony Orchestra in September. In his final hours, he spoke in French to those around him. He was no doubt back in his beloved France with the great cathedrals that had inspired him as a young student.

Virgil Fox was a joyful person who attracted a great following. The Virgil Fox Society, operating out of Brooklyn, celebrated his seventy-fifth birthday in May 1987, and its members try to collect the scant memorabilia that is around after most were acquired by Fox's Canadian heir. Fortunately his most valuable legacy is available on numerous recordings, with new compact discs appearing now and then.

*Colgrass: It's obvious that you carry an unusual passion for your instrument.*

Fox: The organ has been the most mechanized and the least effectively played instrument, because these characters that are attracted to the organ somehow are often not people of real talent and they hide behind the historical. They say "We don't care whether you like it or not—it is correct!" and I feel like getting a shovel and removing them from amidst the conversation. Imagine talking about correctness at a concert of music where vision is supposed to be available to the audience! My God. But they are in university centers, you see, and this authenticity seems to carry weight, which is total rubbish. When Horowitz was being interviewed about a year ago he said, "Music is a matter of the feelings"—emotion has to do with the art of sound. We are not concerned with cerebral exercises or some cockeyed limitations. My God, the organs of three hundred years ago had to be pumped by hand and those vast naves of churches were acoustically warm because of the stone. If you make a sound in one end, like blowing your nose, it sounds like Casals playing the cello by the time it gets to the other end! And these same people who are talking about music want to have organs in rooms that have no similarity to those stone churches. With these extremely overdeveloped upper works, it sounds like somebody dumping cut glass on a tin roof—it's ridiculous!

*What is the alternative? In this day and age we no longer build these magnificent churches.*

The alternative is to make the organ beautiful and the player must coerce it until he has arrived at expressive phrases and expressive treatment of the music. Music without expression is a damn fool monotone. Good heavenly day!

*Does any organist appeal to you?*

In certain categories there are organists who will play a certain composer that will appeal to me. When Pierre Cochereau is at Notre Dame and he plays a fiery French toccata, it is hair-raising. However, if he comes to the Peach Tree Christian Church in Atlanta, Georgia, and puts the same stops on a limited organ in acoustics about like this [pointing around his plush hotel room], it's not honest.

We have already approached about six subjects that would require doctoral theses, and I could go on forever and ever. Landowska made the superb remark in her book: "I do not care to play as musicians played in 1600. The people that I'm addressing my art to live in this time. They are used to the accelerated action of the Steinway, the extended range of the flute, the steel struts of the violin and all the magnificent capabilities of the extended technique. I must address myself to people who are now, that's the point of the music." So when a fine organ is being built, there has to be a sensible humanitarian, an honest man, in charge of the directions to the organ builder. Because when this baroque kick, which is what it is, started fifteen or twenty years ago, the organs in America as well as England and France were suddenly archaic. All these historical birds sniffed, put their noses in the air and said, "Oh dear, this isn't correct. We will have to change it all." So the organ builders were delighted because it meant everybody had to buy a new organ. This is demonstrated in Palm Beach, Florida, where I live. The leading church there—if you mention it by name, I'll be run out of town—suddenly had no limit to finances in making a new organ possible. So they went to a U.S. company that makes something that sounds just like long fingernails that keep going like this [scratches his thigh] until the skin comes off and the blood oozes. There was not one honest, warm, attractive sound in it, it was nothing but overdeveloped squeals.

*How can things get out of hand so desperately?*

I'm glad you asked that question. In the world of the piano and the violin they can't—those media are known. The world of the organ has always been a sideline, and the reason is that it has never been in the mainstream of great music-making, with the organ hiding behind woodwork in a sacred place. I am a very strong believer in the power and need of God and all of his creation, but in the house of God where this instrument became known as the sacred instrument, it was covered up and could never go where the people are. It supplied the background at weddings and funerals.

*So the organ is among the endangered species of the instrumental world?*

That is absolutely the truth. When a man like Marcel Dupré, my beloved teacher, came along in France, he brought one facet of his art to the amazement of the entire world. When he had his New York debut, he improvised a full-length, four-movement symphony—the audience was positively aghast! For Dupré, who had been taught from the age of five to extemporize on the Gregorian chant, it was easier to improvise than to pick up a cup of soup and drink it.

*Where do you put improvisation in your own work?*

I do not improvise in concert. When I was organist at Riverside

Church I did plenty of extemporization, because when you have a hundred and fifty canary birds coming down the center aisle and three thousand people singing, there had to be an interlude between the third and fourth stanza in order to raise the pitch of the hymn and get that adrenalin really flowing. All that discipline I had with Dupré in Paris suddenly would come to the fore. I used to be on the bus in Paris and coming around the corner I would think, "That damn fourth chord can come into the third without doubling the third and it can be this in the soprano. . . ." All my lessons were done in strict counterpoint, you see, over many months and it was that discipline that enabled me to bring the singers down the aisle in the Riverside Church.

*What are your thoughts on Messiaen?*

Lovely question. His wife's name was Oriole [a spurt of laughter] and I'm told that at one of his latest compositions she came onto the stage for the premiere with wings fastened to her costume! He is intrigued with the sound of birds, and for the organ it poses a bit of a problem. The sound of an organ is magnificent in the fourth octave of the keyboard—it can reproduce a bird call much more easily than a piano or a symphony orchestra. But I think there has been a slackening of Messiaen's inspiration. The recent works don't seem to have the impact of some of the earlier. I play with great pleasure the *Dieu Parmi Nous* with which I dedicated the Philharmonic Hall organ in New York—pardon me, the Avery Fisher Hall in this day and time.

*Is there an organ?*

There was an organ. Can you believe that . . . oh deary, we mustn't talk about this, or they will send dynamite to your office! [Fox nonetheless goes on to tell about the questionable act of removing the organ from the famous hall.] There have been organ pipes behind the orchestra in Queens Hall in London, in Massey Hall in Toronto, in Symphony Hall in Boston and every big hall of the world. They all worked in with the environment.

Do you know that when we had a performance with the organ in the new Minneapolis hall, we took just for experiment a dollar bill and rubbed it together on the stage like this [demonstrates] and it hurt the ears on top of the third balcony! It sounded like a colossal sheet of iron, so can you imagine what happens when a French horn player has to relieve some spit from his instrument? My God, the front row would duck! The principal idea in Minneapolis is that the room is not connected with the outer world. There is an air space around it and the result is fantastic.

*Your baby is at the Riverside Church?*

To tell the truth, my baby is where the people are. The reason why I'm in a position that is unique in the organ world is that I first of all appeal to the young people of the world. I did it at the Fillmore East [New York rock shrine] where nothing but rock and roll had ever been experienced. At the end of my first concert there, after the sixth encore, I looked at those kids and said, "As a good-night song I will play you Air on the G String," which is not considered encore material at all, and there was total silence in that room!

*How do you connect with such diverse audiences?*

You have to be honest and you have to want them. When I first used to be interviewed, I made a crack that when I come onto the stage, I feel like saying: "Have a seat, gang. I've got something marvelous to show you!" The interviewer was amazed that I had actually said that, but doesn't everybody feel that way? He said that a lot of performers look at the audience and think, "Oh, my God—people!" There was a black man at the top row at the Fillmore East, and just as I raised my hand to hit the beginning of the Prelude, he yelled, "Go, Virgil!" [Delighted laughter.] All of us took off—I said to them, "We soar . . ." and we did.

*You are a religious person?*

I certainly am. How can anybody not think that a greater power brings in the tide of two-thirds of the earth's surface every day, not to mention separating the sugar from the starch in your tummy after you eat lunch? Oh God, people who don't believe in the eternal.

*Do you see your music as a religious expression?*

How does one answer that? There are times when the best music is a religious expression and there are other times when it is an expression of the devil. I prefer to choose the composers that will give a view that the family of *The Sound of Music* had when they were on the top of the mountain and finally saw only sunlight ahead. That is what I wish to do when I give a concert. I see no reason to have the sounds of an iron foundry brought into the concert hall. Stokowski was one of the greatest creative souls that ever walked this earth, and I think these tangents he tried from time to time were certainly to be admired from the standpoint of inquisitiveness, but if I want a pounding I'll go to the foundry.

I have been reading Albert Schweitzer lately. Honest to God, what a divine man! He said, "It has to give a vision, it has to give a cleaning, an uplifting." If I pay money to go to a concert, I don't want to be pushed, I want to be lifted. Do you know what Schweitzer says in his book? He says we are engaged in the eternal process of life and we must be reverent of it. That man was transcendental! I saw a picture of him when he was twenty years old, and he could have been a movie star—he was positively a knock-out! Tyrone Power was no more attractive physically than Albert Schweitzer, yet that bird got on a barge and floated to the heart of the darkest spot of the world and gave service to the world—I tell you! By doing what he did, he made an example to every person that shall ever live after him. He could have been a politician and dripped blood and no one would have been the better for it.

*When you speak to audiences you often make comments of a philosophical nature.*

I can't resist. [Giggles mischievously.] If you are going to play the finale of the St. Matthew Passion and you are in front of people who have never sung it, who couldn't spell it and hadn't the slightest idea of what is going on, you are a fake if you don't offer every single thing at your command to make them understand, to give them the key that opens the magic place. So I spoke from the stage before Leonard Bernstein ever did. It was in the church in Augusta, Georgia, at the inauguration of a new pipe organ. You can't imagine the people who turned out—there were more on the lawn than in the church. Just before the third piece, which was to be the great Fantasy and Fugue in G Minor, whoever is the boss upstairs simply took hold. I sat there staring at those keys and could not play. All at once I turned around and looked at that mob of Georgia crackers, and fortunately I have this loud, penetrating voice, so I said: "This piece has a tune and this is it," at which I turned and played [vigorously sings a few stanzas] and I explained how it moved. I asked them to keep track of my feet, and I said, "You will then hear the greatest architect of sound that ever walked this earth, making a cathedral before your very eyes." These people never before smelled a Bach fugue, let alone heard one, and the piece was the hit of the evening.

When I hit that bed at four o'clock in the morning after the concert, I did some of the tall thinking of my life and decided right then and there . . . [sings a Bach fugue with abandon] . . . just like someone had gone on a picnic and said, "We have to dance." Schweitzer calls it "the pictorial language of Bach." If you are about to play that, how dare you do it without helping some honest soul in Tallahassee, Florida, who doesn't have any particular knowledge? I could not!

*You are truly an extrovert. Did you ever belong to what you call the Tight-lipped Crowd?*

Never. It took a long time for me to mature, of course, but I come from people who make it logical for me to do this. My dad was the best auctioneer in the state of Illinois. He could sell two thousand acres of land, all the livestock and all the machinery in the middle of winter with a beaver coat on, spats on his feet and a magnificent cane and shout so loud that they didn't know what they were buying. [General laughter.] So the extroverted side I get from my father. My mother's people were all preachers from New Hampshire and Vermont. My mother is what I would call a serene human being. If the world totally collapsed at three o'clock, she would say at five o'clock: "Where do we start?" The two people were the most marvelous combination you have ever seen and they made a real success together.

*You began by playing the piano.*

Yes, my mother had decided . . . [Looks skyward, shaking his head.] Well, she was a most extraordinary person who did amazing things. When they thought there might be oil on a section of our land, they got a professional person with a divining rod and all that jazz. This guy sashayed up and down for the entire day and finally said there was nothing. Mama had stood quietly by and when he was ready to leave, she asked to use the stick. My mother took twelve steps with the stick in her hand and it went swoosh. They stuck in the apparatus and the oil shot out of the ground! As a matter of fact, I had a concert manager once who said, "I don't think you are so hot, but your mother is fantastic." I always said that if Hitler had bombed my mother's house in person, she would have stood in the front yard and caught the bomb and heaved it right back at him.

*She was always supportive of you, I imagine.*

Yes, that was the thing. My father said, "You are not going to make a sissy out of him with his music," and she said, "Watch!" I went to Paris when I was twenty and lived with a French family for one year. Every Sunday I heard five colossal organists play—it was like going to the gates of paradise. Those organs are the great symphonic organs that can play the works of César Franck, they don't just play Bach.

*What was your first professional job?*

That was when I was a freshman in high school. The girl who used to play in church left—I was just twelve years old and played every piece by memory. I had a magnificent mentor who appeared just at the right time at the right place, Hugh Price, a pianist from La Salle, Illinois, and a wonderful man. I was drawn to him like a magnet and he took me into his family and kept me with him every moment I was not in school. He opened the gate to the whole world for me. After high school I went to the Peabody Conservatory in Baltimore. My dad, strangely enough, had bought a motion-picture house—auctioneers do tire out, you can't scream all your life. The theater had a pipe organ in it, a theater organ with only six ranks of pipe but there were fifty stops. The Toccata and Fugue in D Minor, which I have played in the Royal Festival Hall in London for a recording that was sold in forty-four countries of this world, was learned by me on that horseshoe console in Princeton, Illinois.

*So you played in your father's theater?*

Never. My mother would not permit us to go, except Friday and Saturday nights, how do you like that? That's what you call discipline, which the present age knows nothing about.

I had four giants for teachers. I had Hugh Price, as I mentioned, then Louis Robert at the Peabody, Wilhelm Middelschulte in Chicago and then Marcel Dupré. The strange thing was that each one said: "I alone possess the true tradition of playing Bach," and each was totally unlike the other. Of course, I was able to know what this meant: you play it alive, not dead, that is the clue. So after Peabody I felt impelled to go to France because it was the spiritual home of the organ, and when I came home, I played in Maryland in a little church. When the Riverside position opened much later, the organist was told he had to get me. It was right after the war and I was in my middle thirties. After a while I knew that I could not stay in New York, when the world is out there—can you imagine chaining Rachmaninoff to one piano in Town Hall and saying "You have to play here every Sunday"?

*What did the Fillmore East concert do to you?*

It was the big step into the world to reach the young people. The one thing that makes it impossible for critics to give me a classification is that I can play a Scott Joplin rag with just as much flair as any rock player—in other words, I never felt confined to just one repertoire of the organ as long as the music was beautiful and uplifting.

The greatest moment in my life was when I met the staggering giant Wilhelm Middelschulte. I was just fifteen, a farm boy from west of Chicago, and this man had been sent from Leipzig! Without even shaking my hand, he looked at me intently and said, "This is the most mechanical of any instrument, and if you"—pointing at my eternal guts—"ever go beyond these mechanics and make truly expressive music with this organ, you will do what few ever achieve." My God, it was as if you stood in the presence of the angel Gabriel and the thing had been printed in flame across your forehead. It became my entire guide.

I am going to play Wagner's *Liebestod*, can you imagine? That Riverside organ has got twelve thousand pipes and I can smear them like the sunset across a colossal palette of tone color—I can't keep from doing it. I made a spate of recordings for Columbia that I called

Veiled Dreams and Songs of Sunset and all this stuff, and every organist in the country said, "Oh, look at what he is playing!" While I was busy going to the bank, because those records sold enormously, these horned toads with their green eyes were standing around sniffing—they don't have the slightest idea of how to discuss me!

*Do you feel that your career is your own creation, or has someone been pulling the strings?*

I do believe that if a human being gives everything he has got, there are all kinds of forces that help as well as those that do not help. I have been in situations where I could feel the dervishes pull me down, but if you really discipline yourself, they can't do it.

*So you are in charge?*

Yes, I really do believe. I am sixty-six years of age and I am going stronger by far than before. When you finally align with what you know is right for your usefulness, it is a marvelous sensation. You really do soar.

*It takes courage to go with it, if it is outside ordinary concepts.*

Of course, because it would be far easier to fall in line with this little coterie that says that correctness is the only important thing. But you know, it is a strange thing, for a period of about twenty years I have been the *enfant terrible* of the organ world, and now they start coming back—by "they" I mean colleagues. They realize that if I can draw an audience of eleven thousand at the University of Illinois, I can't be a fake.

*You always dress in very colorful garb—what importance do you place on that?*

If you are on the stage, you should be dressed as attractively as possible. If I find a jacket with little sparkles on it I am delighted, and I put rhinestones on my shoes because my feet are part of my playing. I think that if Kirsten Flagstad, who was the greatest Wagnerian singer that walked the earth, could wear a perfectly beautiful gown to give a concert, I should be able to wear a suit that isn't like a pallbearer's. I change coats at intermission, not to show off, but because the first one is wringing wet.

*You are always surrounded by people.*

My goodness, you have to have help. David Snyder has been an absolute answer to prayer for me. [His Canadian heir, assistant and creator of the light show.] Every time I came to his home town, he asked if there was an opening on my staff and I said, "Hey kid, you are looking at the staff." Finally I did need help and he has been with me for fourteen years now. I am so grateful, because twenty years ago I could go anywhere at any time without any problems, but in this day and age you can be done in, physically I mean. I have to practice at remote times—I haunt buildings at midnight to practice.

*Would you say that you are a realistic person?*

Reality is not the goal in music—inspiration is the goal. Nobody has to have the bad rubbed in. What we have to do is to impose the good and then that becomes reality.

# Rivka Golani

In an age when promotion and the right connections are shaping many careers, it is refreshing to see violist Rivka Golani's steady climb —like an inevitable, natural phenomenon. Now in her late thirties, she is sought after by the major symphony orchestras—lately those in Montreal, Toronto, Boston and London—and everywhere listeners are stunned by her searing temperament and superb technique. *The London Times* described her as "a performer of spontaneous and fiery physicality, whose command of technique is assimilated to a remarkable degree into the sharply individual character of her musicianship," the *Basler Zeitung* said of a concert, "Body, spirit and soul melted into one at this performance." Golani admits that "maybe I have not heard others play the viola this way," and she is undoubtedly breaking new ground for her instrument.

A very demanding schedule of concerts in Europe and North America ought to toughen her a little, build that formal protective façade, but Golani still meets every situation with all receptors on full alert. In her unaffected manner she observes everything acutely and reacts immediately, and clearly she makes music from her intense Israeli temperament. Her stage presence is so magnetic that an arts patron once offered to sponsor a concert for her after having seen her play— in a photo in the newspaper! When she is not clad in a gown for concerts, she is usually dressed Cossack-style in boots, pants and flowing shirts in colors that compete in intensity with her vivid red hair.

Born in what was then Palestine, Golani is a contemporary of Itzhak Perlman and Pinchas Zukerman. There was music in her family— several relatives from Russia and Poland are musicians—but her parents did not have the opportunity to play. They insisted that their daughters become musicians. (Bella Ekroni, her sister, is a cellist and painter in New York City.) Her search for a good viola changed her life in many ways. She had already bought one instrument made by

Otto Erdesz, a well-known maker of string instruments. For her medium-sized hands it was a large instrument, more than seventeen inches, but she made the extra effort to master it. While on a tour to New York, she went with a colleague to Erdesz's workshop to help him select a viola. As a result, she married Erdesz half a year later in Tel Aviv and the couple eventually settled in Toronto in 1974, where their son was born. The marriage ended in 1983 and Erdesz moved to New Jersey to set up shop.

At first, Canada was a cold environment for Golani in more ways than one. She wasn't used to the cold climate or the reserved Canadians, nor was she used to being idle. She didn't know anybody and says laughingly, "For almost a whole year I walked the streets." She practiced a great deal in preparation for several concerts in Israel, but she says, "I felt very embarrassed and ashamed, because I used to be on stage every night. I just couldn't tell people: Here I am, come and listen to me!" Eventually she was introduced to Morry Kernerman [assistant concert-master of the Toronto Symphony] and through him was invited to play music in a private home. She was offered a job with the Toronto Symphony, but felt that she was ready for something different. As she slowly worked herself into the city's musical fabric she taught viola at the University of Toronto.

Around forty composers have already been inspired to write works to suit her exceptional talent. Among those is an electrifying piece called *Trema* by the Swiss composer, oboist, conductor and pianist Heinz Holliger. The two have performed together many times, in France, Holland, Switzerland, Austria and Israel in repertoire spanning from Schubert to Britten.

At the time of this interview I had already known Rivka for several years, and when my husband, composer Michael Colgrass, began writing a concerto for her in 1982, she became a frequent visitor in our home. Sometimes she would pull up with a carload of her own paintings that he could place around his studio for inspiration, or she would call with encouragement and the need to know the latest variations he had completed. Their teamwork in creating *Chaconne* was first put to the test with the Toronto Symphony under Andrew Davis in 1984, and together they gave the American premiere with the Boston Symphony Orchestra in 1986 to standing ovations.

One of her many subsequent performances of *Chaconne* made a sudden and decisive change in Golani's life. Thomas Sanderling conducted her in a performance of this work with the Quebec Symphony Orchestra in 1986, and their instant mutual attraction led them to share their musical lives and settle in London, England.

Golani's paintings have been exhibited in Israel, Canada and Austria, and she has published a humorous book of drawings entitled *Birds of Another Feather*. A Centrediscs recording, *Viola Nouveau*, won the Grand Prix du Disque and was nominated for a Juno Award. She has also recorded solo works for Masters of the Bow, the Brandenburg #6 on CBC SM 5000 as well as chamber music on Chandos and Conifer. Her next recording project is a CBC disc with Bloch, Hindemith, Britten and *Chaconne*.

*Colgrass: You're an extremely independent person.*

Golani: I feel that nothing can ruin my independence. I think I avoided being strongly influenced from the outside during my childhood. I was very sick much of the time with all kinds of illnesses. The body was hardly resisting. I had to be by myself a great deal and somewhere deeply it meant something to me. Many people can't be alone at all and that changes their whole being.

*When did you start to study music?*

I began on the violin when I was six years old. I had to be forced. [Laughter.] I knew I had to practice, but it was mostly out of guilt. At that time I found Bach impossibly boring to listen to, so I can't be sophisticated and say, "From the very beginning I loved it." I hated it! I found concerts very still and artificial. I went through so much to get to where I am now—not like some of my friends who won competitions and played Paganini at the age of five. For me everything was hard work.

I didn't have very good teachers at first—one I studied with for five years, another for seven years—and they were very personal relationships. People were so hot around me in Israel and parting from the teachers was almost like a divorce. [At the age of eighteen, while she was still playing the violin, she became a pupil of Alexander Moskowsky.] I had to start from the very beginning on my violin. My right hand was one year's work, my left hand the second year. I was so tight, yet I understood that I would have to undergo this change or I would never stay in music.

The two years were almost like a hiding period—you have nothing to show and you get no feedback. Fortunately the teacher was very supportive. That gave me courage.

*Along with music you also showed promise in painting and mathematics.*

I was always afraid to lose my mathematical ability. It was not something that I learned, but something I was born with. For me mathematics on a certain level is a very imaginary and fantastic world—a whole philosophy. If I couldn't solve a problem, I would continue it subconsciously in my sleep and I would wake up in the middle of the night with the answer. Although there was never a problem I couldn't solve, I was never sure whether I could do it the next day.

*After Moskowsky you began studying viola with Oedoen Partos.*

A very great man who helped me perfect my technique.

*Was it a traumatic change?*

Whatever you do on the violin you do on the viola, only bigger. You need more strength to still keep the same speed. Many violin teachers recommend that their students play the viola in order to strengthen their hands. We hold the viola exactly like a violin, but it is a very unnatural way to hold a large instrument. With the cello, at least, the hands are down in a more natural position.

*While you were still a student, you became a member of the Israeli Philharmonic and stayed there for five years. Did this affect your playing?*

Many people would say that they would be set back by playing in an orchestra, but I learned so much. I never stopped practicing and learned from my colleagues in the section. It was at that time perhaps the best viola section anywhere.

*You've done a lot of teaching. Do you prefer a special type of student?*

What is good student material for most professors is another story for me. When I see there is potential, I take it and I put everything I have in me to make it grow. Unfortunately I think the faculty is waiting for Primroses, and if the students are not on a certain level they are treated accordingly. I don't like that attitude.

They want ready-made players and don't believe people can really develop. I know that most of the professors' backgrounds were different from mine. I was never a *wunderkind* as most of them were. To them it is too late if you don't play certain material at age seventeen. I started developing much later, so my outlook is completely different. If somebody is not a complete beginner but has moved his fingers on the viola before, has good hands and a sense of music, I think "Why not?"

A teacher should be a doctor, really. I know that most of my pupils are a result of my work with them—I didn't have ready-made students whom I just taught music and philosophy.

*Yet a student might arrive with a good technique and not much else.*

There is the spiritual side—if you don't have it, you don't have it. Still, I never met anyone with no feeling at all. If you have a student with lots of technique, I believe you can "irritate" them and bring out a lot. If they are very dry, they are usually dry in every way, even in their technique. But again, a teacher should be able to move the almost unmoveable emotions.

*Your own style is unique in its emotional scope.*

My approach to music is very personal and emotional, I can't help it. Most violists approach the instrument in a very classical way, like people who would look at only a certain kind of realism in painting and might not react at all to something abstract. I find that these "classical musicians" go for perfection. I like their neatness, but I like roughness as well. Most musicians don't go for it, they get scared. Roughness is so much part of beauty.

*Why hasn't the music world turned out many great violists?*

For a long time an unsuccessful violinist would take up the viola. But if you aren't talented, you can't make it on any instrument.

*People rarely regard it as a solo instrument.*

Even when composers wrote for viola it was mostly elegies and dull pieces that were slow and very sad. Nobody accepted that the viola can run and be an exciting virtuoso instrument. The very first violist who brought the instrument up to solo status was the Englishman Lionel Tertis [1876-1975] and after him, of course, came William Primrose.

You have to really dedicate your life to the instrument. You also have to be open-minded and accept contemporary music. If you are such a prima donna who will only accept Mozart, Schubert and Schumann, you end up with five pieces. What kind of a career can you make on that?

*A good many soloists will only play original music for their instrument, they dislike transcriptions.*

Good for them. [Laughter.] There are many pieces that you can perform just as beautifully and maybe even more so on another instrument. So why not? I am sure the composers wouldn't have any objections, because it is still their music, their emotion.

*Have you always liked contemporary music?*

Of course I found it impossible to listen to at first. When I started studying with Partos, who was also a composer, I learned a lot about contemporary music. The more I listened, the more I liked it and the more I was able to decide what was good. Musicians in general tend to talk about contemporary music as if it's all one. They don't have enough knowledge and judge too quickly.

*Your performances always seem so alive and focused in the moment.*

I don't play the same way twice. To me a concert is a happening with certain people sitting there. I play for them and we do it all together. I can't say I know exactly what happens between us. When I played in England at Wigmore Hall, the audience reacted to me on a very unusual spiritual level. I felt from the beginning that I could do absolutely anything—it is something you can swim in. When I feel that the audience is inspired, it makes me play so much better. Because I put so much in it, I can't be terrible, but if I get a certain kind of audience that I don't feel at all, then I suffer very much.

*How do you evaluate your standing in the musical community?*

When I played in Gidon Kremer's Lockenhaus Festival in Austria, I was an unknown name among famous performers, and I saw the reaction from the audience and critics. I am not stupid. It all has to happen in a natural way. I would never push anything. I don't think about where I'll be ten years from now.

# Glenn Gould

When the world woke up in the morning, it was bedtime for pianist Glenn Gould, whose busy day usually ended at six A.M. Such nocturnal habits might have raised eyebrows if practiced by ordinary pianists, but for Gould they seemed entirely appropriate. After all, he played in a style all his own and persuaded us to hear the music his way. He abandoned his brief but successful concert career because he found it "an utterly wasteful activity." He played the keyboard and the controls in the recording booth with equal expertise and asked us to accept his electronic wizardry in the name of art, and we did. This unique life came to an end when Gould died of a stroke only days after his fiftieth birthday.

My conversation with Glenn Gould took place late 1980. He very rarely gave interviews and this, to my knowledge, was his last interview in print. During the early years of *Music Magazine* he had been very helpful and encouraging, so we knew each other a bit, yet this conversation, like all the others, was carried out on the telephone. That didn't make it less personal, because Gould was at his most personal on the telephone and happily spent hours entertaining or working with friends in the wee hours of the night. I recall lying on the floor, being too sleepy to sit up holding the phone, while Gould regaled me with his witty impersonations of politicians, actors and other celebrities. He applied the same intensity at work and at play, most likely because he didn't differentiate between the two.

At the time of his death on October 4, 1982, Gould had recorded for CBS with twenty-seven years and released approximately eighty recordings. Yes, *he* released, because he called the shots when it came to choosing repertoire and controlling the editing and engineering of his recordings. CBS even flew to Toronto to record with him in his own habitat. From the abundance of recorded music that Gould left

behind, CBS has issued only a few new discs due to negotiations with the Gould estate (his beneficiaries were the Salvation Army and the Humane Society). Of the thirty-two recordings to appear since Gould's death, most are re-releases and much of his production is now available on CDs. One can only guess at the treasures that are in store once the legal problems are ironed out.

"I play very little piano," Gould said, probably referring to the fact that he never practiced. He did, however, work on writing and editing his own television and radio documentaries, all carrying his stamp of perfection. In his last year of life, he had begun to prepare for a new adventure, this time in conducting. At the end of our talk, he is referring to this plan, but his secretiveness takes on an eerie significance when he says, "My contract with CBS runs a bit beyond my fiftieth year . . after that, there is going to be a major change of gears."

*Colgrass: You began recording for CBS with the now historic Goldberg Variations. Yet you had to talk them into recording that disc—why?*

Gould: I think the objections they had, which were mild and expressed in a most friendly fashion, were quite logical. I was twenty-two years old and proposed doing my recording debut with the *Goldberg Variations*, which was supposed to be the private preserve of perhaps Wanda Landowska or someone of that generation and stature. They thought that possibly some more modest undertaking was advisable.

*Did they realize immediately what they had on their hands with the Goldberg?*

I think they did. Certainly it came out in fairly quick order. I must emphasize that in all those twenty-five years, there have been very few arguments over repertoire and those few were of the friendliest nature.

*I realize now that the choice of repertoire and the outcome of a recording session is far more flexible than I first thought. Some works might be scrapped in the middle of the project and others added. Is that due to your own choice?*

It usually has been. One of the reasons that I have stayed with CBS for so long and never even thought of going elsewhere is precisely because they leave me alone. I think the relationship is quite unique.

*Does that freedom extend to collaborations you have with other artists?*

Well, I certainly have a veto on any collaboration, but very often CBS proposes certain names and I'll say yes or no. You know, I'm one of the senior citizens down there now—only Rudolf Serkin and Isaac Stern have been there longer. That's making me feel rather old these days. [Chuckles.]

Sometimes projects are dropped and picked up ten years later. I have several things sitting in the can from the mid-sixties which probably now will never see the light of day unless they come out in some special package, because they wouldn't stand up to today's electronic standards, but there have always been certain long-range guidelines as to what I wanted to do at CBS—such as all the important works of Bach—and within those guidelines we were free to experiment.

*You have had some celebrated collaborations—were they established on musical criteria or empathy?*

I think the personal chemistry has to be right. There is a recording just out of *Ophelia Lieder* by Richard Strauss, sung by Elisabeth Schwarzkopf. It is absolutely extraordinary, if I do say so myself. I cannot go into the complications that caused it to be released now, fifteen years after it was recorded. I had never worked with Schwarzkopf before, and an extraordinary pair of sessions yielded that recording. Also, she had never sung those songs and we had no time to rehearse because she was very busy at the Metropolitan Opera. We literally used our first take as a rehearsal. But right from the beginning, I felt a shiver going up the spine, you know—there was a sense that no matter how unusual or deviant our rubato might be, we were absolutely of one mind. Actually there are more songs where that came from, but I can't talk about it . . .

*You not only perform, but you edit and sometimes produce your own recordings. Were you invited to expand beyond your role as a pianist or did you insist on it?*

Well, I didn't insist on it. It gradually fell into my lap and I didn't reject it once it was there. As far as editing is concerned, I began in the mid-sixties to take a very serious look at precisely what we were doing in the post-production process, and I found that this work was not nearly careful enough—and here I'm not being critical of the people I worked with. The problem was simply mine. While I was still traveling around as a concert artist—prior to 1964—I simply didn't have the time to really concentrate on the specific takes and inserts, etc. This is not unusual for a concert artist—it is, in fact, the norm. As a result, I find many of my earlier recordings very irritating to listen to, even though they often have great vitality.

Once I was free of the onerous burden of giving concerts, I began to do a pre-edit of all the recordings. From that moment on, I began to realize what the editorial possibilities were and gradually developed certain theories about the way the time could be most usefully expended in a recording studio.

Schwarzkopf told me rather apologetically that she rarely recorded more than three minutes of music out of every given hour in the recording studio, and for me at the time her comment was astonishing, because I was routinely doing six or seven minutes. What I have subsequently arrived at is something under two minutes per hour, so I'm now even slower than she was. It isn't that I do endless numbers of takes. In fact, although I usually record eight hours at a time, during those eight hours I'm rarely at the piano for more than one hour. It is very rare that one eight-hour session yields more than two thirty-minute job reels.

The time is spent almost entirely sitting in the booth listening to play-backs again and again, trying to decide precisely what insert can best cover something you didn't like in a basic take or, indeed, in a previous insert. I do this using a digital stopwatch that measures literally down to a hundreth of a second. Nowadays, I'm positively happy to say there are very few splices that do not work, whereas in the old days a horrendously high percentage failed.

I try to use the studio as a filmmaker uses a screening room. In film terms I insist on seeing all the rushes as they are shot.

*A film director told me that one of his problems was that the end result can conceivably be perfect. Does that haunt you too?*

Not really. There are always peripheral problems which probably stand in the way of perfection.

*Can technical manipulation turn a less than perfect recording session into a fine recording?*

Oh yes, there are all kinds of things you can do. I could tell you stories of manipulation that would curl your hair. I'll give you one, but I won't tell you where it is—your readers can look for it if they wish. In a very recent recording of mine of Beethoven sonatas, two different pianos are used. Three movements of one sonata were recorded in 1976 on one piano, and the remaining movement was done in 1979 on another piano. Two more different pianos can not be imagined in terms of tonal quality. I knew this was going to be a problem, because there would be a dramatic change in ambiance in the middle of the recording. We did some preliminary experiments and got the two pianos into the same general tonal frequency, but we decided that close wasn't good enough. So we rented a very special graphic equalizer unit which had as many stops as an organ and managed to turn piano number two into piano number one, and nobody appears to have detected any difference in tonal quality. [Laughs delightedly at this electronic caper.]

*Do you work with the same crew all the time?*

Not really. I have a group of technicians who work with me as, and when, they are free to do so. I try to keep one or two with me on one project so they keep the rhythm of it going in their own minds.

*How would you define the recording artist as distinct from the concert artist?*

It's a tough question, but I'll take a stab at it since I once was one of those creatures [a concert artist]. I think a concert artist is somebody for whom the individual moment is more important than the totality. This might seem a contradiction, because the true-blue concert artist will tell you that they sacrifice the momentary for the sake of the whole, that they try for some magical, long line that works from first note to last, and even if they miss a few notes it really doesn't matter, because they have achieved a special mood or communication between the stage and the first row of seats or the last row of seats—whatever! I don't believe that is what they do at all, and having given a lot of concerts I know that what one really does in concert is concentrate on an individual collection of moments and string them together to create a superficial impression of a coherent result.

In any case, I personally never felt that kind of rapport with an audience. I felt quite the opposite—that the audience was getting in the way of what I wanted to do, and what I really wanted to do was say, "I think I'll do another take of this work because I didn't like the first one." It was very frustrating that I couldn't do that, and although a small voice inside sometimes whispered, "This is the time to say it," I obviously never did. [Laughs.]

The true recording artist, who really understands the values and implications of recording, is someone who is looking at the totality— sees it so clearly that it doesn't matter if you start with the middle note in the middle movement and work in either direction like a crab going back and forth. The mark of a true recording artist is an ability to be able to cut in at any moment in any work and say, "This works in a way that's only appropriate for this recording."

*Do you think that recorded music has the same aesthetic and physical effect on the listener as has live music?*

No, and I don't think it should have. I think that recorded music ought to have—forgive me for this—the effect of a tranquilizer really; it should not lead to the kind of visceral excitement that one presumably goes to the concert hall to find. I think that recorded music should try to create a one-to-one relationship between performer and listener—one thinks in terms of a certain kind of direction and immediacy, even in terms of the sound that one uses for recordings. The sound of a piano doesn't have to project to the last row in the balcony when a microphone is six feet away—the same way, after all, one speaks very differently when doing a film role than when doing a theater role. But that is a kind of adjustment that many people find difficult to make.

*To withdraw from the audience would for most concert artists be like cutting the umbilical cord.*

I used to have a motto back in my concert days and it served me in good stead for a number of years. In 1958 I was in Berlin feeling terribly depressed, not because I didn't want to play with Karajan, but because I was about to embark on three months of non-stop concert activity in Europe, which I had never done before without a break. Then some inner voice said to me, "Who ever said it's supposed to be fun?" [Laughs to himself.] That became my motto. It wasn't fun and consequently there was no discomfort in cutting the umbilical cord six years later. I was thirty-one when I stopped playing in public, and it was like being finally free to do what I wanted and not having to engage in that utterly wasteful activity . . .

*Did you ever question in your mind whether you could make a comfortable living by recording?*

At that time I wasn't sure. Certainly the particular markets that have become quite wonderful for me—Japan, Germany and so on— were at that time much less developed than they are now. But I had a reasonable suspicion that it would work out, and it was a step that had to be taken if I were to make music the way I felt it had to be made. I really couldn't see going on in that utterly counter-productive environment any longer.

*How was your relationship with conductors?*

I didn't have very many bad experiences with conductors and I had a lot of very good ones. I say all of this with the preamble that I basically do not like playing concertos at all. There is in the classical-romantic concerto a degree of competitiveness built into the rivalry between soloist and orchestra which is foreign to my nature. I don't believe in competition in any form, and the concerto is metaphorically the most competitive system one has in music. But the bad experiences with conductors I can count on the fingers of one hand and I'll name one of those fingers: Georg Szell—and you can quote me on that. He was a remarkable conductor, but our collaboration was an example of a total lack of chemistry. The polar opposite of Szell is Karajan who is a dream to work with and a most charming man—that might seem strange since he is often depicted as a positive ogre.

*You have described a performer as "being contaminated by the concert experience." Would the Szell experience come under that heading?*

Well, I think that a particular feud between a soloist and a conductor is fairly common. It's pretty hard to play under perhaps twenty conductors in one season without coming to dislike two or three of them [laughs], but I certainly did not have the kind of difficult relationship with conductors that many soloists have, and I think the reason for that related to my peculiar distaste for most concertos. I tried to play the solo parts in an obligato fashion, making the concerto a symphony with a piano part of some importance, but no more than that. Needless to say, that does no damage to the egos of certain conductors [knowing laughter]—they quite like that.

I will tell you a very special moment in my concert life. It was with Karajan and the Philharmonia Orchestra in Lucerne, 1959. We were playing the D Minor Bach Concerto and I had a terrible cold with high fever. Somehow we got through it, but because of this terrific cold and specifically because of the perspiration running into my eyes, I literally couldn't see. Then, in the last movement, there was one moment where something so extraordinary happened that I forced myself to pry my eyes open to see what this man was doing. That particular passage in the last movement always struck me as a bit prosaic [sings first the solo line and then the orchestral accompaniment], but suddenly something happened. It was one of those spooky moments, as when Schwarzkopf and I did the *Ophelia Lieder*. As I looked up I saw Karajan standing on the podium doing absolutely nothing! I have no idea of how long he had not been conducting— but we had been playing chamber music. At the end of that passage, he simply signaled and they began to play as a *tutti* group once again. But the magic of that moment had absolutely nothing to do with the fact that there were 2500 people sitting in the audience—that was accidental.

*I know that the romantic repertoire is not close to your heart and that you have strong likes and dislikes. In all fairness, do you think that two people hear the same thing when listening to the same music?*

I don't know. I never really thought about it. Probably there is a certain common vocabulary that one could apply if you and I were to sit and listen to any recording at all. You might like it and I might dislike it or vice versa, but I think we could find some kind of language to describe what we shared. Still, one hopes for a very individual reaction on the part of each listener.

*I rarely experience a piece of music the same way twice, so if it varies that much within one person, I wondered . . .*

Really! Well, I'll tell you about my experience, speaking as a listener. At any given time, I listen to maybe half a dozen recordings again and again and again. The same thing with films, by the way. I tape films on video cassette units—I'm the only person I know who will see a film forty or fifty times and study literally every shot in the film.

*What type of films?*

Oh, *Woman in the Dunes* is one of my favorites . . . but what I'm saying is that I feel comfortable with the experiences that I know and don't have the need to go out and look for new musical or film experiences.

*So if you like a work, the fascination keeps expanding?*

Exactly. Despite the fact that I have a lot of recordings in my collection, there are periods in my life when I seem to need a particular piece of music for many months, the way someone might need a Valium. [Laughs.] To give you one example, there was a period about two years ago, when I was working on my own [Richard] Strauss documentary, when I became so addicted to *Metamorphosen* that I really had to hear it every day. This went on for several months—it so transfixed and moved me and literally became part of my personality.

*To what do you ascribe the intensity with which you go about everything— playing, filming, writing and broadcasting?*

That's a very flattering comment, if it's true. I think it is due to the fact that I only do those things that I really want to do and care deeply about. In that way, you don't work matter-of-factly, but care passionately about each project and get tremendously involved.

*You are very intellectually inclined, but more than intellect goes into musical interpretation. What do you think shapes the distinctive Gould expression?*

That is very complicated. I would like to think that there is—especially in more recent years—a kind of autumnal repose in what I'm doing, so that much of the music becomes a tranquilizing experience in the same way that *Metamorphosen* was for me. I'm not saying that my own recordings achieve that, although I would be very happy if they did.

It would be nice if what we do in the recorded state could involve the possibility of some degree of perfection, not purely of a technical order, but also of a spiritual order. I think one starts out hoping that that will be so. One is obviously limited by the possible spiritual imperfections of the music being recorded as well as by one's own imperfections, but I think much more is involved than simply the exploration of the technical dimensions in both a performance sense and in an electronic sense.

*You jump with ease from Bach to Scriabin and Hindemith. Do you feel close to any contemporary composer?*

I can't say I feel very close. I am fascinated with many things that are happening, but what bothers me in the musical world—it's nothing new, but is as old as music itself—is the idea of a schism—the idea of moving in this direction or that direction according to the fashions of the day and of the combative elements within the factions that represent these schismatic polarities. I would love to see a musical environment in which one didn't have to choose sides. It has loosened up recently, though, and I think that is a very encouraging sign. But as recently as ten years ago there was this tremendous sense that "it's either/or and never the twain shall meet," and during that period, the entire propagandistic machinery of the media helped widen those factional disputes.

*What is your view of Canadian music?*

I recorded one Canadian album back in 1967 at the time of the Centennial, and I think there was in that album one piece of very great importance—Istvan Anhalt's *Fantasia*. I described it at that time as a masterpiece. But I'm not terribly up on what everyone is doing.

*What are your thoughts on Canadian nationalism?*

Well, that is the "in" topic. I think it is rather silly. I really haven't much sympathy with barriers, maybe because I haven't found any objections to my own participation in the musical life of other countries. I think there are tremendous virtues within the country and I personally am more at home with the somewhat reserved, quieter Canadian spirit than with the more energetic American spirit, and being Canadian I therefore understand the wish to preserve it. But I don't think that you necessarily preserve it by keeping those who didn't happen to be born here out of the country.

*Do you find any artistic elements here uniquely Canadian?*

Except for Eskimo carvings? I don't know. I think that in Canadian films—not necessarily films of particular distinction—there is a kind of unwillingness to be embarrassed by the cliché, which I find to be less true in America. Maybe that trait is also Finlandish or Upper Voltaish [laughs], so I wouldn't be willing to say that it is specific to this country and no other. But one tends to look for distinctions between this country and the one south of the border, and I think this might be one and it is valuable.

*Do you think that we are listening to too much music?*

No. There is this funny assumption, especially among professional musicians, that the fact that one is surrounded with wallpaper music is very harmful. I don't think it is harmful at all. I go into elevators that have it all the time, and when I go into restaurants it is usually there. Not only does it not bother me, but I have the ability to tune it out if I want to.

However, for most people it does something absolutely unique in history. However anaemic the music may be, it provides you with all the clichés of the nineteenth- and twentieth-century repertoire, so that inadvertently one is receiving a kind of education. Now, this kind of education would be of no particular value to a professional musician, but the truck driver, who has to stop every two hours at a roadside café, is picking up a mishmash of Puccini and Wagner and whatever else [laughs]—it might be called Mantovani, but nevertheless that's what it is. In the mind of that truck driver there then is a frame of reference—a basic vocabulary—which does not mean that when he hears Beethoven's Ninth Symphony, he will automatically recognize the music, but he will bring to it a certain tacit analytical perception. I think the reaction of most professional musicians to background music is that it lowers the excitement quotient . . .

*Or the ability to concentrate.*

Yes, but it seems to me that it perhaps leads one to want to transcend the clichés by virtue of knowing what they are. I don't think that one necessarily becomes hooked on them.

I am not a believer in this idea that a great musical experience has to be detached from everything else you do—that you make a pilgrimage by steamer and then by dog sled and finally arrive at some remote festival town and hear *The Ring of the Niebelung*, and that— because of that discomfort—it becomes a great moment in your life! It did happen in the nineteenth century at Bayreuth, to be sure, but I do think there is much more pleasure and much more intellectual satisfaction to be had from carrying a lot of information in your head all the time. In my own case, even if I play the piano very little, there is hardly any hour in the day when I'm not, in an interior way, thinking of some musical idea—even now, carrying on this conversation.

*So you think wallpaper music is a form of energy which is automatically escalating into something better?*

Yes, exactly. Mind you, I happen to have absolutely no tolerance whatsoever for any form of rock-and-roll, so if all Muzak systems converted to that, I would go out of my mind. [Laughs.] It would also be pretty difficult for me to get into an elevator with Janis Joplin . . .

*There seems to be a consistent form of criticism of your playing. For instance, I read recently in The New York Times about your new recording of Beethoven sonatas: " . . . infuriating at times, but nothing if not consistent and thought-provoking." Does that annoy you?*

It doesn't annoy me and I don't know if it is consistent—I hope it is—but I think there is a view that many writers tend to hold about my playing, which may be influenced by my rather substantial contact with the electronic media, that it has become the product of a very methodical study. I don't think that's altogether bad or untrue, but I would say, however, that my own aspirations for what I do in the recording studio are rather more than just the reproduction of all the right notes in the right places.

*Do you think that individual interpretation is lacking now more than before?*

In some sort of vague retrospective way it seems that there was a period when everybody was an individual. I'm not sure that was ever the case. There were obviously incredible individuals around the early years of this century. I happen to be a great Mengelberg fan, for example. He was one of the most extraordinary conductors who ever lived, and on the other hand he was also one of the most irritating. [Laughs.] There were also people at that time whom I would regard as maddeningly predictable much of the time.

*Is that because of an unwillingness to take chances?*

Yes. Even as a kid, growing up hearing Toscanini's broadcast every week, I thought of him as obviously a virtuoso conductor, but also a very prosaic conductor, nonetheless. I never found in him those transcendent moments that I found with Furtwängler, Mengelberg and Stokowski.

I suspect there have always been two views of how to make music. Some people have said, "We must find ways to transcend the notes on the page," while others have said, "Once the notes are down, the right playing is all that's called for and that is what the job is." And I'm not sure the ratio of those two kinds of musicians has changed all that much.

*Presuming you have another twenty-five years ahead of you to record, do you have a new direction in mind, a master plan?*

Yes I do. Part of the long-term plan that I developed when I was around twenty years old was to stop concertizing when I was thirty and to record probably until I was fifty. Well, I stopped concertizing in my early thirties and my contract with CBS runs a bit beyond my fiftieth year—but I'm not a stickler for such detail. After that, there is going to be a major change of gears, much as there was twenty years ago—about which I prefer to say nothing at the moment. I have always believed in change, because there are too many things I want to do.

# Christopher Keene

The phenomenon of the successful young North-American conductor is so recent in our orchestral world that a clear image of one is still in the making. Of the several homebred conductors who are likely to inherit some of the major symphony orchestras that are currently led by foreign conductors, the forty-one-year-old Christopher Keene is a most impressive contender. He has been music director of Artpark in Lewiston, New York, since its inception in 1974 and is now also its President. His aim is to challenge the audience to new musical experiences, so no summer pablum is served there. The current major project at Artpark is a Wagner Ring Cycle with *Siegfried* in 1987, and *Götterdämmerung* in 1988; Keene led the American premiere of Philip Glass's innovative opera *Satyagraha* in 1981; and he personally wrote the libretto for Stephen Douglas Burton's opera *The Duchess of Malfi*. Keene also finds time to compose and has written, for instance, the music for Eliot Feld's ballet *The Concert*.

Ever since Christopher Keene began organizing chamber music groups as a young child in his native California, he has been very active in his profession—first as a cellist and pianist, and starting in his teens as conductor, administrator and public speaker. He has been active in opera since he entered the University of California at Berkeley at the age of fifteen, organizing productions with other music students and gaining his first experience as a conductor. He claims that he really grew up when, at the age of twenty, he joined the New York City Opera as Julius Rudel's assistant, and during six years with the company became chief conductor next to him, conducting a total of fifty operas, thirty of which were without even one orchestra rehearsal.

Although he got a flying start as a conductor, Keene did not stand in front of a symphony orchestra until he was twenty-five years old. He had a large operatic repertoire but no symphonies or concertos,

and for some time he carried the stigma of his early specialization. For two years Keene was junior conductor in Spoleto, Italy, and when Thomas Schippers died prematurely he took over as music director. He spent his last three years there also as general manager and chief fund raiser, and he was instrumental in establishing the American Spoleto Festival in Charleston, North Carolina, before he left in 1979. During these exciting years of juggling performers and raising funds on two continents, Keene premiered five operas of Gian Carlo Menotti.

Maestro Keene likes to have a hand in creating the symbiosis of orchestra and public, which probably inspired him to establish tne Long Island Philharmonic Orchestra in 1979. In addition to the Spoleto Festivals in Italy and South Carolina, he was music director of the New York City Opera from 1982 to 1986, and of the Syracuse Symphony Orchestra from 1975 to 1984; he has conducted most major symphony orchestras in North America and opera performances at the Met, Covent Garden and the Hamburg Staatsoper.

This outspoken, cerebral conductor has found that words are a powerful bridge for people who are intimidated by music. Although he knows it is a matter of controversy, he will talk for as long as is needed to introduce an unfamiliar work. Keene does not think it advisable to specialize in a particular repertoire. All the same, he has a reputation for programming contemporary works, and has received awards for excellence in the presentation of new music. He is associated with a number of contemporary composers, including John Corigliano, Stephen Douglas Burton and Philip Glass.

Along with his American colleagues Michael Tilson Thomas, James DePreist, Leonard Slatkin and Lukas Foss, Keene is an ardent champion of making symphonic music a more integrated American experience. He sees his role as being quite different from that of the traditional European conductor's and is a most eloquent spokesman for his own generation in this 1982 interview.

*Colgrass: Have you felt a disadvantage being relatively young and American?*

Keene: There is no question that people are suspicious of very young talents, and with a certain amount of reason. Conducting is a very complicated profession. William Steinberg said it is one you only begin to understand when you are fifty years old, so youth can be a disadvantage—particularly when you deal with an orchestra of people who are all older than you. There is a certain residual resentment towards the conductor in any case, but once the initial resistance wears off and you are competent, organized and efficient, they respond to that.

The American issue is a more complex one. Our country is still new compared to Europe, and I think music is still viewed very much as a European art form. There is a presumption that a European conductor probably knows more and is better. Yet we have thirty or forty outstanding orchestras in America who really play rings around their European counterparts. When you say you are the conductor in Syracuse, New York, it doesn't make much of an impression, but if you say, for instance, that you are the conductor in Marseilles, France, where there is a pretty rotten orchestra, everybody is terribly impressed.

At the level of the ten biggest orchestras in America certainly there is an astonishing statistical lack of American conductors. I think that only one is conducted by an American [Leonard Slatkin in St. Louis]. When you get to the next level of twenty or thirty orchestras, Americans are doing really well. In the field of opera, the two most important positions in the world are currently filled by Americans—James Levine at the Metropolitan and Lorin Maazel at the Vienna State Opera. [Maazel left the Vienna State Opera in 1984 after much controversy.]

*Will this imbalance change in the coming years?*

It's a matter of breaking down the resistance of boards of directors, who are trying to acquire a patina of elegance and sophistication by importing a European figure.

*How does the music director's role differ on the two continents?*

The bureaucracy in Europe is of such long standing and on such a large scale that the responsibilities of a music director in Europe are only a fraction of what they are here. We have to be a combination of fund-raiser, politician, PR figure, talk-show personality, artist and conductor. Very few Europeans are equipped for those responsibilities. They find them repugnant and they also don't have the variety of skills it takes. A number of European conductors would love to play here because our orchestras play so well, are so quick and well organized by European standards, but they simply couldn't deal with the so-called administrative burdens.

*A young talent is more welcome in opera than in front of the symphony orchestra. Also, opera is where several women conductors got their first break. Why is that?*

Opera is a far more pragmatic world. The conductor here is much less the focus of attention than is the case in symphonic concerts. It also takes a very different technique to conduct opera, and many conductors are not equally happy in both worlds. With a symphony orchestra you have to develop your point of view and give the orchestra direction and purpose. In the opera house you are dealing with the points of view of soloists—many of whom have sung the part many more times than you have conducted the opera—there is the stage director's view, the scene designer's and so on. All those have to be brought together in one whole, and it is an entirely different role.

Very often a symphony conductor who reaches the age of fifty wants to try conducting opera and comes to grief, because when the tenor hits the high C and the conductor comes down, who is the orchestra to follow—the tenor or the conductor?

*So opera is a good school for a young conductor?*

You have to be ready for terrible things to go wrong—doors that don't open, people who forget their lines or the chorus that forgets its entrance. Even in the most well-integrated performance something goes wrong.

*What was it like being Julius Rudel's assistant?*

He would say to me: "There is a *Carmen* performance tomorrow night and you are going to conduct it." That's all the warning you would have. Consequently you would constantly have to know everything and be ready. If you didn't survive those concerts, he didn't think you had the intrinsic talent.

*Your conducting debut with the company was in Alberto Ginestera's Don Rodrigo—without a single orchestra rehearsal.*

In a sense it was a safer debut than it would have been with *Carmen* because nobody really knew what it was all about—including Mr. Ginestera who must have sat through one of the worst performances that his opera ever sustained. [Laughter.] It was a wretched performance—the brass wasn't with the strings, the stage wasn't with the orchestra and the chorus wasn't even in the same act! At the end I stumbled into my dressing room and said, "This was shameful." There was a knock on the door and in came Ginestera! He said, "It was a wonderful performance, I heard things for the first time." I don't know whether it was his way of telling the truth.

*Is there an ideal way to tackle the vast repertoire for symphony orchestra?*

The repertoire is truly endless. It is very difficult to imagine how trying the life of a conductor is from that standpoint—you have a stack of music five feet tall next to your piano and it never gets smaller. Maybe by the time I'm eighty I will have that repertoire under control, and I am looking forward to that day!

*With all that, how do you find the time to discover worthwhile new works?*

You have to develop a relationship with composers in whom you believe. Far more important than playing every composer who comes along—which is nearly impossible anyway—is to be able to say to certain composers: "You write it and we'll play it." This is a lifetime relationship which enables the composer to have a steady home for his music. You will find such relationships in the lives of most of the great composers in the past—they had certain conductors to whom they entrusted their premieres over and over.

The problem with programming new music is that the conductor is in constant middle ground between how much music he can get his audience to swallow before he begins to erode his own power base. I premiered a work by Roger Sessions, his Ninth Symphony. To me it was a great honor to have a Pulitzer Prize-winning composer like Sessions create a work for our orchestra. He came to Syracuse and spoke, and it was a wonderful occasion. The rest of the program, I might add, was Tchaikovsky and Handel, so it was hardly difficult to swallow—but I have never had such an uproar! At least twenty or thirty people canceled their subscriptions as a result of these twenty minutes of music. I had letters and editorials in the newspapers and was admonished by the Board that "no wonder the orchestra was broke when I played music like that."

I was very shocked and stunned by that. For one thing, I never quite figured out why it is music that arouses such hostile responses. After all, people go to an art gallery and look at paintings that they might find even obscene or disturbing without threatening never to go to a gallery again. You can go to a movie which lasts for two and a half hours, decide you have been swindled or bored, and you don't stop going to the movies. So I don't know why it is that a contemporary symphony, that takes twenty minutes, can arouse such tremendous hostility.

*Are musical audiences so conservative because their knowledge of music is slight?*

One of my great concerns about the future of music in the U.S. is that amateur music-making is declining, so that our audiences are less and less educated. It's true audiences are growing, but they know less and less, and therefore the pressures upon us to restrict the repertoire are greater and greater. It concerns me desperately. I am involved also in broadcasting in Syracuse, and we receive regularly the entire broadcast schedules of all the big ten orchestras. Generally, the larger the orchestra the less imaginative and more predictable the programming is.

*Sometimes you introduce unfamiliar works.*

I try to keep it light, I try not to lecture or give analyses—but I talk about the composer, what to listen for.

*What made contemporary music so out of step with audiences?*

The moment the composer was removed from having to please his audience in order to feed his family and could be subsidized by academic institutions, which have little or no interest in performance, we took a wrong turn.

We have often felt that the academic establishment is the enemy of the professional musical establishment within the community. Far from being the ardent supporters of one's orchestra, they tend to be the first people to put down the orchestra and complain about its standards and the musical tastes of its conductor.

I will never forget one of the really revelatory experiences in my life when I was fifteen and went to college. The first thing I wanted to do at the University of California was to start an opera company, because there was not even an opera workshop in the music department. The head of the department was Joseph Kerman, a man famous for having written a book called *Opera as Drama*, and I went to him with my project which was to organize my friends into a performance of *The Crucible* by Robert Ward. Kerman looked at me and said: "Mr. Keene, would you not encourage the performance of music in this department. It inevitably lowers academic standards."

*You've worked with Menotti. How did you meet him?*

Menotti called me up out of the blue when I was nineteen years old. He had been looking for a young assistant to Thomas Schippers for the Spoleto Festival in 1967. I had been recommended by Kurt Herbert Adler of the San Francisco Opera, who was very anxious to get me out of town since he didn't like any other operatic activity in San Francisco at any level, even my small college productions.

*Do you enjoy premiering new works?*

To bring a piece to life for the first time is tremendously exciting. I have conducted premieres of operas by Hans Werner Henze, Thomas Pasatieri, Carlisle Floyd and Stephen Burton. There is the great argument whether the conductor is a creative artist or a recreative artist, but if there is ever a time when he approaches creativity, it is when he is bringing a new work to life for the first time. The responsibility is tremendous. After all, Beethoven's Fifth is here to stay, *Aida* is here to stay no matter what kind of conductor is going to conduct them, but a new work can rise or fall on the basis of a first performance. However, one can't possibly tell the value of a new work by one hearing—I never form an opinion until I hear a work two or three times.

But I also want to perform obscure works by famous composers. As for new works, there simply is no such thing as "modern music"— there is simply music. It has chronological relativity, but what most people refer to as "modern music" was written around 1913-14, long before our present audience was born.

*You seem to suggest an anti-intellectual bias about music in the United States.*

There is no point in kidding ourselves that it is otherwise. Statistics of symphony concerts are simply frightening. Between one and two percent of the population become steady patrons of the symphony orchestras. To survive the economic crises that are certain to afflict orchestras in the next quarter century, we are going to need a much broader basis of support.

I have been fascinated by studies of American audiences. One shows that there are two main reasons why people go to concerts: by far the smaller reason is that they are professional musicians or play an instrument or went to concerts with their parents . . . that is about twelve to fourteen percent. It is also the most knowledgeable and sophisticated segment. The remaining eighty-four percent go because it is a social thing and because they have a good time. Now, you realize this when you get into the problem of contemporary music. The people who know very little about music enjoy it as long as they feel everyone else enjoys it. The moment they feel that others are disturbed or angry or bored, it affects their own perception of what they are hearing. They don't simply listen and say, "I like it" or "I don't like it."

*So you think that simply listening can make listeners confident in their own taste?*

It is as if eating a meal—you don't require an analysis of it to know whether you enjoyed it or not. You are also capable of trying something interesting and saying that you don't want a second helping without being offended or feeling you have been swindled intellectually or taken advantage of.

Unfortunately there is this tremendous gap between the audience and what happens on the stage, which appears mysterious, arcane, erratic. What musicians are and what they do is almost incomprehensible to a vast portion of our audience, and that is one of the reasons that I speak. Just hearing that a musician can actually speak the English language, and that he can make fun of himself and be human, can dispel the image of the musician as a tall, austere person with white hair.

*Are music critics and reviews helpful to audiences?*

The response of the audience is very much determined by critical reviews. However, I think that careers are very little beholden to reviews. The general level of music criticism is terribly low. Most critics are not trained in music and they are not even trained intellectuals.

It is not fair that the performers should have a negative press release before they enter the hall from a person whose credentials I don't acknowledge. I have two reviews here from the same concert—the morning paper says we played disgracefully slow and the evening paper that it was disgustingly fast.

*What prospects do you see for classical music in the United States?*

The current stance of the regime and President Reagan's attitude towards arts funding in general is going to set things back at least a decade in America. It was only after the war that we began to educate simultaneously the corporate sector, the private sector and the government, and by 1975 very encouraging strides had been made in all of those fields. Each one was beginning to recognize its responsibility, beginning to institutionalize it and to make it possible to rely on certain elements of support. Now what has happened is that the President is cutting back, which was supposed to stimulate local support for local arts groups.

It has had the opposite effect! For one thing it has withdrawn the endorsement of the government for the arts in general. It has announced they are not a priority, they are an expendable luxury, and "if you want them in your town, fine—go ahead." For the trivial amount of money that was expended on the arts by the federal government, its withdrawal has had a disastrous rippling effect. Municipalities have said: if the government with its vast resources can't support the arts, how can we be expected to? The corporations, who were just beginning to be convinced that perhaps this was a legitimate cause, now have it all dumped upon them, and they don't want any part of it-- they are having their own troubles.

It is a very severe situation and several orchestras are faced with extinction. It is a tragedy, because an institution takes decades to erect and it can be demolished in a single season.

# Anton Kuerti

An exotic-looking, weather-beaten van has been seen across this continent, from the eastern provinces to the southern states. It has a curious triangular space protruding from the roof to accommodate something. A race horse? Machinery perhaps? No, it is a Yamaha grand en route to the next concert to be played by the driver, Anton Kuerti. To him this is a normal procedure; he prefers doing things his own way. These long treks, which would daunt most performers, simply assure him that he will perform on a reliable piano. He will also be asking for a modest fee at his destination, because he finds it unethical to squeeze the concert presenter too hard for his evening's work. If this sounds like a performer on the fringe of the main circuit, nothing could be further from the truth. Kuerti is a first-rate pianist, acclaimed for his concert performances and recordings. He has recorded the complete cycle of Beethoven sonatas as well as Beethoven's piano concertos with the Toronto Symphony, under Andrew Davis, on the CBC label.

Aside from his musical integrity, Anton Kuerti is known for his involvement in political and environmental causes. He is a vegetarian who places large "No Smoking" signs in his two adjoining houses in downtown Toronto, where he lives with his wife, cellist Kristine Bogyó, and two young sons. One of his houses was acquired for running the Festival of the Sound, which he founded at Parry Sound, Ontario, in 1980. No wonder this intriguing, outspoken performer has built a following among serious listeners. He was born in Vienna in 1938, arrived in the U.S. shortly thereafter and came to live in Canada in 1965. As this 1983 interview points out, he is known not only for his music, but also as a speaker who gives his audiences introductory talks and occasionally asks them to leave if they can't be still while he is playing.

*Colgrass: Your technical strength and intensity make you a challenging pianist.*

Kuerti: Well, I don't try to make my performances either difficult or easy to digest. I try to follow the spirit of the composer as best I can determine it. Everyone is convinced that their own interpretation is the correct one; I'm convinced of the same thing. We can't all be right—and on the other hand, maybe we all can be right. Like viewing something through a prism, you can get different reflections of music, and I don't think my playing is more difficult to listen to than that of other people. I may tend to play music that is somewhat more challenging intellectually than others, although very much of my repertoire is not particularly challenging, certainly in comparison to people who make a specialty of playing new music.

*Often I have to guess who is playing in a concert broadcast, but I usually recognize you.*

I read an interview with Detlev Kraus, who is emerging as one of the major German pianists. He spoke about the search for individuality among pianists. Because there are so many pianists playing the same works, there is almost a disease of trying to make it super-personal for the sake of being different, and often to the detriment of music. I agree with him that it is a very real danger, especially with the proliferation of recordings; you are constantly hearing the well-known repertoire played in different versions. One can develop this horror of sounding like anyone else, when in some cases the consensus interpretation could be correct. Also it may very often not be. That is one reason why I tend to listen very little to records.

*When you do listen, what is your preference?*

I am absorbed by music very much of the time and therefore I will not tolerate Muzak or background music. When I listen to records, it is very often something I can't play myself—symphonies or great choral works. With all these recorded performances of piano music available, one has the constant opportunity to compare one performer with another. You may say: I've got to make it different, I can't be one more faceless interpreter. This can end up in perversity and in distortion of the music for non-musical reasons. It's perhaps also a question of an unnecessary degree of vanity. Right or wrong, I like to feel that I have developed my interpretation without help, that this is something I have gotten directly from the composer.

*Could performance tradition point you in the right direction?*

I'm not really interested in tradition, because very often the tradition was poor. In the late nineteenth century the tradition became outrageously improper with all sorts of additions which distorted and colored the works of great composers with individual and usually not very convincing insights of the particular musician. These editions were then used by whole generations of pianists.

Even Czerny [a pupil of Beethoven] didn't transmit the Beethoven tradition correctly. A few days ago I was looking at a piece that I have never played—a rondo by Beethoven for piano and orchestra. It is full of figurations that are absolutely not Beethoven's style. When I looked into it a little further, I saw in a reference book that it was probably completed by Czerny because it went way beyond the range of the piano of Beethoven's day.

Beethoven himself went into an absolute rage at Czerny who one day played his Quintet for Piano and Winds (op. 16) and added a few little cadenzas of his own. Beethoven stormed out but wrote a letter to Czerny the next day apologizing for his boorish behavior and explained that performers should have pity on the poor composer who simply wants to hear his music as he wrote it.

So when the tradition was already broken in Beethoven's day, I think there is very little we can learn in terms of authenticity from the tradition in how to play the great works. That is not to say that we can't learn something from other great interpeters, and certainly it would be a mistake to isolate oneself totally, especially during one's formative years.

*Do you expand your repertoire with ease?*

I have a good memory in the sense that I can learn pieces very rapidly. If I have a clear week, I would certainly not shy away from learning a medium-sized Beethoven sonata and performing it at the end of the week. But I also forget very rapidly. The first thing I forget is my interpretations. I'm actually quite happy about this, because a great part of my pleasure is listening carefully to how it can be played in a more meaningful, more authentic way. If I could just rattle off what I had decided ten years ago, I think it would become stale and I wouldn't enjoy it.

*I read that Aldo Ciccolini would work out a piece completely in his head before playing it.*

I have done that as an exercise a few times. Surprisingly, it is quite an efficient way of working. I made a point of doing it a few years ago when I learned the fugue to the *Hammerklavier*. The piece had always made a very weird impression on me; I thought it didn't sound quite coherent. It then occurred to me that Beethoven was totally deaf when he wrote this, so he was hearing it internally, and I decided to learn it internally before I got my fingers moving through it. I would work at it very strenuously away from the piano a couple of hours a day, and I don't do that very often because I'm just a little bit lazy.

One of the wonderful things about being a musician is the combination of the intellectual, the physical and the spiritual, and it seems almost artificial not to enjoy the mechanical part at the same time as the musical.

*You are often described as a musician of intellectual bent. Yet there are many fine musicians who achieve excellent results without a keen intellect. To what extent do you think your intellect guides your musicianship?*

If you want to put me into a category, I'm not sure that I would belong in one of intellectual musicians. I'm a little suspicious of that term. Certainly much great music has wonderful intellectual content, but sometimes that can be arrived at instinctively. Some great performers would play magically when young, like Menuhin, and I think it is very unlikely that his performances of Mozart at the age of ten were led by his intellect. So I think it is a danger to over-intellectualize music, just as it is a danger to pretend there is no intellectual content.

I try to understand music as far as it can be understood, but I think one is more successful by understanding musically and not verbally. As Mendelssohn said, the thoughts and themes of music are not too ill-defined—on the contrary, they are too precise to be put into words.

*When did you first zero in on Beethoven?*

There is hardly a musician who is not interested in the music of Beethoven.

*But not necessarily being as successful an interpreter as you are.*

If there is any special turning point, it was when Alan Toff at Hart House [University of Toronto] asked me to play the thirty-two sonatas in concert. I had played all of the concertos by that time, but not even half of the sonatas.

*Did you find it more difficult to perfect your interpretation of Beethoven than other repertoire?*

No, I didn't think that it took more effort to arrive at my Beethoven interpretations than it did at my Schumann, Schubert or Brahms interpretations. Perhaps, in fact, these composers are not different enough. I do see them as being in a certain linked tradition. Indeed, in a few measures you might be confused between them if you didn't know who wrote them.

*What makes music worthy of being included in your repertoire?*

I have to be able to respond to it and to love it genuinely. I don't like to play something as a duty. Yet I will confess that in playing the thirty-two Beethoven sonatas there were one or two that I would just as soon not have played and which I won't play except as part of the cycle. Sometimes I think it is worth one's while to absorb and learn a work that doesn't really appeal to one. For one thing, as an exercise, and for another thing, to see if one just hasn't seen the true light.

*And have you turned around in some cases?*

With Schubert my attitude has shifted quite remarkably over the years. I remember as a student in my late teens reading through all the Schubert sonatas and thinking: really, this music is over-rated. It often seemed repetitive, awkward and long. Over the years I have certainly come to adore Schubert's sonatas and I don't find them too long at all—on the contrary.

[Kuerti has recently completed recording all of Schubert's sonatas—"except the unfinished, juvenile ones"—on his own initiative in the Theater of the Arts in Waterloo. He is now looking for a label that will market the five or six CDs.]

*How about his lieder? I remember you once stated that the texts cannot be properly appreciated by listeners who do not have an intimate knowledge of German.*

Not all of the poetry of Schubert's lieder is of a high standard. It is a well-known fact that the best poems for songs are usually not the cream of the literature, and Schubert drew from a wide variety of sources, including some poems he wrote himself. Often the very twisted, complex German is not renderable in English—either you lose the meaning or it sounds hopelessly opaque. Also, there are often texts of great simplicity that lose their charm in English and end up sounding trite.

*Is there music that you played and loved in your younger years and have now dropped?*

Well, I used to play the Weber *Konzertstück*, but I can really live without that today. I also used to play Brahms' opus 5, the F Minor Sonata, but when I programmed it a few years back I found that I couldn't quite believe in it anymore—it's a little inflated and doesn't quite ring true.

*Is there any composer today who writes music you find worthwhile?*

I'm going to be taking a year off in 1985 to get a chance to do some of my own composing again as well as learn some new works. One composer I'm very interested in is Tomáš Svoboda, a Czech living in the U.S. I have played Messiaen, but I have a certain inhibition against making myself part of his Catholic mysticism. It doesn't bother me at all with music of the past—by Bach, for example—but this is really music that expresses a profound religious fanaticism of today, one that may be very valid and beautiful, but one which I can't identify myself with. Maybe I'm being a bit foolish and should forget about the titles and regard it as simply music.

*Do you think it is conceivable to be both a composer and a pianist?*

It always used to be. Look at Chopin and Liszt. It may be more difficult in the twentieth century. Still, there have been a number of distinguished composer/performers—Scriabin was one. As music gets harder to perform it takes more time to write, so it may be that this complexity makes it more difficult to combine. Eventually I would like to write a piano concerto.

[Kuerti did produce a piano concerto during his year off. The half-hour work was well received at its premiere in Victoria, B.C., in the spring of 1987. Being very interested in computers, he used one to copy the work and the parts, and he is going back to both keyboards to make revisions before the next performance.]

*You are known as a man of principle in music as well as other areas of life. Do you find that artists have an obligation to take an active part in the issues of today?*

Not just artists! I think everyone should do their utmost to see that this planet endures and also to try to help alleviate the suffering of their fellow human beings. In a certain sense the artist, perhaps, has even more of a duty to fulfill this obligation, first of all because he is to some extent in a position to be influential. Also, whether I like it or not, I often find myself playing in the presence of government people, although I haven't played for any of the supreme leaders of the world. I'm just as happy about that and would probably refuse invitations to play in either the Kremlin or the White House.

*Would you consider Trudeau a supreme leader?*

No, I wouldn't, although he might disagree with me. [Laughs.] If one does play in front of these individuals and does not say anything, then in fact one is supporting them and their policies.

*Would you actually address them at a concert?*

That would perhaps be in questionable taste, although at a certain point taste becomes unimportant. I think if I were playing in front of someone whom I considered a mass murderer, yes, I might surprise him and say a few words. Once, during the height of the Vietnam War, I was doing a big performance in Aspen, and the then Secretary of Defense, Robert MacNamara, who was in personal command of the napalm bombings and poisoning of the Vietnamese countryside, was in town. It was rumored that he might show up at this concert, so I was planning to ask for a minute of silence in memory of the victims of the American war. But he didn't arrive.

*Which causes have you been active in?*

Amnesty International, Oxfam, The Canadian Committee of Scientists and Scholars. I'm going to give a benefit concert for the NDP [New Democratic Party] this season. Going back a few years I was involved in the Committee For A Sane Nuclear Policy, Operation Dismantle and medical aid to Vietnam, North and South. I was music editor of a recent book on whales with the proceeds going to Greenpeace.

*Do you think the current demonstrations around the world to contain nuclear weapons will carry enough weight soon enough to have an effect?*

I don't think you can look at demonstrations from that point of view. You can't not demonstrate. You must try to exert whatever pressure you have in whatever way you can, even if it is only to resolve your own conscience. Mind you, if everyone would resolve their conscience in this way, it would certainly change the policies. Demonstrations did help to at least shorten the Vietnam War, and the massive demonstrations in Europe are not going to be ignored. People may argue that there is no peace movement in the Soviet countries, so what's the point of demonstrating here? That is fallacious. We have seen very large upheavals in Eastern Europe, and people there would act if they were convinced that their government was the obstacle to peace. They have such a horror of war there.

*There seems to be both ignorance and arrogance concerning war on this continent.*

It is intolerable and at the same time very surprising. Aside from the moral question of invading countries just because one doesn't agree with what is going on in them—which, after all, is one of our main gripes against the Soviet Union—Americans seem to be extending themselves in a dangerous fashion from a strategic point of view. They seem to be under a sort of cowboy illusion of omnipotence.

*Having two young children, do you ever despair over the future?*

I think the future looks terrible. That is one reason why the current nuclear-deterrent policies are so impermissible. If there is even a five percent chance that they won't work—and the reality is probably closer to ninety-five percent—they are so obviously suicidal. The risks of starting to disarm would be so much smaller. But I'm far from optimistic. It is really very likely that mankind is not going to see the end of this century, at least in a form that is recognizable, but that shouldn't keep one from doing everything possible to change the situation.

*Do you see any possible event that could turn the tide?*

There are lots of events that could turn the tide. This may sound factitious, but if the greenhouse effect of carbon dioxide warming the planet could raise the level of the oceans a few meters in the next twenty years, we might save all the major cities which are situated at sea level. Possible alarm over this and other environmental issues could distract mankind from the stupidity of the arms race.

*It would boil down to being simply a matter of finance?*

One could easily say today that one ought to direct a large portion of the arms build-up to the shameful poverty, illiteracy and lack of development, but it is not being done.

*How do you find time for all these activities?*

Well, I simply cut into my sleep.

*People who work with you say that you drive them and yourself pretty hard.*

I sometimes regret it, and that is one reason why I'm taking a year off. I will have the time to catch up on some reading and spend more time with my family.

*You are also a teacher.*

I don't teach privately at all. As a member of the music faculty at the University of Toronto I have only two students at the moment.

*How do you select your students?*

I'm not very skillful at it. Some of the finest students I ever had I wanted to turn down at first—for instance, Jane Coop and Kathryn Root, both of whom turned out to be marvelous students and very accomplished artists. I audition students, but I still haven't discovered quite what to listen for.

*Of course, your ability as a teacher has a lot to do with the students' development.*

It is a mutual thing. Some students have gotten along with me very well, others I haven't been able to help so well and I'm sure it is not all their fault.

*How did your own teachers shape you, particularly Arthur Loesser and Rudolf Serkin?*

Loesser was the most extraordinary teacher I ever had because he had both artistic ability and tremendous breadth of knowledge, and not just in music. He spoke many languages and knew Japanese so well that after the war he helped decode Japanese secret documents. He was a man who played *The Well-Tempered Clavier* from memory and all the student repertoire plus salon music. When this man died, I'm convinced that some music disappeared with him that doesn't even exist in print anymore. His psychology as a teacher was so wonderful. He really was your friend and ally, and if you played well his eyes would sparkle.

Serkin, whom I respect on the same level as Loesser, served more as an inspiration by example and by his total integrity. But—with all due respect—as a psychologist he was not the best teacher. When someone played something that didn't suit him, he would make this terrible face and not say anything for fifteen or twenty seconds, as though you had really wounded him to the core of his being. Yet he is a terribly friendly and warm man.

Perhaps he shares the idea of teachers like János Starker, with whom my wife studied, that the performer must become hardened and must become able to face difficult situations. This may be valid for some students, but I'm not sure it is the most productive approach. It's not one I try to pursue.

*Talking about hardening the performer—you have been distracted by audiences. Can you enumerate the ways?*

Well, it is certainly not a thing I'm terribly proud of, because I think that in the same way a teacher should be seen as a friend of the student, the performer must also be seen as a friend of the audience. It is very bad to create a hostile atmosphere where people are worried about shifting their position slightly. On the other hand, music can't exist in anything but an ambiance of almost total silence, so if there is a continuous disturbance then I feel I must say something. I try to do it in a humorous way so I don't embarrass people, but I feel I have not always been successful at that.

*Looking at the positive side of talking to audiences, you are known for your informative introductions to music. When did you start doing that?*

Actually, it is the rare concert where I talk. I detest the idea of talking just to prove that you are a jolly old fellow and you are just like everybody else, cracking jokes like a disc-jockey who sits on the edge of the stage. I only like to speak when there is something to say.

Most of my speaking has been done in connection with my complete Beethoven cycle, where it seems to me that it makes the experience so much more valuable if you have a sense of what is happening in these sonatas. Usually I come on and speak, then leave the stage and wait a few minutes. I am not sure I necessarily play better when I have given an introduction, because I sometimes become too conscious of some details I have just spoken about.

*Are you still in the habit of taking modest fees for playing?*

I think my fees are high, other people think they are modest. This is a difficult battle to fight for many reasons. It is true that the concert presenters simply refuse to believe that anybody will take less than they can squeeze out of them, so they assume that there must be some lack of quality. Even a quite idealistic management would be super-human if they could ignore that another artist would give them double the commission for a concert. At the same time I see the terrible plight of the symphony orchestras and I know how hard it is to raise money.

*How about accepting the higher fees that your colleagues get and using the funds for your numerous causes?*

That is certainly a possible point of view. But as a former concert promoter I resent the few occasions when we had to pay a really high fee. It is supposed to be an art, not a business. A musician arrives to do what he claims is his mission in life, sharing emotional and philosophical insights with us. He spends twenty-four hours and takes $6000, for which we would need to hold twenty-five bake-sales or go another six months without a professional administrator.

*There are some soloists who get around $50,000 per performance—that is even more absurd and ruinous for the music profession.*

Horowitz goes on a percentage basis, I think, eighty percent of the gross ticket sale. It is a corruption of the art. Even $25,000 for Perlman and people like that just doesn't fit in with what art is supposed to be.

*Do you think the piano repertoire has diminished in recent years because of this?*

Oh, I think other tendencies have pulled in the opposite direction. There is the recording industry that wants every work recorded, whether it deserves it or not. Also people have become interested in quite a few composers who were before unsalable. Look at Mahler and Schubert some years back.

*What caused you to come to Canada?*

A combination of factors. I lived in the States and had become relatively better known in Canada than in the U.S. Also I wanted to escape the throes of the Vietnam war and live in a country where most of my money would not be used for armaments.

*Do you think the rapid growth of music in Canada in recent years has been worthwhile on every level?*

Yes, one can't have a musical life that is all on the top international level. You also have to have minor leagues and amateur activities. I think amateur music-making is the thing most missing. It used to be the base on which it was all founded. People would play for their own enjoyment and then go to concerts for inspiration and learning.

Any music is worthwhile as long as it really absorbs the attention and is not overly loud or totally trite—like "Hooked on Classics," which I think is the supreme perversion. I can't understand that any orchestra will play it even if it meant the crucial difference between survival and extinction—that's the point where I would rather go and farm than do this to my musical art! Aside from these extremes and Muzak, which goes in one ear and out some other opening [laughs], music can be a valuable experience even if it is not a style that I love.

*Our attention span for music seems different from that of reading, for example. It is easy to be absorbed by a book for hours, but listening like that is more difficult for us. Why?*

When you are reading you can choose your own speed, you can go back and reread something and choose the moment to read. In music there is the whole ritual of going to a concert. If you doze off you can't turn back. The fact that it happens only once can be a positive thing, sharpening your senses and making it a unique experience.

*How much are you aware of the audience during a concert, coughing aside?*

You can feel when you set up a real atmosphere, when you have been able to cast a spell.

*Were you a born performer?*

I got started in a way which almost seems invented in the retelling. I went to my nursery-school teacher and asked her to give me piano lessons. She thought that my parents had sent me, but they hadn't. In fact, my parents didn't think I had a very good ear because I couldn't carry a tune. Also, we were very poor, having just immigrated to the States. Yet they agreed to let me try lessons for one month — and I'm still at it.

# Erich Leinsdorf

Erich Leinsdorf's demand for concentration is almost intimidating. A few distractions that caused my eye to wander during this interview in 1978—such as a stranger peeking into the hotel lounge or a quick check to see if the tape recorder was working—immediately brought a startled look to his face and interrupted our conversation. However, when the maestro is used to holding the undivided attention of eighty orchestra musicians, it must be a nuisance to face an undisciplined interviewer who can't look him straight in the eye for even one hour.

Born in Vienna in 1912, Leinsdorf is among the last conductors of the old European school. His solid musical background has some tried and true ingredients—studies in composition and theory, of piano, cello and conducting. He went through a stint as a singing coach and rehearsal pianist before becoming Bruno Walter's assistant in Salzburg in 1934. His American affiliation began at the Metropolitan Opera in 1937 as assistant conductor, and he subsequently spent the bulk of his career as music director of the symphony orchestras of Cleveland, Rochester and Boston. Since 1969 Leinsdorf has spent his life as a visiting conductor of major orchestras on both sides of the Atlantic, leaning towards large German works and occasionally lending his quick learning ability and excellent memory to the performance of new works. At the age of seventy-five, he recently celebrated the fiftieth anniversary of his American debut by leading the New York Philharmonic in Haydn's *Seasons*.

*Colgrass: You have said that musicians should do their talking in private, especially when they become so famous that their words carry too much weight.*

Leinsdorf: Oh, I speak publicly with the greatest pleasure about my field. What I referred to was private indiscretions, as in Artur Rubinstein's book. I do not care with whom Rubinstein slept—it has nothing to do with his artistry. I'm sure that Mr. Rubinstein, in issuing

his book with the silly business of his youth, made some people embarrassed. Another thing I don't like is for a public figure, who has a certain standing in his field, to give his public endorsements in other areas where he is supposed to have an automatic expertise. In my book there is very little about my private life. [*Cadenza*, Houghton Mifflin Co., Boston, 1976.]

*You said in your book, "Mellow I'm not."*

That is true, and in musical questions I'm getting more and more intolerant. At the moment I'm writing a new book strictly for professional performers—to teach them how to study, to learn and read music. [*The Composer's Advocate: A Radical Orthodoxy for Musicians*, Yale University Press, 1981.] The performer must study the music without middlemen and without recordings.

*You have mentioned that orchestra members very often are under-trained and unsophisticated, and that a conductor's "traffic signals" are about all they see. Opera singers you have often found "innocent of musical culture" . . .*

Yes, and unfortunately it has come to the point where even conductors, through abuse of recordings, are innocent of musical sophistication. Two things decline through abuse of recordings: the literacy in music, and the ability to read music. The individual ways to interpret composers decline if people become influenced by other performers to such an extent that they will hardly be able to detach themselves. If a young person has listened to sixteen versions of the Fourth Symphony by Brahms, he doesn't necessarily know what is going on in the symphony. When he can't answer my questions, it means he has learned by rote, but he doesn't know the work. I proved this years ago in Tanglewood, when I asked a group of young conductors certain basic questions about well-known scores—they were just guessing and didn't know the score. But when I asked questions about something that could be learned from recordings, everybody knew the answer.

*What do you consider the Golden Age in music?*

The Golden Age is with us right now. Some people say, "Oh, you should have heard so-and-so in 1949!" We have excellent talent today. When you hear Jon Vickers, whom I performed with recently in New York, you know we are in the Golden Age. We have Horowitz and Brendel and so on—there is no shortage of great performers. But there is a decline today of several elements in music, such as the literacy of conductors.

*Isn't part of the problem that there is no set background for a conductor?*

That is inevitable—you see, there is no way of practicing this craft.

Today we have a surprising number of conductors out of the ranks of instrumentalists, both orchestra players and soloists, such as Rostropovich, Eschenbach, Oistrakh, etc. That means a number of things. For the soloists I think it means a discontent with the ways the orchestra accompanies them, or perhaps an attempt to produce the same thing in the orchestra which they produce as soloists. That, I think, is a delusion. The orchestra players who take up conducting do it, I think, because of what they endure with conductors—that's understandable. In general, though, there can be no previous preparation for a conductor, because you can't teach this art. The preparation of a conductor is a purely contemplative one.

I remember a new guest conductor who came to the New York Philharmonic. At the first rehearsal he asked the stage manager to remove "the monument," meaning the music stand with the score. He then proceeded to rehearse Tchaikovsky's Fourth, and in a few moments it was clear that he didn't know the work. He was standing there counting his bars with a glazed eye staring fixedly at some point. Fellows like that are trying to impress Mrs. Grande in the gallery and are concentrating on themselves. What the musicians do—perhaps reading the racing form—the conductor doesn't know, because he is busy counting his bloody bars and periods.

*You have a remarkably clear beat . . .*

The way you conduct physically cannot be taught. It is a very difficult thing to show a twenty-year old how to use his body—in sports some can't manage to swing a tennis racket or golf club. In conducting, the body motion must come out of the personality, so a conductor must develop himself in relation to the music, with the least interference.

At this point in my career I'm humoring a bad right arm—doing less with it, since it hurts me too much.

*You still do a vigorous windmill. [Hearty laughter behind puffs of cigar smoke.] You have talked about your childhood's rich cultural world in Vienna. Do you think there is a way for a natural talent to overcome growing up in a barren cultural environment?*

No. If you take a plant and try to grow it in unfavorable soil, no matter how strong the seed is, the plant dies. I'm not a horticulturalist, but I know you can't expect to grow an orange in a cold climate.

I like to equate living organisms to works of art—both have a life expectancy, some longer than others. During my career I have seen how certain works perish practically under one's eyes . . . just pass away.

*You are perhaps the only major conductor who will look at a new score.*

Yes, and I look at plenty. When I started freelancing ten years ago, there was the assumption that I would settle for a few standard programs, but instead I have done a number of first performances, such as commissioned works by Berio and Schuller. It is essential that I don't limit myself, and I enjoy doing new works. Some orchestras come to me when they program new works, because even guest conductors won't deal with them. This situation is partly why I'm writing my book—the conductors must learn better and faster. They have to read music. It is not enough to read notes or listen attentively to records.

*After years as permanent conductor for orchestras such as the Boston Symphony, you are now living out of a suitcase.*

Life is much more pleasant since I started to tour constantly. I don't go in for any crazy schedules, flying from continent to continent. After I go over three or four time zones I leave three days to rest, and I will refuse an engagement rather than work against jet lag. I like to be healthy and enjoy what I'm doing. Traveling has become less pleasurable than it was ten years ago, the flights are more crowded, and the hotels are all getting worse. [Which was just emphasized by a waiter who refused to walk five extra steps to serve us coffee in the hotel lounge.]

*How can a conductor and music director divide himself between two major orchestras in opposite ends of the continent?*

I'll tell you how: by fraud! When you find that an old concept has died, it takes a long time to come to terms with it, but the position of the music director must be detached from that of the conductor. The music director of an orchestra today can't be a conductor because a conductor who is good enough to be head of a good orchestra, an important orchestra, must travel since his career is an international one. A local conductor isn't even going to suffice for the local public! The only solution is to separate the music directing from the duties of the conductor, but this is such a radical subject that nobody even listens to me. It will only change when people realize that the absentee music directors can't fill their jobs. As it is now, with no one person in charge, the department heads of orchestras dominate to the point where they run nearly wild. So any appointment of a music director in the form of a conductor is an illusion.

Talking of administration, I would rather deal with a North American symphony board than the European government agencies that subsidize the orchestra and opera companies. The advantage of the American boards is that the members are replaceable, whereas the government officials are not. If Mr. Smith on the board turns you down, you go to Mr. Brown—that's the great difference. The more

I travel, the more I have come to believe in the American system of support of the arts. It is struggling, and it will struggle worse, but it will prove superior.

*You have decried the low social status of musicians on this continent.*

Yes, a great deal has been missed here. I believe the American system has contributed to the relentless grabbing for financial improvement among musicians as the only way for them to assert themselves. Europe has done better—musicians there are called professors, they are considered to be somebody, they have proper spaces to park their cars. I remember in San Francisco when I was still conducting there, that the intermissions of the orchestra rehearsals were arranged so that the musicians could put their dimes and nickels in the parking meters! These problems in the social status of musicians in America should have been ironed out long ago and weren't—now the hostility is so great and it is too late.

The greatest threat to American orchestras is that the gaps between the top and the second and third echelons is growing by leaps and bounds. Everything depends on the management of orchestras, which is far more important than the music director, because the management can always engage the best available conductor, but the conductor cannot engage the best available musicians.

*You have pointed out that there are no artists' managers and agents, only brokers.*

That is in the nature of the business. People like old man Hurok are very rare. He had the combination of buccaneer and adventurer, he took risks and had money, which only he could gamble with. The conglomerates that have entered the world of management will certainly not gamble the stockbrokers' money to see if Mr. Somebody is going to make a hit. There will be no more Huroks—the margin for winning is too small.

*You seem to be a thoroughly disciplined musician. What is the most frivolous thing you enjoy?*

Oh, I might tell off-color stories to the orchestra, but always with the purpose of keeping their concentration during rehearsal. I always tell them: You have a tremendous artistic discipline, but what you do must come out in the end like play, and not like work. That is the essence!

*You are still talking music—I'm trying to find out if you ever put your feet up in front of the TV and watch a football game while eating popcorn and drinking beer . . .*

Certainly not beer, because it is fattening. Certainly not popcorn, because I don't like it . . but this you will not believe, and only my wife can bear out this truth: I'm actually a very lazy person!

*But when you work, you work extremely hard.*

I never consider a performance work.

*What is the bottom level of orchestra that you will conduct?*

You mean the altitude above sea level? [With a smile.]

*Well, your fee probably determines very much where you go . . .*

Now, I think this is really a sad issue! I was very much offended a year or two ago when a very reputable London newspaper began to grade conductors according to their fees. First, their information was entirely wrong, secondly I have never in my life read an exhibit of worse taste! We all go to England for half or less than half of our normal fee, because the country is very poor, and the public is wonderful. We are all paid peanuts! But once you go somewhere for the fee only, then you have ceased to be an artist!

*You claim to be a hero worshiper. At this point in your career, whom do you have to worship?*

I worship my musical heroes—my Mozarts and so on. I find that the older I get, the closer I am to their personal suffering. When I read a Mozart score—not even a Mozart letter—the tragedy of this person's life overcomes me. There is such contrast between what they gave and how they were treated . . .

*Haven't composers always been the bottom rung in music?*

No, our history teaching is faulty. Mozart was extremely successful in his lifetime, but it was not translated into a better life for him. His operas and concertos were the hit parade of his day—even the organ grinders picked up the tunes! When Mozart finished a new work, he had to distribute the score like the CIA in bits and pieces to different copyists, because if he gave the whole work to one copyist, he would sell it as his own work.

*But Mozart had a popular appeal in his time. Today there seems to be a vigorous resistance to contemporary music on all levels.*

Not necessarily. Let me give you an example. In 1967, the Hamburg opera came to New York and performed a work [*The Visitation*] by Gunther Schuller, written on a theme by Kafka. Gunther said that as a result of the success of that opera, he received eighteen commissions. Yet ten years later he has not written a single other opera! [Schuller's one-act opera *The Fisherman and His Wife* was premiered in 1970.] I pointed out to Gunther on his fiftieth birthday, that he had headed the New England Conservatory, directed on Broadway, written a book and so on, but where was the work that he was supposed to have delivered?

*You found sadness in the way that Toscanini, Walter and others ended their careers.*

Great sadness! What we all need is a manager or a friend who some day takes his courage in his hand and says, "Listen here, my boy, phase yourself out." All I can say is: have some other values in your life to prepare for that day. I have seen it time and again, for instance in the last years of Stokowski. It is now going to become legendary that he conducted till ninety-five, but somebody did the splicing to produce—even by the cynical standards of the recording companies—a salable tape. Fairytales! Another of my colleagues endured needless humiliation because he didn't know when to call it quits.

I think that the knowledge an experienced conductor has should be drawn upon as long as he cares to share it. This is why I'm writing my book. We must part with as much knowledge as we have, to be helpful to those coming after us.

# Yo-Yo Ma

When Yo-Yo Ma received his first cello lesson from his father at the age of four, it marked the beginning of a remarkable career. At six, he gave his first recital at the University of Paris, in the city where he was born in 1955. The program included one of Bach's unaccompanied suites. When the musical Ma family moved to New York City in 1962, his unquestioned talent led him to Leonard Rose at the Juilliard School. He studied there—occasionally venturing out to play concertos and recitals—until, at age fifteen, he decided to expand his horizons by getting his degree from Harvard University. He managed to avoid the often critical transition from the intuitive playing of a child prodigy to the deliberate expression of a mature musician. To no one's surprise, he won the 1978 Avery Fisher Prize.

Today, at thirty-three, Yo-Yo Ma has a world-wide following, and practically every major concert hall has witnessed his exquisite artistry on a 1712 Stradivarius, the cello loaned to him by the late Jacqueline du Pré. His recording career is well established; CBS Masterworks has a dozen discs completed and more under way.

Despite these amazing accomplishments, Yo-Yo Ma is no insular striver, but a relaxed and approachable person with a keen sense of humor. At our 1982 meeting he combined youthful charm with a distinguished worldliness. His young musician friends are often helped in their careers by his insistence on their collaboration in concerts, and he seems well liked by all his colleagues. At this stage he and his wife Jill, a teacher of German literature with whom he lives in Winchester, Massachusetts, are busy with their daughter and son. They are one reason why he has vowed to take time off every year.

*Colgrass: How can a musician advance beyond his years, apart from having a tremendous talent such as yours?*
Ma: Isn't that a lifetime goal for any musician—trying to under-

stand things with more clarity and explore new things? A constant re-evaluation goes on, at least on my part, in which you try to achieve some breakthroughs in the areas you want to work on. A lot of them are psychological breakthroughs beyond the physical act of playing the instrument. I like to approach it in words as well as in sound, although I am closer to sound than to words. To be able to also articulate something gives you one more thing to latch on to.

*You have succeeded in becoming a mature artist in a short span of years, which not many achieve. With your comment about verbalizing your intent, I was wondering if the key to maturity might lie outside music in some way.*

I think in many ways it does, because the constant struggle of a musician is to get beyond the notes. When you start interpreting what a *forte* or *crescendo* means to the composers, then you start talking their language.

*You made an unusual move by changing from Juilliard to Harvard in the middle of your education.*

At that time I basically wanted to leave home. A more serious reason was that I was quite young and had a lot of time on my hands, so I wanted to do something different, and it turned out to be the best thing I could have done. As an instrumentalist one always tends to start young and one's life is immersed in music, it's focused and disciplined. Going to college you are suddenly exposed to many other different things.

*Would you have become the same type of musician had you stayed at Juilliard?*

That's hard to say. You are asking if the environment makes a great difference. I think I would possibly have learned different things at Juilliard, but I met some very interesting people at Harvard. They talked about music outside of the instrument, while people at Juilliard tend to talk about music with the instrument—that's a very big difference. If one thinks always physically, one develops a more physical approach.

At Harvard there were people like Leon Kirchner; there was a wonderful teacher, Louise Vosgerchian, who is a really great teacher in the Socratic sense—always asking questions. By building a very basic vocabulary she taught a lot of people how to think and to trust their own instincts and their own ears. Once you start trusting yourself, you develop a whole vocabulary that applies to music. That is extremely useful.

*Of the two extremes—the musicians who find everything in the score, and the musicians who tend to regard the score as a springboard for their own interpretation—which do you find yourself closest to?*

It depends on the composer and the type of music. There are composers who write very freely. With time I have developed more respect for the craft of composers. If you are dealing with a work that you want to play many times, always learning from it, you are putting all your resources in the service of what you think the music is. That doesn't mean that composers can't make mistakes, or that performers can't do the same. There is always tremendous freedom within the discipline of following a score.

*You have said that in certain works by Schubert the music felt almost as if it were floating by. Was there a certain time when you felt that playing became easier?*

Very early in the morning. [Laughs.] Through experience, the more you play a composer such as Schubert, the more you gradually begin to understand the language he is using and what he is writing about.

*Are there times when everything seems either effortless or very hard due to your disposition?*

Absolutely. I struggled for years to try to understand the Fourth Beethoven Sonata. When I was fifteen I played a recital and Leonard Rose, who was my teacher then, said, "I'm going to give you a piece you have never seen before and probably never even heard, and I want you to think about it." It took years before I first got some kind of breakthrough and said, "Aha! That's what the piece is about." You have to keep trying. I don't believe you can give up and say, "Well, this is not my cup of tea and I can't play this type of music." I think if you try hard enough there comes a point when things fall into place.

*Playing Paganini's Caprices on the cello [CBS Masterworks recording 37280] seems comparable to going over Niagara Falls in a barrel. What made you do this?*

It was a challenge to myself and I'm not sure how well I met the challenge.

*Magnificently.*

It's nice that you think so. I grew up hearing a lot of violinists— my sister was one—and I was always hearing them play these Caprices. The recording was an attempt to say, "Okay, the cello is as good an instrument as the violin and has maybe a wider range—it's not impossible to do anything that a violin can do." It was something I dared myself to do for fun.

*You might be analyzed as suffering from violin envy . . .*

*Geige* envy! [Laughs.] As for the Kreisler pieces on that same record, that's gorgeous music, the type that is just pure, great, wonderful and entertaining. Stylistically it is very demanding to play. Some people say, "We'll only play Serious Music—this and that!"

*Could there be a touch of snobbishness in programming?*

It depends on where you are and what type of audience you are playing for. Some audiences go because they want to be entertained. Others go because it is part of their diet, and if you have an audience that really needs music, as opposed to one that wants to be entertained, you can do all the late Beethoven Sonatas, for example. Most audiences, though, are a mixture of both.

*How much say do you demand in programming?*

For recitals pretty much anything goes in terms of what I want to do. I have done all-Bach programs or all-twentieth-century programs, all-romantic repertoire, and so on. If you can convince the sponsors that it's okay and that people won't leave at intermission, it's all right.

*You can obviously fill a hall anywhere now. How do you keep from getting caught up in celebrity status?*

Well, in classical music there is not much of that. On the plane I might get recognized by people who point and say, "Oh, there's that man with the cello!" Beyond that you get lots of requests to do things such as sending recipes to cookbooks. If that's what you call celebrity . . . [Laughs loudly.] About the constant traveling, I have come to the conclusion that it is important to take time off. I just started last year taking the summer off and it was ideal. If one gets tired of playing—doing it every day for weeks on end—one loses interest.

*Do you ever refuse to play a certain concerto because you have played it too much recently?*

I never seem to play a work more than three or four times in a year. What I do is submit the whole repertoire, and orchestras decide a long time in advance.

*Does your management [ICM] respect your wishes?*

They don't mind what I play. Taking time off is always slightly difficult. You get into a groove and there is a certain snowball effect— you have to balance out American/Canadian commitments versus European, then there are Israeli and Japanese tours. Once you commit yourself it is hard to say, "I won't do this." As long as there is a good dialogue and trust between me and the management and they are not out to overwork me, I won't complain.

*Do you think it is desirable to be in a position like, for instance, pianist Maurizio Pollini's, who can play when and where he wants and still have people clamoring for him?*

I don't know. Part of what makes musical life interesting is being in a place that you least expected and finding something delightful. Obviously, to have the freedom to call the shots is great, but you miss out on the unexpected.

*Do you prefer a specific type of audience?*

You can find great audiences in any country. If people really listen and know the music, there is a certain level of concentration. On the other hand, it's just as exhilarating to play for an audience that is going to a concert for the first time. I like German audiences a lot—they come armed with scores and—*ja*—they concentrate. [Laughs.]

*Unlike southern Europeans who tend to meander in and out of the concert hall . . .*

But that's great, too. It's like being in a family room somewhere. It takes a while to get used to every type of audience. French audiences tend to be visually oriented. The English are very auditory and they applaud less, but you can feel the warmth. In Europe you get a more homogeneous group, while audiences in North America can vary greatly.

*You often perform with your contemporaries. Do you think young musicians have a different attitude towards their art?*

We are living in a different era where life moves faster and there are no restrictions to travel. I was talking to Pinkie [Pinchas Zukerman] the other day. He was telling Heifetz stories. Every day Heifetz was on tour, he practiced for two hours, and he would rehearse for one month on a program before taking it on tour. Nathan Milstein did the same. They would take fewer pieces in their repertoire, but they achieved with them exactly what they wanted.

Younger musicians may play more chamber music, and maybe they have a slightly different approach, playing with more people and playing a wider repertoire.

*Perhaps today's musicians are better equipped for that.*

The training is different.

*Is there any aspect of the teaching of cello today that you take exception to?*

Not really. I think teaching is such a fascinating profession. One used to have a master-apprentice type of relationship with the teacher, which may still exist to some extent. I don't believe in absolutes: This is the way to do it! On the other hand, in learning one has to go through a period where one has to approximate as closely as possible something that a mentor asks. That's discipline.

I think that music is a lot more than playing notes on an instrument. What I would like to see in music schools is a greater emphasis on chamber music as opposed to learning an instrument and playing in an orchestra. I feel that chamber music is the basis of any musician's craft—it's thinking about the music, working it out with your colleagues in the friendliest way. Orchestral playing doesn't always offer this, although an orchestra at its best is great chamber-music playing.

If more musicians had good chamber-music training, it would carry over into all other aspects of music-making.

*It teaches you to listen.*

Yes, to listen and to react, to articulate and to communicate with a colleague.

*Are you playing in a quartet?*

I am going to do some string trios next year with Gidon Kremer and Kim Kashkashian. The following year we'll add Daniel Phillips to play quartets. [The four have already produced a CBS album of Schubert Quartets since this interview took place; recorded performances of Dvořák's trios with Ma, pianist Emanuel Ax and violinist Young Uck Kim were forthcoming at this writing. So far, Ma has received four Grammy Awards.]

*Is there a trap in playing an instrument that is so beautifully lyrical?*

The instrument is capable of doing a lot of other things. It is important to develop a repertoire of sound and character as wide as the music calls for.

*Do you play other instruments?*

I play the viola holding it between my knees [laughs], and I pound away at the piano. My wife, who was teaching German literature at Harvard until recently, is not a musician, but she is my best critic and is probably the person who has heard me the most.

*Your programming is sometimes a bit unorthodox. Aside from doing many of your own transcriptions, I was wondering how you have managed to extend the somewhat limited cello repertoire.*

I have recently started to ask composers, such as the young English composer Oliver Knussen, to write me a piece. Throughout college I had friends write works, I have participated in chamber pieces of new music and even dabbled in electronic music. I think soon I'll be ready to approach commissions in a more serious way. I like the system in Canada where arts councils often pay for commissioned work, and I also like the fact that Canadian orchestras play Canadian works so often.

*Do I dare ask you about the problems of traveling with a cello?*

Sure, go right ahead . . . [Chuckles.] I was so happy some years ago when a reporter asked me about this, and suddenly all the stories I had buried in my subconscious in order to survive all came out and I got that off my chest. It continues, though.

I don't mind paying for a seat on the airplane for my cello, but each airline has different rules about it. There are some airlines that don't take cellos—luckily, one that didn't, Braniff, is now out of business. There is a rule at American Airlines that the cello has to go in the window bulkhead seat, but because they have tables, the cello has to face backwards and I have to apologize to the passenger opposite because of the obstructed leg room. You just have to be prepared for it psychologically.

And the people with the X-ray machines! The cello does go through and is not harmed by it, but recently in Texas a woman insisted that it wouldn't. She opened the case to inspect the cello and started scratching it with her long fingernails.

I think my favorite cello story is about Paul Tortelier, who was very dynamic. He walked on the plane with his cello and was told that he couldn't take it with him. He asked the attendant, "If a singer comes aboard with his vocal chords, would you let him in?" "Yes, certainly, sir." "Well, this is my voice," he said as he walked on.

*I have heard there is a special camaraderie among cellists, which you don't find among, for example, pianists and violinists.*

I think that is true. It may be because all cellists do pretty much the same things. Every cellist has probably played in an orchestra, has played chamber music, taught, and plays perhaps as a soloist with a rather small repertoire. There are cello clubs all over the country.

I am glad you haven't asked me why Oriental musicians can play Western music . . .

*Well, you are an American. I suppose the flood of string talent from the East must be a product of the educational system.*

If a culture emphasizes education, music will fit in somehow.

# Wynton Marsalis

Wynton Marsalis hardly needs any more publicity. At age twenty-seven he has stirred up more excitement and awe during his few intense years on the music scene than any other recent newcomer in the fields of classical and jazz. Marsalis excels in both. In 1984 he became the first musician to win two Grammys in the categories of jazz and classical music—and went on to win both again in 1985 and 1986! Accolades pour in every time Marsalis sounds his horn. A few critical remarks are even creeping into the press, which is a sure sign that he has arrived. The classical trumpet virtuoso Maurice André said, "He is potentially the greatest trumpeter of all time." On the other hand, his colleague Miles Davis has remarked, "He's got a lot of technique, but that's about it."

Although Marsalis claims that "there is only one right way to play Mozart," there is nonetheless a distinct Marsalis sound that can be detected whether he plays the Hummel Trumpet Concerto or a Thelonious Monk composition. He covers the gamut from raspy to flute-like, but prefers the smooth, subtle and flawlessly intonated sound. John Pareles wrote in the *New York Times* that "his tone carries a sense of quiet melancholy that makes his slow movements luminous." To the jazz public Marsalis is known as a puritan rooted in the be-bop style, yet an exponent of many styles. It upsets him when "pop is sold as jazz," and he sees himself continuing the traditions of Dizzy Gillespie, Charlie Parker, Miles Davis and Ornette Coleman. Three years ago, *Newsweek* pronounced him the new wonder boy of mainstream jazz, with a formidable technique and encyclopedic reference. Wherever he plays jazz, he looks impeccable in suit and tie, because "serious musicians shouldn't look like they're playing street football."

Marsalis was born on October 18, 1961, in Kenner, Louisiana, the second of six sons. His father Ellis is a jazz pianist, and Wynton grew up in the close-knit Catholic family, proud of his black heritage and

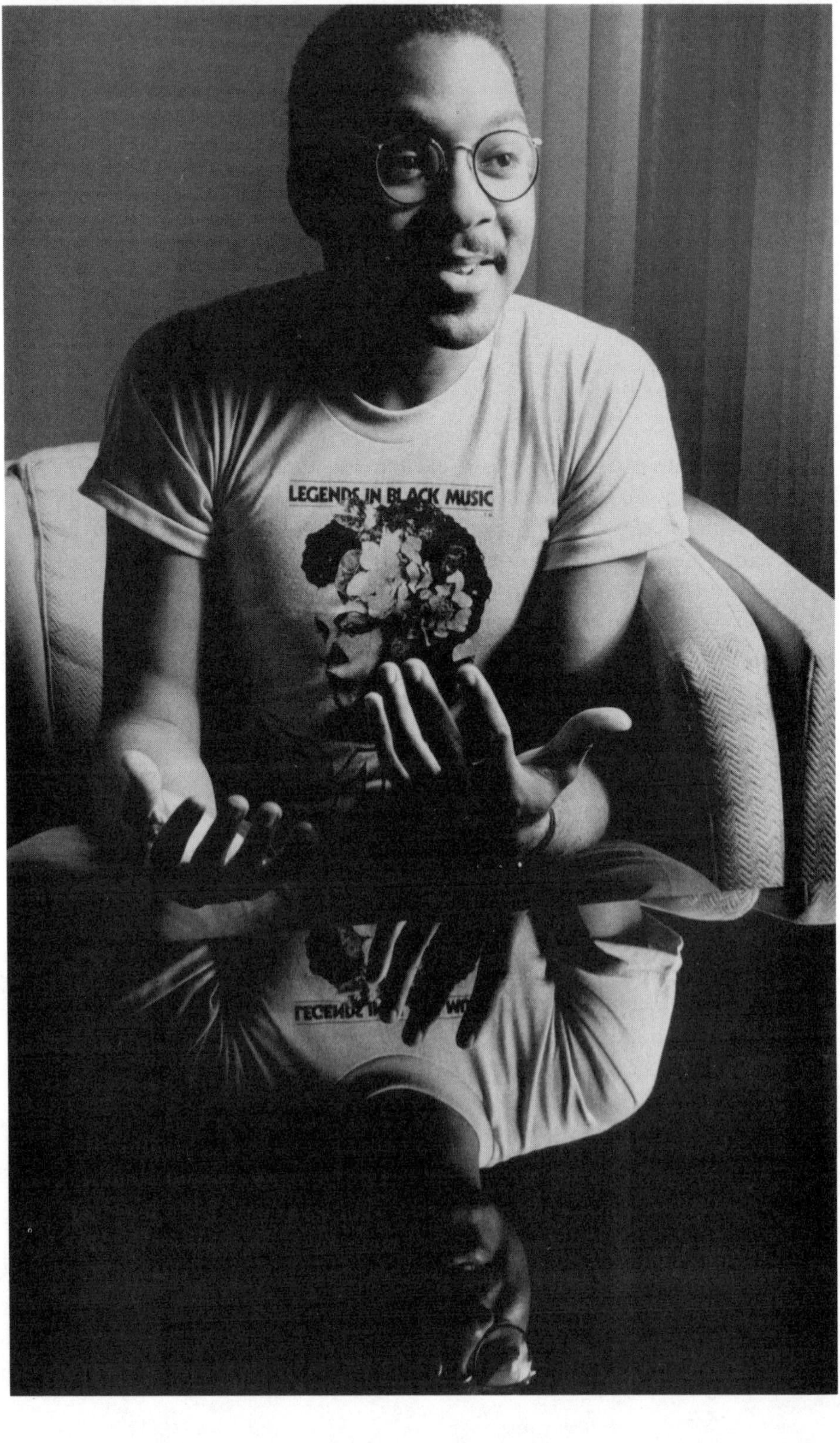
LEGENDS IN BLACK MUSIC

of jazz especially. With the family home just a few miles from New Orleans, the birthplace of jazz, and being surrounded by the sounds of his father's piano and his older brother Branford's precocious clarinet playing, Wynton seemed destined to become a musician. Once when Marsalis senior was playing with Al Hirt's band, he asked for an advance to finance the purchase of a trumpet, but Hirt made a gift of the horn to the then six-year-old Wynton. The following year, the boy made his first public appearance blowing the Marine Hymn in a recital at the Xavier Junior School of Music.

But Wynton was too immersed in academics to concentrate on the horn. Music became his first priority after the family moved to New Orleans when he was twelve and he entered the New Orleans Center for Creative Arts as a gifted student. As a teenager he went through stages of funk, fusion and other "in" styles, yet classical music was very much part of his early training. "I resent these stories that call me classically trained. Training is training—you practice scales and exercises and control, and you use this experience to play anything you want," he once protested to a Los Angeles interviewer.

At age fourteen, he played the Haydn Trumpet Concerto with the New Orleans Philharmonic Symphony Orchestra. Competition with another boy who played trumpet in his school was apparently a major incentive, because Wynton told his older brother, "Man, I'm gonna practice until I zip this kid." As a national merit finalist in high school he was approached by Yale and other Ivy League schools, but by then music had become all-absorbing. At the age of seventeen he went to Juilliard on a full scholarship.

Enjoy Wynton Marsalis while he is playing the classical repertoire. He has proved his point that "a black cat can do it," but in his heart he is a visitor. Besides, there is not nearly enough repertoire to keep him happy in the long run. The Haydn Concerto, which appears on his Grammy-winning album [Haydn/Hummel/L. Mozart: Trumpet Concertos], was the very first concerto he performed. Composers such as John Corigliano and Krzysztof Penderecki are writing trumpet concertos for him, but Marsalis himself is not interested in expanding his composition to the classical field.

Marsalis set the condition that we cover both of his specialties in this interview, which is why we were joined by composer Michael Colgrass, who is well versed in jazz.

*U. Colgrass: Did you always lean toward classical music?*
Marsalis: No. When I first started, I didn't really want to play clas-

sical music. In high school we listened to Beethoven's symphonies—it was hip, yeah—and like everybody else I liked Tchaikovsky first, then Mahler and others that are easy to like immediately. Later I started liking more contemporary composers like Bartók and Berg.

*UC: Did you always feel as welcome in classical music as you did in jazz?*

Not really. Not that many brothers play classical music. But the people are nice and I always felt at home with brass players.

*M. Colgrass: You are unique in that you play both classical and jazz. Do you think it would be possible to educate both types of musicians in the same place?*

I don't know. First, a musician has got to want to play both. The information is out there and they just have to go and get it.

*UC: What did the teachers at Juilliard say about your jazz playing?*

They couldn't have cared less. They were trying to get their own thing happening.

*MC: What do you think about the way we educate musicians and the attitudes in music schools?*

I don't like the way it feels, because it's not geared towards education. It's geared towards performance.

*UC: Technical brilliance?*

That's such a cliché. Technical brilliance is not even geared towards performance. We have to remember that technique encompasses all aspects of music. When people talk about technique they often mean velocity—but sound is technique and so is a sense of style.

*MC: As a jazz musician you embrace many different styles. Do you consider yourself a jazz-repertoire musician the way a classical musician plays all classical styles of the past? Or are you passing through past styles of jazz in order to get to your own original, new style?*

I'm looking for my own original style. In order to go to the next step you have to understand what went before. That's where jazz musicians get lost. Our history is not taught with respect for tradition like it should be. If you read the letters of Beethoven, you won't see "I'm Beethoven and I don't care what anybody else is doing." No, he was studying Bach, Haydn and Mozart—that's where that music was coming from.

I'm always coming under fire. Somebody says, "Well, that sounds like Miles," when it sounds like it was influenced by Miles! It's like listening to Beethoven's First Symphony and criticizing it for sounding like Haydn. Well, it's obvious that he listened to Haydn, but there's a difference between submerging your personality in Haydn's and trying to take what Haydn did and develop upon that.

Now, the music that Miles and Trane [John Coltrane] and Monk laid out in the sixties is very complex. You don't just come up and play that. People still don't understand how great and innovative Coleman was. Generations of musicians have come up uneducated, thinking they are going to be Ornette Coleman—kids who don't know how to play their instruments on a virtuosic level and have no understanding of music and its traditions. They just say, "Man, I'm into the creative thing, playing what I feel." That's ignorance hiding under the guise of soulfulness.

We all know that true soulfulness and emotionalism comes from awareness, and among the first stages of awareness is technical competence. We have a long history of musicians, starting with Bach, Beethoven, Mozart, Haydn, Brahms, Bartók, Bird [Charlie Parker], Duke Ellington, Louis Armstrong—the list goes on and on. It's ironic that they were the greatest technicians on their instrument. Nobody ever thinks about that connection.

*UC: People are probably not willing to make the effort.*

It takes great effort. In our society we have the problem of self-justification—that is, in our democracy everybody is equal. So you look at a genius and figure out how you can equate yourself with him—and I'm not talking about myself now. Miles Davis is one of the greatest trumpet players that ever lived and I hope I'll be able to play just one-tenth of the music he has played, but that doesn't mean I want to be Miles Davis.

*MC: Do you think an artist has a responsibility that goes beyond making music?*

Definitely. To me that's looking for the truth socially, spiritually and in every way.

*UC: Where did you seek out your own education?*

It was all around me—other musicians. I read all the time and I don't read just for enjoyment but to learn something. Recently I have enjoyed books by Thomas Mann and *The Invisible Man* by Ralph Ellison.

*UC: Have you influenced your friends in these matters?*

No. I don't try to do that. You have to be real careful with other people. Sometimes I get fanatic about something, though, and get up on my soapbox.

*UC: Who set this example for you?*

The musicians I knew. I listened to them and knew they were smart.

*MC: When you were a kid, who were your models?*

Miles. And I used to have a big Malcolm X poster over my bed. That man was totally misunderstood. People still get scared just at the mention of his name, but the last thing that was on his mind was hurting people. Of course I was always around my daddy, who was a big influence. I went to really good schools. In grade school there were only two blacks and I didn't like the vibes we had to deal with. But I had all A's, so the education was good.

*MC: How about music education—jazz?*

There was no jazz education. I got that from my father.

*MC: So the level of teaching jazz in American schools is about equal to the teaching of black history?*

Yeah—none. But you know, I don't think there should be a course in black history, just American history taught the right way. To separate black history keeps it from becoming general knowledge.

*UC: I remember listening to jazz as a teenager in Europe, and I was quite shocked to find on my first visit to America that young people here didn't care for it. It seemed more accepted in Europe.*

That was then, not now. That European interest has been overstated. The situation was racially better in Europe then because there weren't many negroes. The climate today in Europe is not so healthy for jazz—it's like a circus. Besides, Europeans don't understand jazz as well as Americans do—they regard the musicians as noble savages, judging from the uninformed questions they ask.

*UC: Some of the most original and beautiful jazz came out of a society riddled with conflicts. As American society improves, do you think jazz will ever regain that vitality?*

Society is not improving in the States, not from a black American's standpoint. But I don't think the music will become less vital, it will just change. Louis Armstrong's music is not necessarily about conflict, it's more about the joy of individuality. In Bird I hear a lot of conflict, but different musicians find different things. Their awareness makes them great, and the truth of what they perceive comes out in their music.

*MC: Considering where jazz has gone now, there is a tremendous amount of conflict—no rhythm, no harmony.*

That's in keeping with what is going on in society—the breakdown of established norms, no acknowledgment of past masters. Democratic principles are being distorted now so the responsibility of democracy, which is mainly education, has been neglected. We now distort freedom of speech to mean "whatever you have to say is worth saying and hearing," and something is valid if it makes money. The real concept of democracy is about individual freedom and not having to be subjugated to another person because of one's birth, rank or wealth. That's the real nobility of the concept. The distortion of it is that if you make enough money it will elevate your character and your stature as a human being.

*MC: That, of course, is how status is gained in America.*

And that is reflected in music—that's why music is real unhealthy.

*UC: The mass media isn't helping the situation by giving a person the chance to be famous for a few weeks.*

Everyone is trying to make money. The fast turnover is appealing to the lowest element in human nature. Of course, the largest number of people will get into the lowest expression of anything, music included. As you demand more comprehension and awareness, you appeal to fewer and fewer people. That represents less money.

*UC: What's happening to you? You won six Grammys in three successive years, which is unprecedented. What financial schemes are being built around you?*

Not many, because I don't sell that many records. Only one-hundred and fifty to two hundred thousand per record. That's not big in the recording world. Michael Jackson sold forty million copies! I mean, people who are hardly known sell a million copies.

*MC: But your sales are big in jazz.*

Jazz has no economic clout at all—none!

*MC: Charlie Parker came and went and nobody ever knew he was here— I mean the American public. He was one of the greats, like Schubert.*

Absolutely. That's the tragedy. It's tied in with prejudice.

*MC: You mean jazz is seen as black and classical music as white music?*

That's definitely the perception. European music is visible, jazz is not. I hear classical music on TV, radio, and there is a steady stream of good musicians and composers' legacies are being preserved. And jazz, man—who knows who Bird was?

The public's perception of jazz is so distorted. Take a figure like Louis Armstrong. There is no concept at all of what he was. There is some understanding of the genius of Beethoven. But Satchmo? Oh yeah—"Hello Dolly!" They have no idea, none. Some people don't even know he played the trumpet, they thought he just sang.

*UC: Do you think people's taste will eventually improve so they will get a bit more demanding?*

In America you run into problems. You say, "improve people's taste" and people will say, "Who are you to tell me what's improved? I think this music is just as good as Mozart's." If you do something wrong nutritionally, your teeth might fall out and your body would stop working, but music is not like nutrition. With music, your brain cells might decay but there'll be no physical manifestation. Spiritually it's hurting you. I definitely think that we are in a bad shape spiritually—we need something spiritual to be happening.

*MC: You play classical music with a flute-like lightness, almost a liquid*

*sound. That's different from what I have heard before from the trumpet. I
would guess that comes from your experience in jazz.*

It's just trying to play music the way it sounds to me. Music has
very strict laws. I can't stress that enough. The more freedom you
have in music, the more restrictions are placed on it. Total freedom
is chaos.

Jazz is the most defined music, the strictest to play. When you have
a hundred possibilities, you have to know all hundred possibilities,
harmonically and rhythmically. The reason it is so unique an art form
and can't be compared to European music, is the time element in jazz.
Jazz uses harmony in motion. I heard someone say that Duke Ellington
sounded like Debussy—to me he sounded nothing like Debussy! Those
composers worked with static harmonies, but jazz is harmony in motion.

*MC: Do you think playing jazz gives you a special insight into European
music? Could Louis Armstrong's lyricism, for instance, give us a different way
of playing Mozart?*

He could have heard it in another way. But there's only one way
to play Mozart right. The music is written to sound a certain way and
is written precisely enough for you to know how it's supposed to
sound. Armstrong would probably know the rhythmic pulse. I think
classical music has lost some of its rhythmic pulse. Everybody is so
caught up in the theory of harmony that they forget about the theory
of rhythm. And a great deal of listeners don't even hear harmony—
they are mainly touched by the melody and rhythm.

*MC: Rhythm is the most important element, and I think the most violated
element in performing.*

Definitely.

*MC: Have you ever felt limited by what the trumpet can do?*

No, I'm still trying to use all the potential it has.

*MC: Do you use imagery when you play?*

I just try to fill the horn up and get the metal out of the sound. A
metally sound is one thing I hate in a trumpet. Louis Armstrong didn't
have any metal in his sound, nor does Miles. I want it to come out
nice and smooth, warm and round like a voice.

*UC: Do you see a lot of good jazz players coming up these days?*

No. People have too many economic considerations. It's a rough
stage. Guys of fifteen or sixteen say to me, "Man, I can't make any
money—when will I get a break?" They are not thinking about making music, but about getting a break.

*UC: Did you ever worry about your own future?*

No, I never did. Perhaps I worry more now than I did at first.

*MC: What kind of non-musical experience do you think is important to become a well-rounded performer?*

A woman. An artist really benefits from having a mate, someone to relate to on a higher level to gain another perspective on life.

But the most important thing for an artist is awareness and the search for truth. Imagine a car crash that was witnessed by thirty people. All thirty have a different story. Only one person saw what actually went down. I want to be that person.

# The Orford String Quartet

In the summer of 1965, Andrew Dawes was a young violinist waiting to take the next big step in his career. He grew up in western Canada, where he had studied with Murray Adaskin, and on the advice of Isaac Stern was shipped off to study with Lorand Fenyves at the Conservatoire de Genève. At the age of twenty-five, he found himself at Jeunesses Musicales' Quebec headquarters at Mt. Orford with an impressive collection of international music awards and an ambition to build a solo career. Yet in the back of his mind he heard Fenyves's advice: "Playing in a quartet is tremendous training for anybody." Soloists were no exception.

Fortunately, three other young musicians were interested in sharing what Dawes intended to be a brief experiment. Together with violinist Kenneth Perkins (a fellow westerner), violist Terence Helmer and cellist Marcel St.-Cyr he formed the Orford String Quartet. Their first concert was such a success that Jeunesses Musicales immediately sponsored their first tour, consisting of eighty concerts.

As readers will know, the Orford experiment never abated. With the twentieth anniversary long gone the Quartet is vigorous, internationally acclaimed and often referred to as a national treasure. A few difficult moments mar the Quartet's history. In 1980, St.-Cyr left to pursue his interest in early music, and for a while Dawes considered joining another quartet. Fortunately, the crisis was averted when the young cellist Denis Brott filled the empty chair, and the Orford String Quartet picked up with renewed energy.

[Shortly after this interview in 1985, Helmer left the quartet and his place was filled by American violist Robert Levine. Such a jolt to a quartet can be compared to an organ transplant—will it take? Well, in the case of Levine it didn't. He longed for the secure world of the orchestra and left after a year to become principal violist in the Mil-

waukee Symphony. Dawes admits that facing yet another new member and working that person into the repertoire made him flirt with the idea of giving up. "But if you truly love playing string quartets you keep going," he said. A most unlikely candidate turned up in the shape of English violist Sophie Renshaw, only twenty-two and a product of the Yehudi Menuhin School in London. The three Orford members found her so outstanding and compatible that they immediately invited her to join, and they set to work on preparing a cross-Canada tour and performances in Europe and the U.S.A.]

*Colgrass: Your sound has more in common with the subtle European tradition than it does with the more vigorous American style of quartet playing. How was it arrived at?*

Helmer: It was not a conscious agreement. Over the years, this kind of finesse of searching out has evolved. I think we have weeded out a lot of those conscious efforts to "fix" things. Each has an individual sound and together we sound maybe on the sweet side—at least that is the concept people have of us. Above all, we are striving to make a beautiful sound and avoid excitement for excitement's sake.

*Do you in fact have a European ideal?*

Dawes: I don't think we have ever tried to sound like a specific group or to make a specific sound. When Denis came in, he added his sound to the amalgam.

Brott: I had never heard the Orford live until we played together. I was building a career as a soloist and teacher and had never even thought of making a living as a chamber musician, although I had played a good deal of chamber music at Aspen, Marlboro and other festivals.

*How long did it take you to settle into the Quartet and the repertoire, which I understand includes nearly two hundred works?*

Brott: Quite a while. For the longest time I was playing too loud because I had played as a soloist, which is altogether different. But playing in the Quartet has been a tremendously rewarding experience both as a musician and as a human being.

*How did you tame him?*

Perkins: We kept pulling the plug to his cello.

Brott: And they put soap on my bow.

*You are well received on your many tours. I'm reading from the major cities that your playing is "full of passion and mystery . . . virtuosic excitement . . . quick intelligence and excitingly fresh." Why aren't you next to quartets like the Juilliard or the Tokyo in the public eye?*

Brott: Just playing and playing well is not easily marketable.

Dawes: One of the problems is that there is no Canadian recording company that compares with Germany's Deutsche Grammophon, for instance. Companies like that do a lot for their own artists.

Brott: We constantly run into sponsors who think very highly of the Orford but virtually have to introduce us to their audiences because of our lack of recordings outside Canada.

*But a quick glance shows you have produced between forty and fifty recordings, and your complete set of Beethoven's quartets on Delos was the first on CDs.*

Dawes: It is often a problem of marketing. When our Mozart set on the CBC SM 5000 series won a Juno in 1985, the company never so much as put a sticker on the double album to attract sales.

*So royalties from recordings don't keep you in caviar?*

Perkins: Just one portion of caviar for all of us to share.

*How many concerts do you give each season?*

Helmer: Around eighty. We just did twenty-three concerts in thirty days in eastern Canada, and before that we played fourteen concerts in Europe.

Dawes: And we are playing the Mendelssohn Octet with the Cleveland String Quartet in Brussels in a couple of weeks.

Brott: No! would you believe on Tuesday? [Laughter]

*Have you observed an increasing interest in chamber music?*

Perkins: I think so. Music became perhaps a little too glib. Along with a desire to do your own carpentry or grow your own vegetables came the need for a more simple and intimate experience in music.

Brott: Many young musicians are turning to chamber ensembles because the orchestral situation has become more competitive and the sense of self has deteriorated in large orchestras.

Dawes: In my view the tremendous upswing in ensembles is seen much more in the U.S.A. than in Canada. There aren't that many more groups in Canada now than there were ten years ago, and the only countries with a large number of quartets are England and the U.S.

*Since 1968, your quartet has been in residence at the University of Toronto, where you teach your art to the next generation. Is it rewarding?*

Perkins: It is strange that none of the graduate students have formed groups that stayed together. Some have played together for a year or so and have then for some reason gone to orchestras. It has always been a goal of ours to produce a functioning string quartet.

Brott: It can be said in favor of teaching chamber music that a well-trained chamber musician always will turn out to be an excellent orchestra musician. The reverse is not true.

*Perhaps none of your students have stuck with it because quartet music is the mature musician's repertoire.*

Dawes: There is no question that for a quartet to arrive at a musical expression requires a lot more interaction than one finds in an orchestra. In that sense it is also more stimulating.

Brott: In a string quartet, even in rehearsal, you always have a responsibility to your colleagues. It is a stimulus to improve and we always have to practice. It's funny, but for some reason my cello has recently been plagued by these wolves, with vibrations hitting each other and I have no idea why.

Perkins: Oh, it's just because we have played too much up north.

*What is your instrument?*

Brott: [Laughing.] It's a Giovanni Batista Ceruti from 1799.

*The others are high-premium as well?*

Dawes: I play a J.G. Guadagnini from 1770 and Ken has a Matteo Gofriller from 1726.

Helmer: Mine is the latest model from Massey Ferguson. Actually it's a viola built in 1957 and I'm quite pleased with the sound.

*You must spend as much time together as you do with your families. Do the sparks ever fly?*

Dawes: When we work on interpretation we all have input and we get along well. I certainly don't play "big boss." When we settle practical and less important questions we might resort to something as inane as flipping a coin.

*Do you easily agree on the repertoire?*

Brott: We have to think about getting the complete works by major composers out to the public on record—Brahms, Beethoven, Mozart and so on. Sometimes we have made terrific miscalculations about people's taste. We might have planned one major quartet followed by a number of shorter, lighter pieces for a small-town audience, and then found that they wanted to hear only major works.

*Do you give the concert presenters a wide choice?*

Dawes: On a recent tour we took about twenty works along, not only for the presenters to choose from, but we would occasionally ask the audience at intermission what they would like to hear in the second half of the program.

*You have a reputation for playing new works. Has your appetite for new repertoire diminished over the years?*

Dawes: We have about twenty contemporary quartets from several countries in our active repertoire and several of them were commissioned by us. It is true, though, that we play less new music than we used to, because we play so many concerts where people want standard repertoire.

*To many listeners quartets are as serious as you can get in music. Have you ever entered the twilight zone of cross-over repertoire?*

Perkins: We have recorded an arrangement of Beatles songs on Fanfare. The popular performer André Gagnon once wrote a piece for us called *Four Tangos* with himself at the piano—a sort of great classics tied together. We went on a tour together.

Dawes: We usually play for an audience of five to six hundred, but here there were twelve hundred. We had never played anything so pop before.

Perkins: At one point we did an audience survey, and a great many people said they would be interested in coming back to hear the Orford alone.

Brott: Marketing is a terribly important part of a musician's career, and we usually go along with what is needed. Recently someone wanted to photograph us in a sleigh pulled by reindeer, but it started to rain and do you know what? Reindeer absolutely refuse to go out in the rain.

# Arthur Ozolins

Pianist Arthur Ozolins has two equally fascinating sides to his career. First, the obvious—his introspective yet high-wire virtuosity on the keyboard. Second, his life story, which is so fantastic that it strains the imagination. The forty-two-year-old soloist is a third-generation concert pianist. Perhaps he is so genetically programmed that nothing could have deterred him from becoming a pianist, although his formative years were a disastrous string of events that took him from refugee camp to slums to affluence over three continents.

Ozolins has been "discovered" repeatedly since his debut with the Toronto Symphony in 1961. Ten years later, Winthrop Sargeant wrote in *The New Yorker*, "I suspect that Mr. Ozolins will become one of the great virtuoso pianists of our time," and followed up five years later stating that Ozolins "has become the master that I predicted." In 1987 he was the Critics' Choice in *High Fidelity*, which described him as "one of the greatest young virtuoso artists in the world. André Gavrilov, move over!" Despite a constant track record, Ozolins has not yet found a secure place among his peers; his busy concert schedule bounces between venues high and low.

Perhaps the hurdles that have been placed in Ozolin's path from his first day of life are an essential part of his artistry. Smooth sailing might reduce the fiery, crystalline touch that often echoes the early years of Horowitz. In order to understand Ozolins, one must go back to pre-revolutionary Russia, where his grandparents lived in glittering St. Petersburg. The family saga continued in Latvia, Germany, Argentina, New York City, Paris, and Toronto, where Ozolins lives today.

*Colgrass: Your life story reads like over-heated fiction. Not even a Hollywood agent could dream up such heartbreak.*

Ozolins: I know, I know. [Smiles apologetically.] The musical side

of my family was my mother's parents, Oskar and Emilia Bertholds, who lived a very comfortable life in St. Petersburg. My grandmother was a concert pianist and my grandfather was the first importer of automobiles in the city. They held a salon where Chaliapin and Caruso came, and my grandmother became a good friend of Rachmaninoff. He was crazy about cars and bought one from my grandfather.

*Did you hear your grandmother play Rachmaninoff?*

Oh yes, when I was five or six years old I used to hear her practice both the First and Second Concertos. I have a copy of the First, in its first edition, which Rachmaninoff autographed for my grandmother. She was much more romantic than me. As a matter of fact, Rachmaninoff himself was very romantic, almost schmaltzy in the lyrical parts, although he was one of the modern romantics who kept track of time.

*What did the revolution of 1917 do to your family?*

It was a disaster for them. My mother was just two years old. The Bertholds family originally came from Latvia, so it was natural for them to flee to Riga. This is where my mother went to the conservatory and she also studied in Berlin with Edwin Fischer, who was quite famous.

*Now there were two concert pianists in the family. Where does the name Ozolins come in?*

My mother, whose name was Sylvia, met my father, Gottfrieds Ozolins, who was a lawyer, and they married over my grandparent's strong objection. I now understand why.

*I read in your biography that you were born in Lübeck, a town that is now in West Germany.*

Yes, in a refugee camp. When the Russians entered Latvia during the Second World War my family was forced to flee again, and like all Latvians we were placed in the camp by an order from the Allied Occupation Forces. The family stayed there for two years and that's where my brother [one-year-older Imants] and I got our start.

*How did you get out?*

Well, my mother's brother, Marcel, had managed to escape to Argentina where he studied medicine. It was in those days a rich and promising country. He arranged for our emigration, and everyone was probably looking forward to returning to a lifestyle that resembled what they had known in the past. Somehow my grandparents had managed to bring with them oriental rugs and eight pianos of excellent quality, and that gave them a bit of money.

*So you got your start at the piano in Argentina?*

I was taught by my mother and grandmother, but things didn't go well for us. My father found it impossible to learn Spanish, so he couldn't go back to his profession. Instead he succumbed to a life-long problem of alcoholism. My mother returned to the concert stage, but after a few concerts in Argentina and other South American countries she had a thyroid operation. Only a few hours after the operation she died. I was six at the time. Soon afterwards my grand-father also died, and he had been the breadwinner of the family.

*What happened to you?*

Just four of us were left. My grandmother blamed my father for the premature death of my mother, there were money problems and my father drank. By the time I was nine, my father had completely lost control of the situation. My brother and I were living with him in the slums of Buenos Aires — dirt floors and no running water.

*Did your grandmother save you?*

No, actually, my uncle Marcel. He got us into a German-Lutheran orphanage for three years. It was strict but pretty decent, and every few weeks I managed to visit my grandmother and practice the piano.

*How did you get to Canada?*

One of my father's old fraternity friends from his university days offered to sponsor us as immigrants. By that time I was twelve years old, and I immediately went to the Royal Conservatory in Toronto for piano lessons. At home, though, we continued living very badly. My father had become a sweeper at Princess Margaret Hospital and was still drinking. Fortunately I began making some money by giving recitals when I was fourteen.

*One of the numerous patrons who watched over you in those days told me a charming story about your debut with a symphony orchestra.*

Well [an apologetic smile], my English wasn't quite perfect when I was fourteen, and I read a notice in the Musicians Union's publication that the Toronto Symphony was auditioning players. I thought that included me, so I asked to audition. They explained to me that they only wanted string and wind players, but I insisted, and Walter Sus-skind, who was then music director, overheard the discussion. I guess he felt sorry for me, at any rate he agreed to listen to what I had prepared. At the end he handed me the score to Dohnányi's *Variations on a Nursery Song* and asked if I could learn it in six months. I though I could learn it in a couple of weeks, so in February of 1961 I made my debut with the orchestra. I was immediately re-engaged and it opened a lot of doors for me.

*Did you become financially independent?*

I could have been, but my father decided to spend my cheques his own way. One day I came home and found that he had sold my piano and my bicycle to buy liquor, and I decided then and there to leave home as soon as it was legally possible, at age sixteen.

*A frightening thought, I imagine.*

Something miraculous happened. The Women's Committee of the Toronto Symphony had kept an eye on me and knew about my situation. They contacted Marjorie Jackson, a social worker who specialized in child placement. She also played the piano and lived alone in a comfortable house where there was a grand piano. She gave me a home, first for a trial period, and eventually we became close and I began to think of her as a mother.

*You still do?*

Oh, she is my mother. When I became twenty-one she was able to adopt me legally, although my father was still alive. I changed my name from Arturs to Arthur, but I kept my last name to hang on to my artistic and Latvian identity. My mother always helped me a great deal, both with school work and by playing the orchestral accompaniment to about thirty of the forty piano concertos in my repertoire.

*Who were your piano teachers?*

First Talivaldis Kenins, who is also Latvian and a composer. We are very good friends and I have often played his works. For a while I studied with Alberto Guerrero, who also taught Glenn Gould at the Conservatory. When I was sixteen Pablo Casals recommended me for studies with Nadia Boulanger in Paris, so my mother and I took a small apartment near Mademoiselle, as Boulanger was called by her students.

I was so used to hearing people praise my technique but criticize my musical immaturity, but Mademoiselle said, "You are a born musician, but you have no technique." I'll admit that we were often at loggerheads—to her technique was everything, and I thought at that time that performers were in such ecstacy and torment that they never thought of structure. [Laughs.] I also had to be ready day and night for her call to come and see her immediately. She said that a true musician could afford only one hour a week of private life and that she herself took only five minutes a day to consider her problems!

*In other words, she gave you a rough time.*

Well, I finally realized that Mademoiselle was right. Everything is built on structure. After my Paris studies I played a little cooler. It is important to even plan the emotions—the humor, the charm and the passion. I visited Boulanger shortly before she died, and by that time we were friends.

*You also studied with the legendary Nadia Reisenberg in New York.*

Yes, I went to Mannes College on a full scholarship, and among my classmates were Murray Perahia, Frederica von Stade and Richard Goode. Madame Reisenberg was a tiny, dynamic woman who had been a protégée of Joseph Hofmann, the famous Polish pianist. She was much cooler and more modern than my grandmother. Sometimes she found my playing too volatile, but she liked my tone—remember, in those days I was still finding my way. My five years with her was the greatest influence on my playing. However, as a pianist I consider myself a perpetual student.

*Counting on my fingers, you are the product of seven nationalities and speak Latvian, German, Spanish, English and French. Did you ever suffer an identity crisis?*

No, when I'm with Latvians I feel Latvian, and when I go to South America I really feel at home too. Now I'm a Canadian and my adopted country has given me so much. I suppose I have the advantage of feeling at home wherever I go on tour—England, the States, Spain, Sweden, Germany, and do you know I have had six tours in Russia? In the Soviet Union you are immediately aware of the tradition fostered by the great pianists like Richter, Ashkenazy and Gilels. Even the young people there are knowledgeable about music, because they don't get sidetracked by all the distractions we have here. When I first played there, in 1975, I got quite worried. The audience was very cool, waiting for me to prove myself. But once they warmed up, they got so hot that they demanded encore after encore and finally carried me away on their shoulders. I have since experienced that many times, in Moscow, Leningrad and Riga, where I have lots of relatives.

*Are you ever distracted by the audience?*

Sometimes they cough a lot and it can be distracting. My concentration was really put to the test during a recital in Alice Tully Hall at Lincoln Center. It was in 1978, at the height of the protest against the Canadian seal hunt, and someone had phoned both the box office and the Canadian Consulate in New York to inform them that I would be shot onstage! The concert still went on, though each member of the audience was searched at the door. The entire recital was played in a brightly lit hall and I had two of New York's Finest standing solemnly next to the piano, guns at the ready, staring at the audience. Fortunately I was alive to read the reviews the next day.

*Most successful soloists insist that outstanding talent always rises to the top. Do you agree?*

Yes, in the long run, but who you know can help a great deal too. Some say that it helps to live in New York or London.

*Are you getting tired of being "discovered" again and again?*

Ha! I think everybody wants to feel that they personally have discovered you, and it does make sense that an artist prove himself in every territory. The real test is whether they re-engage you, and I have been lucky in that regard.

*Did you ever win a major international competition?*

No, and that might have held me back. I have been a juror on several competitions, though, and I always look for someone who could be a star, who interprets the music, recomposes it and makes it art. To me music is drama—I don't mean making theatrical faces—and people who take chances can miss notes. It is very easy to deduct marks in those cases, as I have seen it happen. Sometimes the winners of competitions disappear after a few years because they didn't have enough personality or drama to interest the audience.

*Does that make you a popular juror?*

It depends on where it is. At the Teresa Carreño Competition in Venezuela some audience members didn't like the results and blamed me, coming from a neutral country. They screamed and even threw chairs at me! [Laughs heartily.] Further north we are not so volatile, fortunately.

*In your own work, have you changed your approach to learning over the years?*

Yes, first of all I'm able to learn works so much faster. I understand the structure of music better and memorization, thank God, I have no problem with. Learning by ear is the easiest way, but to perform music you must analyze it in depth and try to make it a dramatic entity. Also, learning a piece of music is not enough. For that I could just stay at home and enjoy myself, the way Glenn Gould did. He finally didn't even have to play the piano, but could just look at the score and enjoy it. I still do play, however, and have to interpret and memorize and be able to play on all kinds of sometimes awkward instruments.

*Your temperament sometimes threatens to make you disappear from the stage in a puff of smoke. Do you ever feel close to the brink?*

Sometimes I surprise myself, especially when I listen to a tape after a concert or recording session, and think, "My God, what speed and where do I get this fire?" Even though I'm forty-two, I still feel young. I remember being fascinated by Rubinstein in his forties when he also had the flamboyance and energy. When he became older, he was more aristocratic and elegant, so maybe I'll get more serene with age too.

*Are your moods as volatile as your artistic temperament?*

No, I'm rather steady. Only if I'm sick or terribly tired can I feel blue. But I can get irritated by spending a lot of time on the tiny details that go into a concert career, like getting up in the middle of the night to call East Germany.

Recently I wasted a lot of time because I was audited by the tax people. They just can't understand why I have to go to the west coast three times in one month. When I explained to them that I had concerts on the east coast in between, they insisted that my days without concert engagements were holidays. Can you imagine? When I explained that I practiced on my days "off," including Saturday and Sunday, they evidently thought I was completely crazy. They concluded that I played at home for my own enjoyment and therefore could deduct only half of my expenses. Well, I fought the case and won, but that kind of thing takes a lot of energy.

*What keeps you going with such relentless energy?*

Well, playing is very hard work and I sometimes wonder how I got into it. I had to sacrifice so many things, mainly friendships and sports. But I suppose I'm an artist at heart and I have a sense of duty to continue the family tradition.

# R. Murray Schafer

While most people struggle to make a success of one career, R. Murray Schafer usually has half a dozen projects going at the same time—in different arts, that is. He is a composer, a writer of educational and scholarly books, a visual artist, a reluctant teacher, and the director and producer of his own shows, which are often wildly original in their epic theatrical proportions.

It would be impossible to mention Schafer's entire output, but some milestones are in order. His 1977 book, *The Tuning of the World*, documented the findings of his World Soundscape Project, which had turned the international music world on its ear during the 1960s. The controversial opera *Ra* took place between sunset and sunrise variously in Canada and Holland, a giant encounter with insomnia and Egyptian mythology. Among his over seventy works are more conventional compositions for ensembles and orchestras, such as his Flute Concerto of 1984 and two string quartets from the 1970s. Recently he received the first Glenn Gould Prize of $50,000 for his music and ways to communicate it. However, it is as the conjurer of magical events that Schafer is at his most original. A typical Schafer event was *Music for Wilderness Lake*, which he co-directed with nature in 1979 around O'Grady Lake in southeastern Ontario.

Some concerts tend to blur in one's mind after a while. We go to the concert hall and spend a couple of pleasant hours, and at the end of the season only the very best or the complete disasters are remembered. So when the invitation came to drive for four hours into the countryside, stay overnight and get up at 4:30 A.M. to reach a remote wilderness lake where a concert would be performed at dawn, it sounded very much like an event that would be remembered.

The lake was close to where composer Murray Schafer lived, in the village of Maynooth. No other cluster of humanity was in sight, but

on the map it seemed close to Peterborough, Ontario. For the past four or five years, Schafer had been thinking of writing a piece of music to be performed under certain outdoor conditions, taking its cues from nature. His duet with nature brought out twelve trombonists, a film crew, sound people, photographers, several boats, a raft, and various media people. It was a fall morning, the frost was biting, and the stars were still bright in the sky.

In the fleeting night light everything initially seemed white, with mist moving gracefully over the black surface of the lake. The shores were invisible and marked only by the haphazard sounds of trombones coming from several directions. At first sight, the slightly bizarre combination of a peaceful lake surrounded by trombones warming up and hectic film people scurrying for position brought a smile to our lips. A boat came out of the mist and whisked us to a favorable location on the shore where we could take in the show. As it turned out, the three people who shared my boat were not music buffs at all, but nature lovers. To my surprise, their enthusiasm continued unabated through the music—indeed, it lasted till we were shipped back to the only habitation around the lake five hours later for a much-needed breakfast.

What did take place, then? Well, there were many people at work, first of all the twelve trombonists situated in three groups around the lake. They were members of Sonare, a trombone choir of sometimes thirty players that has premiered numerous new compositions and will play anything from Bach to ragtime. The spectacle was recorded in five locations. One of these was a raft in the middle of the lake, which also served as the vantage point for the conductor, Murray Schafer, who cued the players with colored flags. As the contours of the surroundings became defined by the morning light, the raft looked much like a spaceship with its colorful cargo floating in a white mist. The birds seemed to take their cues with uncanny precision, the serenity emphasized by rustling leaves and fish making small splashing sounds. The trombones fitted perfectly into this setting, but then the music had the organic flavor of nature, as if twelve animals of the same species called across the lake in unhurried, simple voices.

Since the wilderness lake adventure is not likely to be often repeated, the entire happening was filmed by Fichman-Sweete Productions [now Rhombus]. The film crew had worked with Schafer on every detail.

It is not surprising, of course, that Schafer produced his *Music for Wilderness Lake*. He invented the word "soundscape" to describe his work with recording and investigating the sounds of nature during his tenure at Simon Fraser University in British Columbia, from 1965 to 1975. Schafer's is a lively, obstreperous mind. His ideas break apart the cultural establishment with a crowbar, but he also sees it coming together again, albeit in new ways.

In recent years he has created theatrical events of even larger proportions, an interest that began in his rural environment during the late 1970s when he found himself an outsider in Maynooth, where family roots go deep. Like most artists, Schafer is a communicator, and he needed to become accepted in order to reach the local population.

*Colgrass: What made you write Music for Wilderness Lake?*

Schafer: The idea was to do a piece of music around the lake with the trombones positioned on the shore, and to make use of the special change of sound at dawn and dusk when the temperature of the air on top of the water is different from the air higher up. This gives certain defractions, bending the soundwaves.

It was a collision between a human group and the natural environment. In the score the pauses are marked with "Pause until the last echo has decayed" or "Stop until you hear the birds again."

*The second part was produced at dusk.*

The sound was very different. Not nearly as full or reverberant as at dawn.

*When you settled in Maynooth, how did you get involved with the community?*

I looked for an existing social organization that would welcome a choir, and obviously that would be the local church. The Lutheran church at the corner accepted my help with their singing, and the first week eight people joined, none of whom could read music. Some even had problems reading print. They learned everything by rote.

*This must have been an exciting challenge.*

When I taught at university I frankly got bored for the simple reason that everyone you encounter there is of moderately high intelligence, usually of upper-middle income, and all of the same age group. I also found the university intellectuals quite predictable. In my choir here, which grew into a community choir, we had a complete cross section of the community with the youngest eight years old and the oldest about sixty-five.

*Did you teach them hymns?*

I also made them sing hard music—English madrigals, plainsong in Latin. In fact, we learned a whole Latin mass which we sang several times in both the Catholic and Lutheran churches—they don't care.

*What made you settle in Maynooth?*

I like things primitive. You can have this illusion at least that you are living close to the elements and nature.

We have adopted southern kinds of culture as our model—types of entertainment like the guitar are not indigenous to Canada. I think there are certain features of the environment that can't be ignored and people will finally have to accommodate themselves to them no matter where they come from. It is hard for some newcomers, for instance, to understand that the concept of space is very important to Canadians. We have a need for space and for wilderness uncontaminated by human settlements, and when you destroy that, you are destroying a myth. I'm sure that is in the Indian head, too. This is not an inhospitable environment if you know how to go with it, instead of fighting it all the time.

*Was there any cultural life in Maynooth?*

There is such an artificial attitude about culture and where it orginates. There is this idea that the really valuable enterprises exist in the big cities and are pumped out across the country. When I went to an arts council and asked for some assistance for Maynooth, they said, "Oh, you want to start a summer festival and get string quartets and ensembles?" I told them no, I just wanted $1000 so I could have an assistant choir master, a local person. They asked about his credentials, degrees and the like, and I said there were none and that I just wanted to train this person who could not afford to do the work for nothing, as I can. The arts council's idea is that the really important culture comes from the city, and that their goal is to find summer employment for musicians and actors out in the sticks somewhere. Would these people, for instance, extend an invitation to my choir to come to Toronto to present their work? Of course they wouldn't!

*So the cultural establishment discriminates . . .*

I would say that there is some kind of culture anywhere in the country you go, and if I can't see it, I'm at fault. It's always there, even if it's just in the way a man picks up a piece of wood and starts to whittle it.

Why does every community aspire to getting a symphony orchestra and then a ballet? I have often thought that for the same amount of money that's put into the Victoria Symphony, you could have the world's best string quartet. It could be called the Victoria String Quartet and play both in Victoria and elsewhere, giving valuable publicity to the city. Why have a so-so symphony orchestra when you can have something first-rate? But it never occurs to a single community—they all want to have the same sorts of things.

*Could all the new immigrants change this?*

The kinds of people coming here today, being so different from those of past centuries, are going to bring very different cultures.

Once they get integrated and strong, they'll confront the arts councils and want the money for Chinese opera and the hell with the Canadian Opera Company and European influence, because they now represent the majority of clients for culture. So things will change. [With a smile.] The only thing one can do in approaching a foreign culture is try and detect excellence and craftmanship. Even then we might not have any idea of what emotions are stimulated by them.

*You've experienced this in your travels?*

When I was in Australia I met some aborigines. They were beating on the ground with their sticks—very primitive—and some were playing a flute that's just a tube without holes. They went on forever with their hollow, monotonous sound, and I thought: my word, this is like the beginning of music. However, it suddenly occurred to me that they weren't breathing. That tone never stopped. They were doing circular breathing [a method of breathing that allows the flutist to play continuously while taking in air at the same time]. Suddenly what appeared primitive became very sophisticated. Later I talked about this with some oboe players in Sydney and they said, "Oh yes, we are trying to learn from them how to do this."

*Despite our foreign influences, do you think that a unified Canadian character will emerge eventually?*

I'm shaped by the Canadian climate and ecology, as I think we all will be. Ultimately that's the thing that will give the real character of the country. We will, of course, be influenced by different peoples, but in the end we'll be shaped by living in this cold climate and coming to terms with it.

# Richard Stoltzman

"I try not just to play the clarinet, but to play music in a vocal fashion," says the celebrated clarinetist Richard Stoltzman. His wish is to make the listeners forget that a clarinet is between them and the music, and it must have come true. *Washington Post* critic Paul Hume calls him "an artist of indescribable genius," and audiences at the end of his performances have been reported to "come to their feet as though someone had hollered 'Fire!'"

The youthful Stoltzman, forty-five at the time of this interview, was born in Omaha. After music training at Ohio State University and Yale, he soon gravitated towards the pinnacle of music-making, the Marlboro Music Festival in Vermont. During his ten summers there, beginning in 1967, he played with the very best musicians in North America and met his future founding partners in Tashi, a highly acclaimed and innovative ensemble. The group was named after pianist Peter Serkin's dog, Tashi [i.e., auspicious coincidence], and although Tashi's master eventually left to go his soloist ways, the ensemble still lives on in different groupings with Stoltzman at the center.

In the course of playing with practically all the major orchestras and finest chamber ensembles, Stoltzman has garnered many honors, among them the Avery Fisher Prize and a Grammy Award for his Mozart/Brahms recording on RCA. On the crossover album *Begin Sweet World*, he added jazz to his usual repertoire so successfully that the record was on the *Billboard* charts for over thirty weeks. But despite his remarkable career and association with other famous musicians, Stoltzman still views it all with a sense of wonder. How can this be deserved? When must I get "a real job?" Although he plays with profound musical insight and great finesse, he still seems as vulnerable as a precocious child.

The following talk is probably more casual and candid than usual

because I had known Dick Stoltzman for many years. We met this time before a Tashi concert at Toronto's CentreStage, celebrating the ensemble's tenth anniversary in 1983. Stoltzman had just spent a month with his violinist wife, Lucy, awaiting the birth of their youngest child, Margaret Anne; the couple also has a son, Peter John. Lucy has since become a member of the Muir String Quartet and the family has settled in Winchester, Massachusetts.

*Colgrass: You considered becoming a dentist at some point. Did you doubt your musical ability?*

Stoltzman: I guess so. I don't think anybody had confidence in my making a living as a musician. Why would they be optimistic? The only jobs open for a clarinetist were either in an orchestra or teaching.

*By now you must have come to terms with living as a soloist and being constantly on the road.*

Yes [sigh], I suppose I have come to terms with it. It's a funny thing with me, I have never really thought I would be doing this for a living. I still keep thinking that I've got to get a job one of these days—I've got to start doing something serious. I don't know what is going to happen to me from year to year.

*Nobody really does.*

No, but if you have a job and a contract it's different.

*I understand that the technical aspects of the clarinet, especially the reed, can be rather daunting.*

I sometimes get upset with myself for being so removed from these technical things. I don't know much about them at all and it makes me sort of embarrassed. Often people will come up to me after a concert and ask, "What reed did you use?" or "What mouthpiece did you use?" I just don't know these things! I pay almost no attention to them and I like it that way. On the other hand, if something doesn't work, I don't know how to fix it, so my attitude can create problems.

It often bothers me about clarinetists that they are constantly searching for reeds, mouthpieces and fingerings. These are all subservient to doing something with the music. When the famous clarinetist Carol Reich once played in the Brahms Quintet at a gathering of clarinetists, they all sat with their scores listening to "the clarinet part." Afterwards somebody came up to him and said, "Oh, Mr. Reich, it was just so fantastic. How do you play so long without getting a squeak?"

*How do your colleagues react to you?*

A lot of players don't really like the way I play. They don't even consider me a clarinetist.

*What do they say?*

Nothing. They don't come backstage, so I don't have to worry about what they say. They may have heard that I'm some kind of "big deal." Then they hear me and say, "He doesn't even play like a clarinetist."

*Why do some clarinetists get such a piercing, reedy sound, when you can make your sound so smooth and velvety?*

There are teachers who emphasize that quality of sound as being appropriate for the instrument. I remember studying with a teacher who said, "If you don't change your sound, you are never going to fit in." He was concerned that I was going to try auditioning for orchestras and would be immediately eliminated because my sound is not of the certified quality. He was right—I never got into one.

I did play a bit in the New Haven Symphony at Yale, though. It was great playing the orchestral repertoire. I also played a little in the Marlboro Festival when Casals was conducting, and that was very exciting. Later I played a few pick-up dates with New York orchestras, but there was an interesting attitude among the musicians of tongue-in-cheek cynicism about the whole business. I was worried and didn't want that to happen to me. Just by default I didn't get enough engagements to become jaded.

*You have an almost jazzy, spontaneous feel to your playing. Have you worked hard to develop that?*

I think that came in my childhood from playing with my dad. He was an executive with a railroad company and also played jazz on the tenor saxophone. He loved Lester Young, Ben Webster, Coleman Hawkins and people like that. When I was in seventh grade he bought me those "Music Minus One" records where you fill in the solo. Both my parents encouraged me and I began to get the feeling for going beyond the notes.

*You are one of the few classical musicians who can improvise.*

Well, I'm trying to. I don't want to be so presumptuous as to say, "Oh, I play jazz too." If I heard a jazz musician say that he played classical too, I might wonder. I love jazz and I respect the musicianship that comes out of it, and sometimes I try to emulate it. You have to pay your dues and I don't think I have done that in jazz yet.

*How do you keep up with such a variety of music?*

I have worked a lot with pianist and composer Bill Douglas and he acts almost as my mentor by sending me cassettes with music that I should know about—both pop and jazz and perhaps a special hot section from a Martha Argerich recording. He has very eclectic tastes and sends me these care packages so I can keep up with what is going on. Unfortunately I get too immersed in my little world of the clarinet. I don't go to enough concerts or hear enough recorded music.

I recently did a CBS show where Eugenia [Zukerman, flutist] asked me what I would do if I didn't play the clarinet, and I replied, "I think I would be a much better musician." I really think that if I didn't play I would study more.

*I saw that TV special. Did you like the end result?*

After it was over I just looked at Lucy. It was done over the summer and took many days and hours of filming. It seemed like such a big deal at the time, and then this little microscopic show came on!

*I have seen you depressed when things didn't go exactly right, but in this program you seemed much more anxiety-ridden than I know you to be.*

They apparently decided to make the angle of the story the "dark side of the musician." So whatever was light-hearted they cut out.

*They also portrayed your teacher, Kalman Opperman, as some sinister slave driver—"Every minute you are not playing, there are other clarinetists out there practicing," and so on.*

There is that aspect to him.

*Is that a good way to teach?*

I think he was a good teacher at the point I found him. I thought I was pretty well set and just needed a couple of touch-ups. But he dragged me down and put my ego way low, and I started over.

*How about a more joyous approach?*

This is his way. He makes such an impression on you that—like a child breaking away from his parents—you have to break away from that force to establish your own playing.

Keith Wilson [of Yale University] taught from a different place. He taught from the joy of the instrument and a tremendous love for chamber music. He was the one to make me realize that chamber music is a true gold mine for the clarinet. But Kalman Opperman is sort of the dark side and that quality attracted me.

*What is your own approach to teaching?*

I used to teach a little at Cal Arts [California Institute of the Arts], but I don't have time for it anymore. My only teaching experience now is in master classes. Still, it is difficult because I'm the kind of teacher who tends to hear something good or wonderful in every person's playing, even when it's not all that great. I try to find out why they want to play and then reinforce that.

*Even a player like you needs stroking.*

Yes, sure. I think teaching is a volatile field and psychologically very dangerous, so you have to take it tremendously seriously.

*Your career seems to have developed along with close friendships with certain musicians, such as those in Tashi and at Marlboro.*

Friendships in music-making are very important, because they enable you to say exactly what you want without it being construed as an attack on someone's ego. Your friends know that you are talking for purely musical reasons. Also you can tour in a relaxed ambiance with your friends.

*As long as none of them decide to marry each other. [Two Tashi members were married briefly, yet stayed in the group.]*

That doesn't work too well. There was a thought of having my wife Lucy join Tashi, and my manager said, "Please don't do that; I want you to stay together." At the time we thought it was a rather cynical remark, but now we see that it is very important to have the relationship of husband and wife sacrosanct and apart from performing. It's hard enough just to be with yourself twenty-four hours a day.

*You have broken several barriers with the Tashi group in terms of both repertoire and presentation.*

Yes, we like to search out unusual repertoire. We also decided to just wear the clothes we felt good about when performing. Most jazz musicians don't worry too much about what they wear—they certainly rarely wear identical clothes.

*Do you travel first-class as a group?*

Oh no! Once in a while we stay in a first-rate hotel; it's such a satisfying indulgence. We have just performed in the States and stayed in one of the more common chain hotels where people were partying in the halls at night. After the concert we ended up having take-out chicken wings—ugh.

*You weren't fed after the concert?*

No. That's often the case and it's nobody's fault. Only chamber-music societies that have been in existence for a long time recognize this kind of personal need of the performers. We have sometimes ended up in milk stores buying bags of potato chips, cheese and peanuts. So we really revel in staying at a luxury hotel.

*Did you find a new musical world when you first went to the Marlboro Music Festival in 1967?*

Sure. For one thing I was playing as a clarinetist with people who were at the top of their profession; that is a hard thing to come by for a wind player. It was like moving into a whole new world for me. I was talking with musicians about things that clarinetists don't usually bother with—in other words, we never talked about the clarinet, just about the music. And we spent the whole day, every day, playing.

*That was an unusual pleasure?*

Pleasure and a lot of pressure. You wanted to play better there than you had ever played before. There is a very, very high level of expectation at Marlboro for everyone to make the most meaningful music and the most magical experience possible. "If it's going to be done on earth, it'll be done there," is the feeling everybody has. It's like being in heaven in the sense that there is nowhere else you want to go.

*What do you like most, playing chamber music or concertos?*

I get different pleasures from each one. It is a great pleasure for me to stay in one place for several days, as when I play with an orchestra. I also like being taken care of—somebody meeting you at the airport and so on, as opposed to straggling into town, trying to find the hall and hoping there is a door open when you get there. Sometimes you really are on your own when you play chamber music. As compensation you hang out with the other players.

The nicest thing happened to me once when I was at my most apprehensive. I was playing my debut concert at La Scala. It was a big deal for me to stay on that stage and play for three nights. When I came out for the first rehearsal the whole wind section stood up! I almost started to cry—I had been so worried that they would think "Here comes that dumb guy from the States," so I bowed to them and felt just great.

*Did you ever have a real disaster?*

A thing happened which now seems funny, but at the moment it hit me like a thunderbolt! It was during my Carnegie Hall debut in New York when I was dedicating a suite of pieces to Benny Goodman, who came to the concert. I talked about how much Benny had done for the clarinet in the twentieth century, and as I pointed towards him, everybody turned to look. I was clapping while holding on to the top of my clarinet. Suddenly the bottom part of the clarinet fell off and bounced on the stage! Ironically nobody saw it because they were all looking at Benny, but I saw it as in a dream. There I was at Carnegie Hall seeing my instrument bouncing on the floor. Then I just picked it up, stuck it back together and hoped for the best. Luckily nothing had happened, but if something in the instrument had bent, cracked or split, it would have been the end of the concert right there.

*Fortunately your instrument is replaceable.*

In a way that is also bad. The nicest thing about my instrument is the case. It is a beautiful hand-crafted case of rosewood. I think I got it unconsciously, because I always travel with string players and they are always asked to show their instruments. To me they say, "Let's see your case," because that is all I have to show. The instrument is made on a machine somewhere. I have gone through lots; each one lasts for about five years. I wish that the love and care that went into making the case would extend to the making of the clarinet.

*Do you think it could be improved upon?*

I don't know. We are now getting into the technical things that I don't know about. Sometimes when I overhear clarinetists talk about weaknesses in the instrument, I don't even know what they are talking about.

*Are you more aware of your breathing than you are of technicalities?*

No, I'm really not aware at all of my breathing. People say that I must have tremendous lung capacity, but I don't feel that. However, I do feel that the sound people hear—a composite of my breath vibrating the reed and going out through the air—is very exciting. That is why live concerts are no comparison with other forms of listening; I don't care how great loudspeakers or laser beams or digital get.

*You record for RCA?*

Yes, I did the Mozart Clarinet Concerto and a Brahms sonata that won the Grammy Award. I have something like fifteen records out, most of them on RCA. The Weber Concerto No. 1 is among them.

*Since some musicians have made a living on recordings, it must be rather lucrative.*

Maybe for some people, but my royalty cheque from RCA in 1982 was $49!

*But they don't record anything unless they expect to sell several thousand recordings. What does the artist get?*

I think it is five percent of the wholesale price, and there are pages of clauses in the contract which are all to the benefit of the large corporation. Once the record is repackaged in any way, the royalties are down to practically nothing. RCA decided to take the Tashi Mozart record, repackage it and put a sticker on it saying "Music from M-A-S-H." I was told that the final TV episode of *M-A-S-H* had a couple of minutes from Mozart's Clarinet Quintet, so maybe they will sell extra records, but it won't accrue to the artists. Anything on a budget label is to the financial disadvantage of the artist.

*How much time do you manage to spend at home?*

We try to arrange it so that I can have a week at Christmas, some time around Thanksgiving and the summer to be with my family. It doesn't always work; last year I had my Thanksgiving dinner in the Denver airport. Thanks to my manager I just took off the whole month of March, which meant canceling a lot of concerts. I really wanted to be with Lucy for the birth of our daughter. Most people understood this and could rearrange their plans.

*What are the main pressures on you as a soloist?*

To stay healthy—that's very big. I try to eat a big breakfast . . .

now, that sounds really corny! But there are certain things you have to do, because health is a huge element in trying to have a career as a performer. It is not so terrific for your health to travel around all the time, so it's all the more important to stay away from colds, sore throats and exhaustion.

Another big pressure is to go to each rehearsal and performance fresh and without prejudice about other players or the music. Then there is the pressure of trying to balance the time you have to yourself *vis-à-vis* publicity, interviews and radio talk shows. Finally I must maintain an intimate contact with my family and try to know what is going on and be part of it even while I am away.

The actual music-making is just a pleasure. Getting out onstage and playing is great.

# Teresa Stratas

More than a touch of glamor attends the image of a prima donna. That was evident when I first met Teresa Stratas, in 1980, backstage at the Met after a splendid *Mahagonny*, as the adulation and champagne bubbled around her. The soprano looked frail and beautiful, having given her utmost as Jenny in a televised performance for "Live at the Met." Because of this exertion, our interview the next day was canceled and a new appointment was made at her large apartment in a historical landmark building where Toscanini and Eleanor Steber once lived.

On our second meeting, any illusions about the life of this opera star very soon vanished. Stratas had personally painted the walls of her apartment in dramatic colors, sanded the floors and made the curtains. Even her chic brown dress was her own creation. Not a servant was in sight. After explaining how a small person can handle a sanding-machine without making gouges in the floor, she curled up in a sofa corner and proceeded to set the record straight—the life of a prima donna is tough indeed.

"I don't like giving interviews because basically I'm an introvert. I believe that too much bla-bla-bla says nothing of my work and actions speak for themselves," she said. She also made the prophetic statement: "I won't sing so terribly much longer, perhaps another five years."

Teresa Stratas' early years were filled with emotions and traumas which prepared her well for her thirty years on the operatic stage. She grew up in Toronto as one of three children of Greek immigrants. With a modest income from their small restaurant around the corner from the Maple Leaf Gardens (a large indoor sports arena), the family struggled to survive both financially and emotionally. Fortunately, the arena in those days also hosted the Metropolitan Opera on its spring visits. On Teresa's sixteenth birthday one of the restaurant's customers

couldn't pay for his meal, but he had two opera tickets in his pocket. Though Teresa had been singing pop music already in clubs and radio shows, it was this incident that led her to her very first opera— *La Traviata*. It made such an impression on her that she immediately searched out a voice teacher to prepare for her own future in opera. At the age of nineteen she was singing at the Met.

For the next twenty-five years Stratas sang twenty-five roles at the Met alone, and she illuminated all the world's major stages with her glorious voice and instinctive acting talent. In the last decade she has diversified and reached what was perhaps the high point of her career with the first complete *Lulu* staged in Paris in 1979; her recording of *The Unknown Kurt Weill* received resounding praise; and a public far beyond the opera crowd saw Franco Zeffirelli's sumptuous film of *La Traviata*, with Stratas wooed by Placido Domingo. During this period she also backpacked through India and worked a stint with Mother Theresa in Calcutta; she nursed Lotte Lenya on her deathbed and witnessed her father deteriorate and finally die from Alzheimer's disease. She also saw the musical *Rags*, in which she sang the lead on Broadway, reach its final and premature demise.

At the moment Stratas has completed a recording of *Show Boat*. There is always talk of what this extraordinary artist will do next. Perhaps she will return to the Met—and perhaps not.

*Colgrass: You are a small person, yet you have a big voice and emit a lot of energy.*

Stratas: The energy we transmit has nothing to do with the size of the person. It's something from within—well, it's actually from somewhere else. I'm the instrument for transmitting that energy. You can have a great big blubber on stage with absolutely no energy, no waves or electrical force.

My voice was always enormous. When I was a little child I spoke with this dark, deep voice. In my parent's restaurant in Toronto everybody was shocked at this skinny five-year-old who spoke like an old man. The speaking quality was always this dark, resonant sound. Sometimes in hotels when I ask for room service over the telephone, they answer "Yes, sir!" You can imagine that can be very upsetting on the day of a performance. Usually someone my size does the soubrette repertoire and stays in that very light sphere of singing. Certainly my voice was always larger than that.

*Were you ever in danger of being type-cast as the pretty young girl?*

Never. I started out doing Mimis, Micaëlas and Madama Butterfly—

already a different kind of repertoire. The people involved with the development of my singing were fortunately highly intelligent and perceptive. They saw the many facets of my personality so that I was never confined by "Oh, she is a marvelous comedienne, so we will only have her do comic, light parts," or "She is a Puccini singer." No one ever tried to put me in a box and tie a pretty ribbon around it.

*But you must have a favorite repertoire?*

I must say I don't like that question. I will only do a role when I'm convinced of it. If I'm doing a film of *Salome*, obviously that's my favorite role at that moment—I lived and ate and breathed that music and those words. If I'm doing *Bohème*, I think, "What a masterpiece, not one note too many. What a wonderful, vulnerable creature Mimi is." So I can't answer that question.

*Do you ever tackle a role that's opposite to your natural temperament?*

What's natural temperament? I don't think a person has only one temperament. People are not one-dimensional characters. Opera singers are no doubt blessed with more dimensions and I don't say that out of arrogance—we are blessed with that. So I don't think I have ever done a role that has gone against my temperament.

*In that case, what type of role might you have turned down in the past as being unsuitable?*

I took Butterfly out of my repertoire and I'll tell you why. It was very hard for me to be convinced that she couldn't help herself get out of that situation. There is something a little too passive in her, maudlin and whiny, so it's very hard to be instilling honor, belief and trust and all these other things that one could also interpret in the role. I found I was not convinced, so how could I convince the public? For these reasons I took it out of my repertoire, although it's suited to my voice and I'm always asked to do it.

*Don't you get to a point when you tire of singing a role again and again and want to take a rest from it or abandon it all together?*

It has never been that way with me—in the *Salome*, the *Lulu* and now Jenny in *Mahagonny*.

*How did you approach the role of Jenny, being aware of the cabaret style established by Lotte Lenya?*

Well, I used to sing in night clubs and I brought all that with me.

*That opera was telecast from the Metropolitan Opera. Isn't it nerve-racking to know there are close-ups all the time as opposed to having four thousand people neatly arranged at a distance?*

Well, I tell you as long as what you are doing, you do honestly . . . I love the camera, I love film and I love television. It gets into your brain and your soul and it says everything that is inside you.

*You obviously take acting seriously. It would be well if all opera singers did the same.*

I never think of one part of it being singing and another part acting. It's all one thing. We are here to give forth emotions, ideas, thoughts. You know, the vocal cords lie in a very strange place, right here in the throat just a little bit above the heart, a little bit above the soul. I sincerely feel that however you are feeling spiritually definitely affects the performance as a whole.

*How do you keep yourself in one piece in a profession that's so demanding physically and emotionally?*

One of the difficulties has been that I was always sick from a very young age. I had tuberculosis and it was not properly cured, so it's now chronic consumption and I have to be extremely careful. It's very difficult to live under the strain of this profession with all the traveling and staying in hotel rooms, changes of climate and time schedules, the long hours—plus the fact that I'm an insomniac. I'll go nights without sleeping, perhaps sleeping half an hour one night and an hour or two the next, and then suddenly it catches up with me. On top of this I have trouble keeping weight on. I started rehearsing *Mahagonny* at a good normal weight and everyone said "Gee, you look great." After three days, the weight was going down and down. Finally Jimmy [conductor James Levine] started to send me home early from rehearsals, so they were very sweet and considerate.

Keeping myself fit has always been precarious. I love to cook and do things for other people, but I'm not likely to do things for myself. Still, I'm in better control now and know the symptoms when the consumption is getting worse—the sweats and this and that. For years I ignored it and suddenly a doctor would say, "Young lady, you have to take six months off." They never have any other answer than rest, and that's exactly what I don't get in this profession. The last few years I have given up on doctors and administer homeopathic remedies to myself. I also do yoga, which helps a great deal.

*Where do you feel most at home?*

I don't feel at home anywhere.

*But your home is in New York . . .*

Well, I'm here two months of the year. I'm everywhere two months out of the year. I hate cities. I do what I have to do—singing—and don't ask me why I do it. Opera houses are in cities and I really despise cities with the high buildings and being surrounded by cement slabs, not able to see the sky. I do believe that cities are the enemy of people, and I will eventually buy a farm. I won't sing so terribly much longer. Perhaps another five years.

*That seems a shame . . .*

There are so many other things to do in life!

*Would you leave the profession entirely?*

Oh, absolutely! I might occasionally come out of retirement to do a film or two, but I would cut off abruptly and not just fade out.

*Would you teach?*

Never!

*You have appeared in several films, among them Salome, and you love the medium. Could you see yourself as a director of opera films?*

Yes I could, but I won't. I want to leave opera all together. I'm a voracious reader, and there is much I want to read and reread. It's wonderful to do absolutely nothing, just sit and let the thoughts come to you. It's a luxury. That's why I live alone.

*You were never married?*

No, I don't think I could have a normal married life, but not because I'm an opera singer. On the one side I'm so idealistic that if I did marry, I would believe in the whole thing—till death do us part and the total supportive partner. I'm also so realistic that I know that such a situation could never really exist.

*Are most of your friends singers too?*

Friends—I think if you have one friend you are very blessed. "Friends" is a term we use very loosely, like the word "genius." There are a lot of acquaintances, so-called friends. The moment I would lose my voice or be in trouble, that would be the end of those friends, no doubt, and I'm very aware of that. Maybe there are one or two friends that will still be friends when I stop singing.

*It's also time-consuming to have friends.*

It's energy-consuming to be around people as I am a good deal of the time. If I must be of service to myself and to others, I have to have time to refuel.

*Do you take rests between engagements?*

I always work. But I don't do anything very regularly. Perhaps I'll get up at three in the morning when I can't sleep and work to the extreme on my music and then perhaps not open a score for the next several days. I don't work with an accompanist, but always on my own at the piano.

*How long did it take you to get under the skin of a part like Lulu?*

You know, I hate analyzing what I do, because I think a person can talk and talk a thing out until it's talked away. So my work is like my religion: I don't like to verbalize it. Learning a role is a very natural thing. I start wearing the "skin" immediately, drawing on life experiences. I've had a lot of experiences and therefore putting on different skins is probably easier for me than for others.

*Do you prepare a role like Jenny by reading around the subject from books of that era?*

Do I do thousands of analyses? No! If something comes to me, like this book, *Brecht's Berlin*, I read it, but I don't go to the library to find literature. One has to have faith in the work, the words and the music. The problem with a lot of directors nowadays is that they are all looking for something scandalous or interesting—new, new, new! If people would only be secure enough to let the work speak for itself.

*Do you ever have disagreements with your directors?*

Oh yes, definitely, and that's the only place where analysis comes in. My instincts tell me what to do. Most directors are smart enough, like Franco Zeffirelli, to leave me alone, or if he sees the development of an idea he'll say, "That's wonderful, take it a step further." If he sees something that he doesn't like, he'll also tell me.

Then there are people who believe that being a director is being a dictator. When I did the film *Salome*, the director, Götz Friedrich, and I had totally different opinions of the role. He thought the whole thing was about sex, and he asked me to do really ridiculous things on camera. Well, something sexual might be a secondary result of that opera, but it's not the primary motivation. That was an out-and-out war, because I just wouldn't do what he asked of me. I kept asking why?—maybe the man could convince me that he was right.

In that one-and-a-half hours this woman lives a whole life time, so that by the end she would have died anyhow. So I found it went much deeper than sex. The director yelled: your job is to sing and my job is to direct! I finally ended up doing what I wanted. Fortunately the producer was totally supportive of my ideas and that we hadn't set out to make a pornographic film.

*Are there directors you refuse to work with?*

Yes, there is Götz Friedrich. Every day he would run out of the studio frothing at the mouth. I told him life's too short for that, so let's spare each other the agony. That we had problems on the film, though, doesn't mean the man is no good. He must have built his career on something.

*People often think of opera singers as being essentially temperamental. Is there any truth to that?*

I know I'm known as being temperamental and difficult, although I don't think I am. I think it has to do with not being comfortable. It would have been much easier for me to go through life always agreeing, but I couldn't live with myself that way. If I believe in something, I have to say what it is. If I'm in a room where somebody says something I really disagree with, I'll voice my opposition rather than just be quiet. Maybe that's being difficult. We have gone through life expecting ladies to act like "ladies," and that usually means not having an opinion.

*How do you enjoy performing with Jon Vickers?*

He's my favorite partner.

*He's quite adamant about having things his way.*

Yes, that's why we love working together. I love that man as a human being and as an artist. He's our greatest singing actor on the stage today. No doubt about it.

*Had you not gone through a difficult childhood as the daughter of poor Greek immigrants in Toronto, do you think your career would have been easier?*

I was singing at the Met at the age of nineteen. How much faster could I have gone? If you had taken me out of my background and put me elsewhere, I wouldn't be me. Whatever person I am, is because we had a difficult life. Therefore, if I'm sitting here in a fancy, enormous apartment in New York City with Lincoln Center down the street where I am a "star" of the Metropolitan Opera, and of every other opera house of the world, it doesn't mean a thing because that's not really what life is about. Because of my background I know that those material things are not really very important. I came from this very poor background, and certainly there was a conflict, suddenly finding myself in the glitter and glamor when I first came to the Met. I wasn't sure what was happening to me, but I did sort it out thanks to my background.

*If this isn't the real life, what is?*

Certainly not the glitter and the glamor!

*But the essence of the art is real . . . .*

That's what's important, the art itself. If you can get all the other things out of the way and find it. Sometimes it's buried behind all that.

*Vickers has called opera "a search for truth."*

Art is a search for truth, isn't it? The arts are an indication of what's better and elevated in mankind. I think it's very interesting that Khomeini has outlawed music in Iran.

*What do you think would happen if the arts were taken away from us, outrageous as it may seem?*

I think that the world would be filled only with our worst qualities— that's apathy and alienation. We border enough on that as it is and should be very careful. But there is always a low before there's a high.

I would like to think we have reached that low and are now going to pull up our socks.

*Going back to the opera world, have you found it tough and competitive?*

If there is a talent it will be heard. What's competition anyhow? Everyone has different qualities to contribute. I never felt threatened and I never questioned my talent.

*How important is the audience to you in regard to giving your best?*

You are asking if it is a matter of feedback from the audience? [Long pause.] I don't know if it's electrical—this vibration, that intangible thing that Vickers has—again that's something singers have been blessed with. [When a ringing phone interrupts her thoughts, she merely lifts off the receiver and drops it on the floor.] It comes from somewhere, whether it's God or the center of the universe, and certainly in my case it comes and goes in different strengths. Let's call it an aura which has something to do with the spirit, and it transmits those pulses out to the audience. Some days are very positive in golds and pinks, and some days are in grays and blacks. I firmly believe that whatever I am on a given day is what's going to affect the audience and not vice versa.

*So if you don't feel up to performing some day, does it make you nervous or dispirited?*

I always feel that we artists hold such a responsibility because of what we represent. If I'm less than one-hundred percent capable, whether in spirit or in voice, then I'm handicapped and I'm frustrated. If I feel so bad that I have nothing to offer then I cancel, but a lot of singers would just go ahead and sing anyway.

*Opera-goers in Canada are eager to hear you. Is there any chance of a visit to your home town?*

When they build a new hall I might.

# Jon Vickers

As we arrived at Jon Vickers' farm in the rolling hills near Orillia, Ontario, the heldentenor was in the shower getting rid of the sawdust and grime from building a couple of four-poster beds. This was his summer respite at his Canadian retreat. The rest of the year, Vickers and his wife Henrietta live at their splendid permanent residence in Bermuda, while their five children now lead their own lives elsewhere.

The celebrated tenor looked fit and healthy on this visit in 1986, and his only adjustment to having just passed his sixtieth birthday was a reduced opera schedule. Nowadays his date book is filled with oratorio and recital performances. Retirement is out of the question since Vickers is driven by an obligation to serve—"the essence of the Christian faith"—and he is a man of granite determination.

When Jon Vickers was a young man in his twenties, singing was "fun," but he says, "Frankly, I never had the wildest dreams of becoming a professional singer." Although he eventually sang as many as ninety concerts a year in Canada, his commitment to singing began to waver, and by June, 1956, he had decided to quit entirely and concentrate on his considerable talent for business. Just six weeks before his self-imposed deadline, the Royal Opera House at Covent Garden asked the then thirty-year-old Vickers to sing Riccardo in *Un Ballo in Maschera*. It was a great success, which he followed up with roles in *Carmen, Don Carlos, Aida* and *Les Troyens* during his three-year contract at Covent Garden.

Thirty years in the international limelight have brought an impressive array of recordings. Among them is *Otello* (Serafin and Karajan), *Aida* (Solti), *Fidelio* (Klemperer), *Tristan und Isolde* (Karajan) and his gripping role as Peter Grimes (Colin Davis). His unforgettable performances and associations with the foremost singers of his time place Vickers among the greatest heldentenors of our century. Of course

his voice has aged, but he is still capable of powerful performances and can rein in his huge voice to fit the miniature of lieder, a talent that is given only few opera singers.

Jon Vickers' first recollection of singing was at a Christmas concert with his family—he was the sixth of eight children—in his home town of Prince Albert, Saskatchewan, when he was three years old. The work ethic and Christian outlook came with the rugged western territory, reinforced by the Vickers family performances in churches, hospitals and mental institutions. In his youth he would sing "for anyone, anytime, anywhere." Vickers' track record as a successful businessman began at age thirteen, when he took over the agency for Fleischmann's yeast cakes in Prince Albert; while still a teenager he increased the annual turnover from $25,000 to $150,000. He subsequently joined Safeway, Woolworth's and the Hudsons's Bay Company, but a scholarship to the Royal Conservatory of Music in Toronto stalled these ambitions as well as his wish to become a physician.

The powerful spell that Vickers casts from the stage is apparent also in a one-to-one conversation. He presents his ideas forcefully and with constant eye contact, weighing everything seriously. One can believe that he has had an intimidating effect on more than a few colleagues and that this was the tenor who for moral reasons refused to sing *Tannhäuser* at Covent Garden.

*Colgrass: You are a stimulating conversationalist, yet you have shied away from interviews. Why?*

Vickers: I think it is such a sham when an artist uses artificial means to puff up his image. An artist must stand or fall on his art. Of course, today that's not the accepted thing. I opened my address at the University of Toronto this summer with a quote from the *Wall Street Journal*. The opening sentence of an article about an excellent company in the U.S. read: "It is no longer good enough to be the best—you have to succeed in telling the world that you are the best." I think that's very sad.

*With your reputation being what it is, you could allow yourself some leeway and offer your opinions.*

You can publicize the art form all you want, but if you allow so-called operatic artists to start publicizing themselves, they take precedence over the opera. I turn down all talk shows and stuff like that, so I stand by my convictions.

*Perhaps by talking about opera you will make more people interested in it.*

That's the argument that is being used by every hype PR man in the opera business. They name certain opera stars who have done great things for opera—they haven't! They destroyed the standard of opera, because people come to opera houses today *not* to see *Tristan*, *not* to see *Fidelio*, *not* to see *Walküre* or the *Ring*, they come to see Miss X or Mr. Y, and the opera lovers have been driven out of the opera houses. We have a hamburger mentality now in the opera houses with no discernment. To prove that there is no discernment, we now have to put up with these stupid surtitles. We have to run them over the proscenium arch so that people can read what's being sung on stage, instead of people *watching* what's going on.

*Have you sung in productions with surtitles?*

No, I won't sing if they are used.

*Do you think that the enormous costs of producing opera are forcing companies to publicize widely?*

That is the excuse. Opera is expensive today not because the art form is expensive. Now, opera won't pay for itself, it never has and it never will. But when the staff of the Metropolitan Opera Company has been increased from a payroll of 700 people to a payroll of 2300 people, without one more seat in the auditorium or more performances added, that adds up to millions and millions of dollars. We have also decided that we have to be spectacular and put on a great big gimmicky spectacle, like having snow falling throughout the whole of one act. What's that got to do with anything? It is the interpersonal relationships of the people involved that is the story, the heartache, the tragedy!

*Perhaps Broadway has heightened people's expectations of staging.*

You put your finger on it! Is Broadway art or is it entertainment? Is opera art or is it entertainment?

*Isn't there entertainment value in opera?*

I see no entertainment value in *Otello*. I see no entertainment value in *Parsifal* or the *Ring*.

*Well . . . I don't see entertainment as something that's necessarily cheap . . .*

You are struggling now, and the way you are speaking is a very dramatic manifestation of what I'm saying has happened. We no longer can define or draw a line between what's art and what's entertainment. We can't define whether Broadway is art or entertainment, we can't decide whether or not the Metropolitan Opera House is something that feeds the best minds. Picasso said it very well in his great confession in 1952: "When art ceases to be the food that feeds the best minds, then the artist can use his talents to perform all the tricks of the intellectual charlatan," and that's what is happening over and over again in the art world. We have talented people using their talent to perform tricks and charlatanism. Why? Because they are serving mammon, running after the almighty dollar.

The young, sincere up-and-coming artists, where are they to look for examples and guidance? I give master classes across the land, and the students ask me how to make money. They never ask me about the interpretation of *Peter Grimes* or the way I sing a phrase in *Otello* or *Les Troyens*—they ask me how to gain experience under camera, how to find a publicity agent or a good personal manager.

*Do you think this attitude is pervasive in all art forms or special to opera?*

I think it's a general movement. You can never separate what happens in art or entertainment or business practices from the basic philosophy that seeps into society. We are living in a society in which this absurd contradiction of equality has crept in. There isn't equality, there never will be, and to pretend there is, is an insult. Plato said it: I do not believe that men were born equal, and furthermore I think it an insult to my fellow man to postulate that they are. I may believe that I'm superior to Socrates and I may even persuade other fools to flatter me by saying that I am, but Socrates is there to prove me wrong.

*So élitism it not to be scoffed at.*

You had better look up the word in the dictionary and find out what it means! "Elite" has become a dirty word today, perverted by this notion of equality. Would I, for instance, put myself on the level of Karajan? Would I put myself equal to Beethoven? If art serves a function, it does not do so by holding a mirror up to society—that's a lot of rubbish. If we only do that, then we have a society that just preens itself by examining itself on the stage, and that's an excuse for all kinds of appalling things.

*Despite these weaknesses, do you think an audience automatically understands, instinctually or intellectually, when something is right on the mark?*

Absolutely! They may not be able to articulate it, but they will.

*You are drawn to powerful roles of men facing great moral dilemmas. Do you identify with these men, or do you see yourself as the messenger of universal truths?*

I'm a tool that is useful. In the entire chain that constitutes an operatic performance, the composer is impotent without the performer. Look at *Les Troyens*, for instance—it has many messages for society. One of them is: It would have been just plain common sense to check out the horse. Laocöon begged them to do it, Cassandra begged them to do it, but common sense was abandoned to the disaster of the Trojans.

In our society today you can look at the confrontation between East and West, and common sense would dictate that we examine our political life. You could examine the motives of the Kremlin and of the U.S., and I assure you that if you had any honesty about you at all, you would go down on the side of America a thousand times. I'm not waxing political, you understand.

Here we have another example from *Les Troyens*: Aeneas is called to do something great. He has the physical and intellectual prowess to do great things—he carries his ancient father and leads his son out of the flames of Troy, he wins the Carthaginian wars. When he is side-tracked with Dido, he has a choice between his own personal satisfaction and love and sensuality, or being called to something of destiny. He chose the harder course, the great course, and left Troy to found the Roman Empire. These messages are universal truths.

*I suppose we are bombarded from all corners till our sensitivity is lost.*

If you bombard people enough, you don't give them a chance to examine you closely. They are so impressed by an image on stage that you blind them. I read a very crude saying in a store window in Dallas: If you can't dazzle them with brilliance, then you blind them with bullshit.

*Isn't it sometimes hard to sit half a mile away from the stage and be intimately involved?*

That's the fault of the performer.

*Is it possible to bridge that distance?*

Is it possible? It has been my whole life! I have involved audiences over and over again with my Tristan, my Grimes and my Fidelio—I'm not bragging, it's fact. When I sang with Maria Callas in Epidaurus, 22,000 people jammed that arena.

*You take great moral responsibility for the portrayal of your roles.*

It is difficult today to use the word "moral," because it has become preachy. If you deal with moral issues, people say: "Don't listen, he's just a preacher." I've read about myself that I'm a bible-thumping jackass.

*You have been criticized for changing certain words in operas.*

That's lie! The person who changed the words was Tyrone Guthrie and it was approved by the composer himself, Benjamin Britten.

*You must have rejected a number of roles because you disagreed with their basic premise.*

I have rejected some. *Tannhäuser* is obvious. Other roles I have refused not for moral or artistic reasons, but because I found them boring or not challenging.

*You have had an uneasy relationship with Wagner.*

Always!

*Do you think his personality imbues every role in his operas?*

Well, everyone who has ever written about Wagner has discussed his works as being autobiographical. He was anarchistic and bad news, he really was.

*Did you feel the same way when you first sang in Bayreuth in 1958?* [*Siegmund in Die Walküre.*]

One grows into greater understanding as one gets older. You read more, you see more. I didn't like Bayreuth, though it was an exhilarating and challenging theatrical experience to work with Wieland Wagner. This man was a genius in his field. Alas, a lot of second- and third-rates tried to copy him afterwards and never measured up to him.

The biggest thrill of all in Bayreuth was the *great* Hans Knappertsbusch, and after 1958 the *only* reason I went back to Bayreuth was because Knappertsbusch would not conduct *Parsifal* anywhere else; that was Wagner's wish and he honored it.

*Some opera houses have upset the public with productions that disregard style and historical context.*

You have to be a little careful about historical context and so-called style. To attempt to lock a work of art completely into the period of history in which it was written is to emasculate that art. I think it was T.S. Eliot who wrote something to the effect that we must change the past as we must be guided by the past.

However, when you have a production of Mozart like *The Marriage of Figaro*, where the entire set is the nude torso of a woman's body and the count makes his first entrance through the pubic hair, walks across the belly and disappears through a doorway under the breasts, this has nothing to do with Mozart.

*But within limits it's acceptable?*

What makes Salieri forgotten and Mozart what he is comes from us not trying to lock Mozart into the period in which he wrote. He was a timeless, universal thinker who dealt with great issues.

*As well as superior to Salieri . . .*

Well, Salieri was what we see today. Salieri was a populist, wasn't he? We have to draw in the crowds and mustn't make it too difficult for the audience. Do you follow me? I think it is a *disgrace* to the music world that it was a film producer or a playwright who wrote *Amadeus* to point out where we are going wrong today.

*How do you stick with the essence?*

First you have to make yourself sensitive to it. Then it is the job of a performing artist to digest a work of art and regurgitate it to the best of his ability. Yet you could take all of the Otellos—Martinelli,

Tamagno, Del Monaco, Vinay, Max Lorenz and myself—and none of us has been able to reveal Otello and none of us could hurt him. You can't hurt Verdi or Shakespeare or Boito!

*They are.*

They are! And the more we wrestle with these works, the greater they are revealed.

*Do any current artists in any art form have the stature to compare with the great artists you just mentioned? [Vickers pauses to think.] Any composers?*

I think composers today are suffering terribly. A wave of nationalism sweeps the world. A new revelation in the search for truth or pursuit of excellence is subjected to Canadian content, for instance, or the American way of life, ethnic problems, ecology and so on. The power of media communication today is so overwhelming and the method of bringing our work to the fore is at odds with the pursuit of excellence. So whether there are composers today who are working away diligently, or painters or whoever, we may not see or hear them because so many flashbulbs are going off.

*It seems to take so long for us to digest music compared to painting or dance.*

It takes a long time for art, too.

*Yet contemporary visual art and dance are generally accepted.*

But everybody accepted Picasso and he was a charlatan and painfully admitted it. He was a great and sincere artist up until Cubism. Now, I'm only going by what Picasso himself said: "I have understood my time and I've exploited the imbecility and vanity of my contemporaries."

*Of course, this does not apply well to music, which has no commercial value unless it's performed. You can't hang it on the wall.*

But there is a political, ethnic and nationalistic value in a Canadian piece of music with a Canadian theme. You can engage government with that.

*Numerous artists do their work day in and day out, being very poorly paid. Why would they do that if they were as interested in commercialism as you say?*

I think people have attempted to be great composers and great painters throughout history. Millions of canvasses never saw the light of day. The obvious example is the one of Mozart and Salieri. Salieri wrote something like 120 operas. People get impatient with me when I'm talking this way and say, "You are wrong in saying that art should stand or fall on its own merit." It *must* for the good of our society. If the arts continue to be corrupted the way they are today, the art form will not die—it can't—but society will get in such a mess. Yet down the road the priorities will be sorted out and art again will rise from its own ashes.

*Have you considered that the audience for music and any other art form is many times larger today than it was just twenty years ago? Our problems could be temporary while the audience is pulling itself up by the bootstraps, and quality will eventually rise again.*

No. People who are going to opera and theater today are going because it's the "in" thing. If we continue to blur the line between what's art and what's artifice, it will become just a fad.

*When you take on a role, how do you make certain that conditions are acceptable to you? Do you sit down with the director?*

Yes. I wouldn't accept *Peter Grimes* with the Metropolitan Opera Company until I had a meeting with Sir Tyrone Guthrie. I said to Tyrone: "I will not play this opera from the standpoint that Grimes is a homosexual; to limit it to that would be to deny the greatness of the work. *Peter Grimes* is a study in the entire human psychology of human rejection. It may have been written by a homosexual for a homosexual, but this work is timeless and universal and it's wrong to think that homosexuals are the only ones who ever felt rejected." Sir Tyrone absolutely agreed with me, and he, Colin Davis and I revolutionized the work.

*Your ability to act is outstanding. Does it stem from the music or have you studied acting?*

It is hung on the music, absolutely. Everything I do as an actor I find a motivation for in the music.

*You seem aware of the emotion behind every word.*

I try to be. So many words have to be defined because they have lost their meaning. Love, for instance, has lost its meaning—"I love pizza" or "I love New York." If I say, "Pig!" you know I'm not talking about the animal, don't you? So the voice has the ability to slice through and reveal the depth of the meaning of a word. Then if you add the color of an instrument, if you add the harmonic structure behind the word phrase and the human voice singing the words, coloring it according to the emotion, enlarged by the tapestry of the symphonic background . . .

*It's a powerful experience. How do you control your own emotion on such a highly charged level?*

You are not there to give yourself a jag. You are there to involve other people, to create the role for them. So in the analysis and in the preparation of the work you surrender your emotions, working from the standpoint of having the audience react to it. You create the emotion, you don't experience it.

*What is involved to make for the exalted moments?*

It happens so rarely. Of course, that's why opera is the most difficult of all the performing arts. It involves everything—mime, dance, symphony, poetry, acting . . . everything.

*Aside from singing from early childhood, what prepared you during your upbringing for the world of opera?*

I have sung since I was a tiny boy and being in front of an audience was normal for me. It became special only when I went through the trauma of charging for it. I was brought up to believe that if one had a talent, it was one's duty to just give it. It took me a long time to discover that a lawyer has a talent, a hairdresser and teacher have talents and we all must give. If we don't, we are not rewarded.

*When did you see your first opera?*

Oh, not for a long time, but I listened to the Saturday afternoon broadcasts quite often. My background is a very, very strong family home life, where it was fundamental in our upbringing that no matter what we did, we did it to the utmost of our ability.

*You have the advantage of having been in the business world for some years. That must have matured you and helped you handle your money later on.*

Yes, I think a lot of my colleagues have made tragic mistakes in believing they made a lot of money. They looked at the gross instead of the bottom line. The Internal Revenue people are the same—they look at our gross earnings and can't believe our expenses, so we pay far more taxes than we should. We are abused, actually, as all artists are. When you submit a tax statement with $38,000 in expenses and air fares they think you are a multi-millionaire living in the lap of luxury.

I have always realized that there is no insurance scheme, no sick pay, no holiday pay, and I'm constantly aware that I'm only as good as my last performance.

*You have paced yourself so well and are still in good voice. Surely you could have made more money if you had sung what was asked of you.*

They wanted to push me in *Tristan* when I was thirty-one years old, and after my first *Otello*, everyone also wanted me to sing Otello. I said, "I'll sing six performances a year and they will go to the best bidder where I get the best conductor, the best Iago, the best Desdemona, the best production and best fee." But the fee was never my prime concern.

*Do you think that your large voice took so long to mature that, despite your impatience, you entered the opera world at an opportune moment at the age of thirty?*

Well, I think there is no question that my career began in the period which is now called the golden mini-period of opera. It's hard to explain now, particularly in Canada, because I don't think Canadians

even know the names when I describe my international career—
people like Karajan, Böhm, Knappertsbusch, Serafin . . .

*Surely people know who they are.*

No, they don't know who Knappertsbusch is. I heard a CBC critic
pronounce Karajan's name as Karadjan. Another critic of my performance in *Carmen* said that I sounded too "Beyrootean," trying to
be very clever but revealing his ignorance.

*When you went to England at age thirty, you had four hundred lieder in
your repertoire.*

Not just German songs, but Italian and French as well.

*Now that you are planning to scale down your opera engagements and do
more concert work, do you feel that you have more to offer as a lieder singer
than you had at age thirty?*

You know, Lotte Lehmann always said that a person should start
with oratorio, pass through opera and end his career with lied. Every
song in German is a mini-opera. If you sing *Der Doppelgänger* or just
the last song in *Winterreise*, there is a whole life in one song. It's not
good enough to just sing the notes and pronounce the words. And
you haven't got a massive orchestra, lighting effects and costumes or
people around you. All you have got is a bare stage, a black piano
and the spotlight on you. With that you have to engage the audience.
Incidentally, I'm encountering great difficulty getting into the recital
field.

*Why is that?*

Because they don't want my repertoire. They say *The Four Last Songs*
of Strauss, the *Diary of One Who Disappeared* by Janáček or *Winterreise*
or *Dichterliebe* are too heavy. "Our audiences aren't geared for that.
Couldn't you also do some opera excerpts?"

*How could you possibly sing opera and art songs in one program?*

That's what I'm saying—see, we have come full circle in our conversation. This is what has happened in the music world!

But don't misunderstand me. There are still places, wonderful places,
where we perform this repertoire. I have sung *Winterreise* in Los Angeles, Chicago, New York, Paris, Toronto, and soon I'll be singing it in
Calgary and Washington, D.C.

*You have a wonderful record out on Centrediscs with Canadian songs that
was nominated for a Juno Award. I've heard you like the Bernard Naylor
songs particularly.*

Oh, I love Naylor's songs. In my opinion—and who cares about
Vickers' opinion—I don't think the world is really ready for Naylor's
songs, but his day will come.

*They are difficult to sing.*

Fiendishly difficult and I did them very inadequately.

*You seem to be singing more in Canada now.*

I find it very sad, actually, that this is happening—very, very sad that in my great years I was not singing in this country.

*What was the reason?*

They wouldn't hire me.

*Were your fees too high?*

When I'm turning down three performances out of four, you can't expect me to all of a sudden come to Canada and give up months of my time to sing for 40 percent of my fee.

*But they invite Leontyne Price, Joan Sutherland and people of that caliber— why not you?*

Because I'm a Canadian. In the great years when I was at La Scala, Bayreuth, Salzburg and so on, Canada wasn't included. In Montreal, though, I sang *Otello, Tristan* and *Aida.*

*When you were in your twenties, you must have been disappointed with your career, since you were considering dropping it.*

I didn't have a hard time getting my career going in Canada. I was singing about ninety performances a year, far more than I sing today. When my international career was established, I settled for between fifty and fifty-five performances a year. Once I sang sixty-five and I told my manager, "No more, that's not living." At that pace you are not geared to give an audience what it deserves. Next year I gave fifty-three performances.

*How do you prepare yourself for the stage?*

I isolate myself and can't be social. In fact, when I enter my season I put myself into a discipline that involves a routine of rest, of silence and of eating sensibly. It is a total commitment. I can't sing a performance and then go out and booze and socialize until the early morning, although some people do. When I finish performing at the Metropolitan, for example, I walk directly to my hotel room and go to sleep.

*You don't have to unwind?*

No, no. People take such a long time to unwind because they are indulging themselves too much in their performances, becoming far, far too personally involved. Sometimes you are grabbed by circumstances. I sang my first *Peter Grimes* seven days after I buried my mother. That was very difficult. When I described the death of the boy—"Picture what that day was like, that evil day"—it was difficult to keep myself emotionally removed.

*What's your life like outside of singing?*

I get involved in physical things like carpentry and farming.

*That must keep you in shape, which is important given the physical rigors of opera.*

Oh, I don't know . . . [A rare smile lights up his face.] I can think of some opera singers who are not in too great a shape.

# Edith Wiens

The sturdy-looking second-grade Vancouver student, dressed in distinctive Mennonite garb, informed her teacher that she was going to be a singer. "The teacher laughed. She was facing this clunky, chubby, braided kid in heavy, navy blue shoes—it was a long way from the stage," says soprano Edith Wiens as she lets out her high-decibel laughter.

If that teacher is following the career of her former student, she will find that Wiens, now in her thirties, is a frequent soloist with the Berlin Philharmonic and other major European orchestras. Her crystalline voice has in recent years been heard on this continent with the orchestras of Boston, Toronto, Los Angeles and Ottawa. With regular oratoria performances in Berlin, and with her career rapidly expanding into opera, Wiens now feels confident about singing in North America.

The robust Mennonite kid who was born in Saskatoon and grew up in Vancouver in a sheltered religious community is now a tall, slim vision of worldly elegance. In personality, however, Wiens is every bit as robust as her ancestors, and she carries with her a large dose of Mennonite discipline and common sense. (Her father was a minister and the family would frequently take off to distant parts of western Canada to serve other congregations.)

Wiens's voice is not distinctive for its power, but its clear, lyrical quality makes her ideally suited for recitals. After her appearance in Buenos Aires' famous Teatro Colón, one critic wrote: "Miss Wiens is without doubt one of the great Mozartien singers of our time." And the *Berlin Morgenpost* reported: "She possesses one of the most beautiful sopranos of our day." The major works by Bach, Haydn and Mozart are among her favorite repertoire (she has recorded Haydn's *Theresienmesse* on MPS, J.C. Bach's Gloria in G Major on Schwann and Mendelssohn's *Elijah* on Erato), but when I talked with her in 1986,

she was anticipating major changes in her career. For the first time she would allow herself to sing opera. The future performances she talks about here have since earned her great praise. After each *Marriage of Figaro* in Buenos Aires, for example, the Countess received a ten-minute standing ovation.

Two strong influences have kept Wiens away from opera until now. First, her Mennonite upbringing, which frowned on the theater—indeed, we won't ever see Wiens as Salome—and second, her family life. Wiens is married to cellist Kai Moser, a member of the Bavarian Radio Orchestra and part of the Moser family that also includes the late musicologist Hans Joachim Moser and soprano Edda Moser. The couple has two young boys who have traveled with their mother since they were born. Munich has been their home for several years—it is a hop and a skip from Paris, Rome, Berlin, London and Vienna where she has made her name as a concert singer.

Edith Wiens says of her career, "It's a very exciting, heady time with things going up and up." Yet a glittering façade alone will never pass her Mennonite scrutiny. She recently sang a gala performance in the arena of Pompeii with Klaus Tennstedt conducting the London Philharmonic. "The Prime Minister was there and it was live on TV. People in the audience could hardly walk straight from the jewelry hanging on them. During Beethoven's Ninth they smoked and clapped between the movements. They smoked!" Oh, wrath of the Prairies.

*Colgrass: How does your Mennonite background influence your life?*

Wiens: When I speak of the center of my life, I do mean a spiritual center. I'm certainly not as dogmatic as most of my church people, but I haven't thrown the baby out with the bath water.

When I was a child, our life was bounded completely by the church. It was very much like one big family. We grew up with singing. At home—we were four children—we would sing a hymn before breakfast, some with twelve verses.

Whenever I speak of my background, I'm always amazed at how the seemingly negative can be so positive. Here is a poor kid, brought up so strictly so far from the world. She has to be different from everyone else, but it has given me courage. When I talk about this in Europe, it's like talking about a different century.

*Weren't you allowed to go to a public school in Vancouver?*

Yes, at first, but when I was ten, my parents got worried that I was becoming too worldly and involved in too many musical activities. They sent me to a private Mennonite school. I was very angry about it, but it turned out to be much better for me, with only eleven of us in a class and young teachers who really cared.

*And after high school you went to Bible school to study music.*

Again I didn't want to go there, but it turned out to be for the best. When I later applied to study in Hanover, the Germans thought I had a university degree and gave me a post-graduate scholarship. That was very fortunate. I studied there for three years and then went on to Oberlin College in Ohio.

*What did your parents think when you decided on a career so outside the confines of the church?*

I don't think they really knew what my world was, but they were proud of me for being successful and they were pleased I was choosing concert over opera. The main thing to them—and to myself, too— was that I would remain clear to myself.

*Do you feel different from other musicians?*

Yes, but it's difficult to explain exactly how. One colleague said to me, "Do you have to be so happy all the time—why are you so damn cheerful?" Wanting to be happy and not being ashamed to express it comes from my upbringing.

*As a singer you have chosen an unusual route.*

If I had said to anyone in America, "I want to make a concert career," they would have laughed. They even laughed in Europe, because nobody does that except Elly Ameling and a couple of others.

*But you fit in there?*

I'm not an American sound but a typical European soprano. I have a very good high C, but it's not an Italian sound.

*One of your first breaks was being invited to sing oratorio by Paul Sacher, a Swiss conductor known mostly for his wealth and generosity.*

He did not make a great career as a conductor, but he was influential by offering great support to young artists. Many European soloists had their first performances with Sacher, as I did. He also commissioned works by Bartók and Stravinsky and gave Rostropovich his cello when he came out of the Soviet Union.

*Aside from oratorio, you have become an excellent interpreter of art songs.*

I like the intimacy and the music being so perfectly suited to the voice. Actually I'm happiest singing recitals, the romantics—Schubert, Schumann, Brahms and Strauss.

*Can you evaluate your own growth as an artist?*

I've sung at my present level for about two years, so I'm far beyond the early years when I would sometimes remind myself that I always could return to a normal life as a school teacher. [Laughs.] Now when

I'm asked to sing at places like the Salzburger Festspiele, I feel that I belong there.

*Have you always been confident?*

I believe deeply in the leading of a person. This year I opened the door to opera, which led to an invitation to sing the Countess in *The Marriage of Figaro*, again in Teatro Colón. After that, I'm opening a center in Hong Kong with the Glyndebourne Festival as Donna Anna in *Don Giovanni*.

*With such a busy career, how do you manage your family life?*

This is the last year before Johannes [the eldest] goes to school. He and Benny are another reason why I haven't sung opera, which would take me away from home six weeks at a stretch.

I'm very lucky to live with Kai. For one thing he lets me go with the children.

*Both dedication and a strong constitution are needed to tour with small children. You must get tired sometimes.*

All the time. I don't overcome it, I live with it. Ask any mother with two young kids if she isn't exhausted even without doing anything else.

*Do your boys get involved in your musical life?*

Most of all the boys love going to Kai's rehearsals. They like the absolute music better than choral music. I was recently singing the Saint Matthew Passion with Peter Schreier and Theo Adam with [Kurt] Masur conducting the Gewandhaus Orchestra, and after the rehearsal, while I was talking with Peter, the boys came running into the hall and shouted, "Mama, that was so boring!"

# Pinchas Zukerman

A performer's true nature is usually revealed in rehearsals. Pinchas Zukerman enters in blue jeans, his unruly mane of curly hair threatening to cover his eyes, and the violin dangling from his oversized hand as casually as a baseball bat. His presence brightens the faces in the orchestra—this rehearsal is going to be enjoyable and exciting. Zukerman, in his role as solo violinist, dances a small jig to the introduction and at the last possible moment swings his violin into position to hit the note right on the button. When not playing he moves about the stage to the music, revving up the orchestra with his body language. This is home to Zukerman, who lives music around the clock, not just as a violinist, but as conductor, chamber musician and violist as well.

When I talked with Zukerman in 1980, he was thirty-two years old and at the end of his first season where he felt he had been around for a long time. No doubt he was already then a seasoned violinist and violist, but as music director of the St. Paul Chamber Orchestra in Minneapolis he was still a greenhorn. The music world is not terribly generous to soloists who decide to pick up the baton, and Zukerman got his share of negative predictions, all of which he has put to shame as he has grown on the job. The orchestra has developed and prospered along with him and is likely to continue doing so till his contract ends in 1990. Starting with twenty-six players, it is now approaching forty-six and is the only professional chamber orchestra in the United States. To complete the picture, the orchestra has a new concert hall and recording contracts with CBS and Philips, and has gained prestige on tours abroad.

Zukerman is on a roll, and he now gets plenty of respect on the podium, as well as when he guest-conducts full-size orchestras. Along with conducting he has continued to deepen his artistry on both violin

and viola, touring and recording extensively. His private life has also changed since we talked. He was previously married to flutist Eugenia Zukerman, with whom he has two daughters. The Zukermans often concertized together and were much in the public eye, which is in sharp contrast to the very private lifestyle the conductor leads today. "Don't even mention that he is married to Tuesday Weld," said his New York manager.

"Pinky" Zukerman was born in 1948, in Tel Aviv, where his father introduced him to the violin at the age of eight. His unusual aptitude soon called for more experienced teachers, and when he was thirteen the small family moved to New York to further his development. During some rough years the child prodigy was transformed into an artist with the help of Juilliard teacher Ivan Galamian and mentor Isaac Stern. He emerged at age nineteen as the winner of the Leventritt Competition, sharing the first prize with Kyung Wha Chung.

He has been closely associated with Daniel Barenboim, Zubin Mehta and fellow violinist Itzhak Perlman, and in recent years he has collaborated with many composers, such as Boulez, Lutoslawski, Schwantner and Takemitsu. This year Zukerman will be forty, which is considered a young age in his profession. It is difficult to predict the next turn in his career, but he will certainly choose his own route.

*Colgrass: Before you were thirty years old, you had reached the top of your profession. Does it ever make you stop and think: Where do I go from here?*

Zukerman: I have some ambitions, obviously. The main ambition in my life is to be able to do as much of two or three or maybe six composers' output, to really learn their complete works, as a servant to music. I think that is an ambition every performer has. In my case it is slightly easier because I play chamber music, I play the viola and the fiddle and I conduct. To be able to go through all of Mozart's pieces is almost impossible. Isn't that amazing?

*You don't ever look around and compare yourself with other performers?*

I don't think of myself that way. I don't have the time and I don't want to. When something is right, it's right, and when it's wrong you know it.

People have asked how it feels when I'm performing and I say, "I don't know how I feel." I don't analyze my playing except in the recording studio where you become like a psychiatrist trying to be as objective as you can. But at the moment of performance, you are feeling something, you do it and you hope that what you are recreating from the page makes sense to the audience.

*When did you take up conducting?*

About eight or nine years ago, but I had been thinking about it for quite a while. It was just an extension of music-making. At Juilliard I went to conducting class, but it wasn't really of any importance to me at that time.

*Do you think many soloists dream of conducting because of what they have endured under conductors?*

I think that's a legitimate feeling, definitely. On the other hand, the moment they try to do it, they see how difficult it really is. The main reason is that you are never in control of your sound.

*As a soloist you are completely in charge.*

Of your own playing, yes. It is a long subject—I can go through all the details and it's very boring, especially to me! [Loud laughter.]

*I have heard you conduct chamber orchestras. Are you more attracted to them than to symphony orchestras?*

Well, I'm attracted to music-making. It all goes back to chamber music. Chamber music is the essence of all music-making. Why? Because it is the most acute form of listening. In all musical expressions, a concerto, a string trio or a quartet, you constantly have to listen. Now, if you understand that as a performer—not just listening to what you are doing, but what's around you harmonically and texturally, etc.— then you already have begun to think as a conductor. In other words, music becomes vertical rather than horizontal.

Now I'll step back a little bit. There are two important principles in music that I go by; one is tension, the other is relaxation. Those two are the human principles. One thing that creates tension and relaxation is harmony, and this affects my playing in so many different ways. You are thinking all the time of what's happening in the score and not just about the melody lines. As a soloist I play a single line, and the single line means *nothing* without its harmony. So my conducting has not come as something from the outside, it has come from within.

The other side of conducting is the actual physical action. There are many different ways of giving a beat, but the basic gesture is a body language that you throw at the orchestra. It can be an expression on your face, a look, the motion of an arm or an elbow. There is no definite correct way to conduct. The beating of time is not a big deal.

*You learn that quickly.*

Yes, you just get it into your blood stream and it's not a big problem. It's the knowledge beyond that you are constantly searching for— that's a need like having to eat when you are hungry.

*Some conductors convey their energy with large gestures and others with tiny motions that can prove just as powerful.*

Exactly. But that's just the physical end of it. The knowledge you must have of a score and how to rehearse it, that's what conducting is about. You may think you are in control of the sound, but you are not. That adds color, though.

*Is it easier to control a chamber orchestra than a symphony orchestra?*

It's the same. With the symphony orchestra, the problem of listening is of course augmented because there are more instruments and more players to coordinate. You have such regulations, such rules in music! Such discipline! We are all very disciplined people. Still, there are no two places in the world where you can play a concerto that will sound the same as the conductor's concept, because there is always an intermediary, a space in between.

*Your emphasis on chamber music suggests that a musician can't develop without extensive experience in that area.*

Well, I wouldn't put it as final as that. I think there are people who play wonderfully without necessarily going through the rigorous work of playing chamber music. On the other hand there is a definite fine line between solo playing and orchestral playing *vis à vis* playing in a quartet.

*How is that?*

A quartet has the absolute four voices that music is about—counterpoint. That's why it's so difficult. It takes great knowledge and experience to play in a quartet—even in a string trio or piano trio you don't have that complete musical form. From my experience, I just don't think many people listen that way.

*If you had pursued your career only as a violinist, would there have been a danger of going around the world playing the same concertos over and over?*

Absolutely!

*What could that have done to you?*

I could never do that because I'm not made that way. It's very boring. Very. I have played chamber music since I was a little boy. To play quartets, though, is a whole different story. You have to meet three other people whom you can work with, it takes a lot of time and is very hard. Very few people understand that.

*In professional music circles they probably do.*

Yes and no—you'll be surprised.

*Did you ever spend a great deal of time on the virtuoso circuit and find that it was not for you?*

No, I have always done so many different things. I play in recitals, I'm a soloist, I conduct and I have just recorded works for oboe and viola. It's all intertwined. Much more work goes into it than the public realizes. I work very hard and the more I absorb the more I hear.

But it doesn't get easier, because the more colors I have the more colors I want.

*Do you ever exhaust yourself doing so much?*

Oh God, yes.

*You don't transfer the energy from one thing to another?*

Yes, in fact I do. Still it's physically very exhausting, and very rewarding.

*Well, conductors seem to live to a ripe old age. Do you foresee giving up the violin and concentrating on conducting?*

I can't. The violin is an integral part of my life. It's like saying: Okay now, you won't see with one eye for the next five years. How could I do that? One thing feeds the other. I'm very lucky. I think I was given a gift of some kind, I don't know by who, and I have a duty to do everything as well as I can. Sometimes, though, I'm pushed against the wall, but it's my own fault. I live music twenty-four hours a day.

*What did you do with the first eight years of your life? You must have been terribly bored without playing.*

That's funny! [Roars with laughter.] Nobody ever asked me that before.

*Were you a brat?*

Oh sure, I still am!

*You seem very calm and good natured, too. That must be a blessing in your profession.*

I would think so. Again, I don't analyze that.

*Do you ever blow your stack in rehearsal?*

Once in a while you lose patience, but I don't really care.

*Is that when people are not doing their best?*

It has something to do with *Musik Kultur*, a lack of understanding of what's correct musically, of what's on the printed page.

*You mean, people don't read music properly?*

Well, *Musik Kultur* is very difficult to analyze, it's so monumental. When you look at a piece of music, it's supposed to be done in a given style—it's natural, like speaking a language. If you don't have all the words then you don't speak that language. A musician is supposed to be constantly entrenched in that language, it is an integral part of our whole make-up.

*Is it conceivable that a musician can go through the motions technically without ever learning that language?*

Again you have hit on something that is rather complicated. I think that before you run you must learn to walk. In other words, you have to know how to play your instrument to the best of your ability and for that we have very good teachers. I think that we have become so proficient in playing that there are some incredible instrumentalists through the whole orchestra. But there is something beyond that. At a certain point in one's life as a musician, in the formative years between thirteen and nineteen years of age, I think a chemical change happens in the body—certainly the emotional process somehow gravitates towards being a musician. With that comes a whole different thinking process that enters your blood stream as something basic for the rest of your life. I was very fortunate in those years to know people like Stern and Casals. These people had gone through it themselves, but I had to experience it myself.

*You had quite a rough time for a while, though.*

Yes, because of those years.

*It must have been tough to have been pulled out of Israel and plunked down in Manhattan, which is so different. Was there some help you failed to get?*

The only thing that would have helped me at that time would have been my parents. They were there physically, but I didn't live with them and after a while my father moved to Montreal because he couldn't get a work permit. On the other hand I learned, I saw and heard everything so quickly. People around me expected me to do certain things and I seemed to know what was right and what was wrong—animal instinct.

*Could you have lost your direction?*

I don't think so. Some people have, but my basic upbringing was already so disciplined and correct that it couldn't have happened.

*Did Ivan Galamian [then Juilliard's foremost violin teacher] take you apart completely?*

Oh, absolutely! That was the toughest part of it all and I think that's why I did all those crazy things.

*Like what?*

I played pool, I smoked and I saw all those incredible people on 32nd Street. It's all part of growing up.

*What's wrong with playing pool?*

Oh, there is nothing wrong, but there is something wrong with staying up until four o'clock in the morning when you know you have a lesson at eight. I used to hang out in the pool halls and go to tournaments.

*You still play pool?*

Nah . . . I used to play okay and could hustle a few people who came to the pool halls just to make a dollar for my breakfast. For seventy-five cents you could get a hell of a breakfast in those days. I was only fourteen, but I was older I guess.

*Did it give you a sense of freedom to be on your own in New York at that age?*

Yes and no. It was very hard. In retrospect, I think, my God, how could I do it?

*Weren't your parents nervous about their only child?*

I don't think they realized how bad it was. I don't think anybody did.

*Do you have other outside interests apart from pool?*

I love sports. I play tennis, in fact I used to play a lot.

*You are not worried about your hands?*

Ah! I won't do crazy things like downhill skiing, that's common sense. But so much is interconnected between knowing where you are on the fingerboard and shooting a basket. Most musicians are sports freaks.

*You really think so?*

Oh yes, the ones I know, anyway. I thought I was going to be the next Laver in the tennis court at one point.

*Your father was your first teacher. Was that a good beginning?*

In some ways. He was a very natural musician and self-taught on the violin. He was a jack of all trades in music, really, so I learned quite a few things right away, like the tango and polka. It all went very fast and he saw it. After a couple of months I got a wonderful teacher, so my foundation was really very solid.

*You said Juilliard was a shock to you. How long did you study there?*

I spent four or five years there doing the basic things everybody does. I hated school. Those formative years are very critical and even more so when you are a talented kid. It's usually the parents who screw everything up—in nine out of ten cases. I was lucky I didn't have my parents pushing me, even though other things went wrong.

*Are you parents still alive?*

My mother is. She lives in Tel Aviv where I go quite often to see her.

*What did your friendships with Stern and Casals do for you?*

Absolutely everything. Stern more than Casals, though. It is a fantastic thing to be able to know someone like Stern who has been through all the paths, performing and administration. It was not only a guideline—you have faith it's going to be okay because he is there. There are many criticisms of the man and that's okay. For me personally he gave a sense of security.

*Do you think you could do something similar for an exceptionally talented youngster?*

Yes, I would make it my business, and I have helped some people, although indirectly. I'm beginning to feel very old in this profession. Yesterday *Newsweek* phoned and said they wanted to do an article on Stern, Perlman and me as the established violinists *vis à vis* the youngsters coming up. I got five more white hairs when I heard that! [A burst of laughter.] For the first time this season I get the feeling of having been here for a long time.

*Are you interested in teaching?*

Yes, I do master classes, but I have no private students.

*Does it annoy you that people always compare you with Itzhak Perlman?*

Nah!

*Do you think it is possible to compare two performers?*

Don't you compare Chevrolets with Buicks?

*I don't drive and I honestly don't compare. I don't sit in a concert, hearing you play and say, "Gee, Perlman does that differently." You can't compare an apple and a pear.*

Oh, but you can!

*Where does it get you?*

To a banana, probably. [Laughs.] Comparison is okay as long as it's dealt with properly—that's how we build things. If you ask me about the difference between Itzhak and me, I can tell you right away, but I can't tell you *how* it happens. When I go and hear him play and he does something good, I'll tell him so and the next time I get to that spot I say, "Hey, I'm going to do that too." Why not?

*Do you find a great difference between the music world here and that of Europe and Israel?*

Oh yes—*Musik Kultur*! When I go to Europe I don't have to explain to anybody who I am. They know. Automatically there is a difference right there. In North America we are still explaining to people what we are and what we are doing. There's a tradition in Europe of music being an integral part of daily life, and rightly so. That is new here. I don't see anything wrong in telling somebody in Iowa what I'm doing if it really solves a problem for that person.

*What can we do to speed things up a bit?*

Television! It's the only medium to do this, and it's okay as long as it's done properly, without cheating the audience. In the next decade I think we are going to see a whole new rethinking of the educational process because of computerized television. I think textbooks will completely disappear.

*What will happen to reading?*

That is a problem. The *Sesame Street* idea is only the sub-basement of what this form of education can be.

*You know that children who play an instrument fare better academically, yet music education is a very low priority.*

I don't think one can persuade anybody to listen to music, go to a museum or read philosophy. It must come from within. We can only guide people, and if they don't want it, that's their choice. If you force it, it will only reverse the process. If you give someone a dollar, he feels obligated to you—that's what is wrong with the Third World countries today. You resent someone who gives you something.

*There are ways to develop young audiences, like presenting music in an environment that is not so stuffy.*

That is just a format, a vehicle to get people to the concert hall. I don't think that it, in the final analysis, is the right way. Again it depends on how it is handled. I don't just go up on the stage and play in jeans, because it is something very special for me to play and I dress accordingly. That has nothing to do with me being stuffy or not—it's my own feeling towards my art form.

*Did you feel any resistance when you entered conducting?*

Only from the critics, not from the public.

*Why was that?*

There are so many things that go into making music that can't be explained and shouldn't be explained. It is an intuitive thing. So I pass through a city and do my thing, and it's just not always comprehended. After a certain amount of time, you expect that they begin to see what you are doing. Objectively speaking, writing vindictive criticism about me I don't like.

*What's the most common criticism you are subjected to?*

That I am impersonal on stage, I look bored. "Obviously it is so easy for him that he is bored and should have been somewhere else if he doesn't feel like being here." Blah!

*But you emit good energy on stage. That it looks easy ought to be a plus.*

In the long run criticism is unimportant. In the beginning it's nice to be appreciated and it might get more people to the concert hall. But in my case it hasn't done anything one way or the other.

*Many musicians feel it is a lonely battle to build a career. Did you ever feel lonely?*

Oh yes. But I always had support. I never thought of building a career—it just happened, and I never thought of doing anything else.

# Index